Praise for *The Witch of Bourbon Street*

"Part ghost story, part myste
the power of love, forgivenes
haunting and uplifting. . . . E
spheric details, making the ecc ourbon Street
and the damp mysteries of the bayou as alive as any of the
cleverly named supporting cast. The use of multiple voices,
including historical documents, will immerse readers in the
world of the story and the eerie legacy of one remarkable and
powerful family." —*RT Book Reviews*

"[Palmieri's] strength lies in the fullness of her vision, immers-
ing readers in the heat and noise of southern Louisiana. Fans
of Paula Brackston and M. J. Rose will enjoy this story of
redemption, self-preservation, and the power of shared history." —*Booklist*

"Suzanne Palmieri is quickly becoming a standout star of
magical fiction. *The Witch of Bourbon Street* may just be her
best yet. Haunting and beautiful, you'll find yourself capti-
vated by the exquisite setting, and the Sorrows themselves. A
must-read." —Sarah Addison Allen, *New York Times*
bestselling author of *First Frost*,
Lost Lake, and *Garden Spells*

"Few writers can create the richly atmospheric worlds of
Suzanne Palmieri's fiction or bring to life such compelling
characters. Caught in the ghostly half-life between their

own bad choices and their tragic history, the Sorrows inhabit a mystical, mysterious world where time is distorted and redemption becomes imperative. A family saga that will linger with readers like the lost souls of the bayou. Palmieri's best so far." —Brunonia Barry, *New York Times* bestselling author of *The Lace Reader* and *The Map of True Places*

Praise for *The Witch of Belladonna Bay*

"About the lies we tell, the love we struggle for, and the way we find our way back to our rightful place in the world, Palmieri's book is a stunner."

—Caroline Leavitt, *New York Times* bestselling author of *Pictures of You* and *Is This Tomorrow*

"Ms. Palmieri's authentic dialogue, and ability to paint a family in crisis, is both charming and layered. If you're a lover of Southern fiction, magic in its many forms, and the kind of storytelling that keeps you turning the pages, you've come to the right place, y'all."

—Lesley Kagen, *New York Times* bestselling author of *Whistling in the Dark*

"Magic weaves its way through this beguiling Southern gothic, swirling from the moss-laden trees around the Big House through the misty and menacing Belladonna Bay, and settling into the hearts of Bronwyn and her niece, Byrd, whose Strange Ways most people just don't understand. Reminiscent

of Sarah Addison Allen's *Garden Spells*, this bewitching tale of ghostly mystery, love and family ties will enchant you from the very first page and linger in the air around you long after the last." —Wendy Webb, bestselling author of *The Fate of Mercy Alban*

"All of Suzanne Palmieri's novels cast a spell, and *The Witch of Belladonna Bay* is no exception. Palmieri delivers a rich and magical story about the two most powerful forces in life: family and love." —Elin Hilderbrand, *New York Times* bestselling author of *Beautiful Day*

"Suzanne Palmieri has crafted a riveting tale that will keep you up late at night guessing what will happen next. It is a story that will intrigue both male and female readers. Guys, don't let this one slip past you."

—Jason Mott, *New York Times* bestselling author of *The Returned*

Praise for *The Witch of Little Italy*

"Palmieri's enthralling debut will make adult readers nostalgic for beloved books from their childhoods. Abundant with secrets, hidden passageways, magic, and several enchanting mysteries, it'll keep you on the edge of your seat until the end. The magic and witchcraft elements are subtle, enhancing the overall effect of this clever, beautiful novel."

—*RT Book Reviews*

"In her debut novel, Palmieri has combined romance and mystery, folklore and psychology to create a jigsaw puzzle of family secrets and tragedies, losses and loves, guilt and forgiveness. . . . Entertaining."
—*Kirkus Reviews*

"Charming and enchanting *The Witch of Little Italy* drew me in from page one. A magical story of family, secrets, loss, and rediscovery written in beautiful prose and sprinkled with effervescent characters you won't soon forget. Palmieri nimbly blends the past and present to concoct a delicious spell of a story that will appeal to fans of Sarah Addison Allen and other fabulously entertaining novels."
—Karen White, *New York Times* bestselling author of *The Beach Trees*

"*The Witch of Little Italy* is a warmly enchanting debut that will have you believing in magic and craving homemade Buccatini Amatriciano."
—Susanna Kearsley, *New York Times* bestselling author of *The Winter Sea, Mariana*, and *The Rose Garden*

"I was utterly enchanted from the first page, and found myself continually marveling over the effortless grace with which this story unfolded. *The Witch of Little Italy* is a complex, richly textured tale that practically sings with magic, and I know Suzanne Palmieri has a long and brilliant career ahead of her. In a word: I was charmed."
—Donna Ball, award-winning author of The Lady Bug Farm series

Also by Suzanne Palmieri

The Witch of Little Italy
The Witch of Belladonna Bay
The Witch of Bourbon Street
I'll Be Seeing You (coauthored as Suzanne Hayes)
Empire Girls (coauthored as Suzanne Hayes)

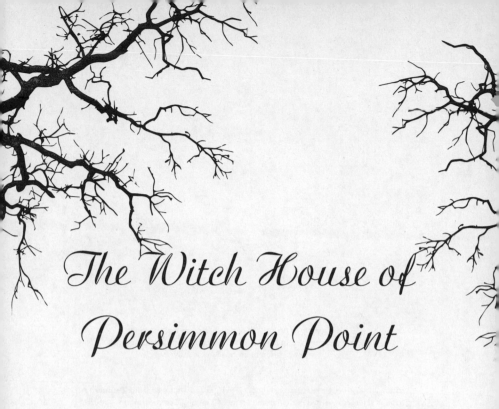

The Witch House of Persimmon Point

Suzanne Palmieri

ST. MARTIN'S GRIFFIN

NEW YORK

THE WITCH HOUSE OF PERSIMMON POINT. Copyright © 2016 by Suzanne Palmieri. All
rights reserved. Printed in the United States of America. For information, address
St. Martin's Press, 175 Fifth Avenue, New York, N.Y. 10010.

www.stmartins.com

Library of Congress Cataloging-in-Publication Data

Names: Palmieri, Suzanne, author.
Title: The Witch House of Persimmon Point / Suzanne Palmieri.
Description: First edition. | New York : St. Martin's Griffin, 2016.
Identifiers: LCCN 2016014364| ISBN 9781250056184 (trade paperback) |
    ISBN 9781250091925 (e-book)
Subjects: LCSH: Domestic fiction. | BISAC: FICTION / Contemporary Women. |
    FICTION / Romance / Gothic. | FICTION / Family Life. | GSAFD: Gothic fiction.
Classification: LCC PS3616.A353 W574 2016 | DDC 813/.6—dc23
LC record available at https://lccn.loc.gov/2016014364

Our books may be purchased in bulk for promotional, educational,
or business use. Please contact your local bookseller or the Macmillan Corporate and
Premium Sales Department at 1-800-221-7945, extension 5442, or by e-mail
at MacmillanSpecialMarkets@macmillan.com.

First Edition: October 2016

10 9 8 7 6 5 4 3 2 1

Dedicated to Fay Barile

1917–2015

My very own "Mimi"

This one's for you, Gram. I sure hope you're dancing.

Author's Note

Dear Reader,

It's raining as I write this, which is fitting. I love the rain. My children and I call rainy days "Brontë" days. I feel as if I'm walking with Jane Eyre through misty fields of heather. Or exploring hidden hallways with Mary Lennox from *The Secret Garden* (it rained throughout her saga, too).

Anyway, without giving away too much of the story, I need to share something that's been weighing on my mind. A warning, if you will.

This book may not be for you. I wrote this book for me. An exorcism of my own demons. My own experiences placed inside a fictional landscape that is safe. For *me*. But maybe not so safe for *you*, my dearests.

In life we all have our triggers.

I've always held the belief that writers should write what they *must* write. That being said, I also believe that if a novel contains trigger material, it is the responsibility of the author to let a reader know.

To those of you who have read my other novels, rest assured this book delivers the things you have come to expect. There are gardens and ghosts and family secrets galore. And magic. Always magic.

However, this is my most deeply personal narrative. Some parts are the closest to memoir I may ever get; though just as many parts are deeply entrenched in make-believe. However, for those parts that may cut right at your soul, I wanted to give you notice. I also wanted to give you a place to call if you need to talk.

If you experience trouble, please call 1-800-656-HOPE to contact RAINN (Rape, Abuse & Incest National Network), the nation's largest antisexual violence organization.

And please know, whatever your difficult journey might be, I travel with you.

Yours,
The Lost Witch,
Suzy

Permanent
Geranium Lake

Journal Entry on the Night of the Biggest Doom

Byrd Whalen

MONDAY, JULY 14, 2025
HAVEN PORT, VIRGINIA

There's a portrait of a woman hanging on the second-floor landing of the Witch House, holding court over the sweeping staircase and crooked, bloated foyer. Her piercing green eyes span the darkness, waiting. When I first cracked open the heavy front door the day I arrived, sweeping back the expected cobwebs, hers was the first face I saw.

And goddamn, I knew I was home.

At first, I thought the house was having some fun at my expense, painting a picture of a future me as some kind of welcome present. A psychic gag gift or what have you. But then, I was fourteen and self-absorbed (as most fourteen-year-olds are wont to be). It didn't take too long for me to figure out she was the lady I was looking for though, dead or not. The keeper of the secrets. Crazy Anne Amore.

My great-grandmother.

We share black hair that's a beast to tame, stubborn chins, and big eyes. I swear until I saw it, I'd never seen another person who wore the same "Do what you want, but cross me and die" look that I wear. And inside that gaze, if you look real close, you can see the real message. "Don't get close to me because I'll love you, and when you leave me, and you will, I swear it, it *will* destroy me. And then I'll have to destroy you, because . . . fair is fair."

She's painted sitting on a window seat with her elbow resting on the sill, not looking out the window, but looking straight ahead with a purpose I'm still trying to understand. The colors melt together in greens and golds and garnets, but it's the lighting in the painting that invokes a little fear.

See, I've always been obsessed with light. Especially the way it falls in late afternoon. Like thick, honey-colored hope. And that's the kind of light in the painting. It obscures half her face with shadows and the reflection of the windowpane makes a blurry glass tattoo of the other side.

You can't hardly figure out where the darkness ends and her figure begins. From what I've learned about her, the painter's perspective suited her perfectly.

So there she hangs, staring straight down the stairs at the wide front door.

Because there was no way in hell anything could stop Anne Amore from guarding her Witch House.

Not even death.

I swear, her gaze follows me each time I walk by—like something out of a Sunday matinee haunted-house movie, shifty eyes and all that mess—but especially when I'm on my way to the third floor. After all these years, I still can't tell if she likes that I took her room or not. And I still canNOT stand how she won't actually come right out and haunt the place. Sometimes I want to yell, "Show yourself, old woman!" but I don't. Because even though I never met her, and even though she won't visit me proper, I know I'm her favorite and that she has her reasons.

But if there ever were a time for her to show herself plain, today would be the day. Because today is the day I die. I could use some advice, really. What good are supportive, loving family ghost witches if they can't come save you when you're about to give up the good fight?

I'm so tired.

I spent the first half of today searching for my mother's wedding dress. I bought the black dye at the Woolworth last Sunday and thought, "PERFECT. I'll dye that fancy frock a deep shade of black and wear it."

I spent the afternoon dyeing it. I don't care that it's not an even sort of color. I don't like anything even, really. Not even numbers, or even lengths of things. Evenness has always seemed like some sort of lie. If I had the chance to give a little girl one piece of advice, it would be, "Don't trust a person who likes things even. Only trust the people who thrive in chaos."

I'm not sure I fully believe that. But it sounds good.

Now I'm sitting here, in my room on the third floor of this terrible, wonderful house, and I'm waiting for the damn dress to dry properly so I can prepare myself for the execution. I'm sure I'll have to wear it damp. But I don't mind.

Can a person call this type of situation an execution? Probably not. Still, I like the idea of taking my final walk through the moonlit garden with the satisfying flurry of satin and tulle all around me.

It's all very dramatic.

I've always loved this room. The cheery wallpaper and wide windows facing the idyllic shoreline of Persimmon Point don't even really hint that a madwoman planned murders here while she brushed her long black hair. The pillowcases she rested her head on after digging that grave out by the juniper trees don't give up her dreams. The sunlight playing across the wide, uneven wooden floors don't echo many tears.

I don't think there's anything more comforting than sunlight on wood floors. And the more I think about it, the more I think that this room, and maybe even the whole house, is hardwired for human comfort.

Which makes sense in ordinary circumstances . . . I mean, a house is supposed to be like that, right? Well, this house is a whole other ball of wax. I'm sure its feelings are hurt as I write this. It fancies itself a horror house. Home of witches and murderesses. Of death and decay and destruction. And here I am, calling it *comforting*.

Because, see . . .

There always seems to be a soft breeze weaving through its salt-marsh-and-juniper-scented rooms, which some poet somewhere should have likened to the way a woman's hair smells when she's in love.

Maybe I should have been a poet. Avoided this whole mess. Poets make livings on unhappy, un-endings. Granddad would say, "Sugar, you missed your calling!"

I'm of the mind that we should expect more unhappy endings than we do. Sure, we say we do. But we don't.

I don't care what anyone says about us, that's something this monstrous family of mine did right. We expected the bad. We created it. We embraced it. Hell, we imagined it and then gave birth to it.

I'm an unhappy ending myself. A whole embodied, unhappy ending of my own mother's life.

But I won't dwell on that. Not today.

My fate is my own. And I own my fate.

So I'm going to sit here and tell this goddamn story while my goddamn dress dries.

I left Magnolia Creek, Alabama, for Haven Port, Virginia, in the summer of 2015. It wasn't an even-numbered year, so I figured it was safe.

When my aunt Wyn tells the story, she says I ran away from home and wove a web of lies so thick no one even knew what was happening until I was good and safe and settled. She was secretly proud of my fourteen-year-old machinations, I suspect. Only I wasn't running away, I was simply moving.

I don't run away from anything.

And God knows I probably should. Like right this very moment, but that's beside the point.

Growing up in Magnolia Creek I always felt like a stranger in a strange land.

I was loved, I can't argue with that, but as I grew older, things changed. Sometimes knowing people love you but also knowing they don't really *know* you is downright lonely.

So, I focused on this house. This side of my family I never knew, from a place I'd never been. One I'd been warned about. My mother's home. My mother's people.

"Stop mooning over those crazy women. You aren't a lick like 'em. At least, not much," my granddad Jackson always grumbled.

"No, Byrd, we can't go there and visit. They're all dead. And don't go on and on about how you can visit with them anyway, because there's no guarantee they haven't gone on to the other side. Besides, I want you to live here in Alabama in the sunshine. I don't want you surrounding yourself with so much darkness, sweet girl. Promise me you'll let that all rest. It's what your mama wanted," pleaded my aunt Wyn who had "strange ways" of her own, but that fact never seemed to stop her from wanting to not let me enjoy them a little.

(That's what they call our "gifts" back home. I grew up feeling like my aunt and I were each something of a human anomaly. Why can't the ordinary people be thought of as the anomaly? Damned unfair is what it is.)

But nothing anyone said could deter me. I'm driven when I want to be. Besides, what's the harm in a little conversation with family? So what if they're ghosts?

By the time I was thirteen I was a regular scholar on the history of Haven Port, Virginia, and the Witch House. There wasn't a book or an article I hadn't read. Wasn't a show I hadn't watched. And I was IN LOVE with the idea that I was one of them. My favorite book on the subject was called *An American*

Haunting: Wild Ponies, Wild Women, and the Invention of Sin in Haven Port, Virginia.

All that research made me feel close enough to that whole, previously unknown part of my life that I decided maybe I'd wait until I was older to visit, like Aunt Wyn said. I figured it'd be easier that way.

But then, as I was about to hit pause on the whole shebang, this big ol' news story broke, and guess what it was about? Yep. Seems a special program was set to air featuring a local journalist who dabbled in paranormal investigation. He was planning to figure out, once and for all, if the rumors were true. And he'd gotten permission from the current owner to do an investigative report.

The Mystery of the Witch House

That man had done a little ill-fated magic himself. He had taken a perfectly intriguing name and managed to make it sound like a middle school reader. BORING. Or so I thought. Evidently, America found it fascinating. The interest surrounding the show, some silly show that at the time didn't even have an air date, was overwhelming. Ads were selling by the billion or some such nonsense.

That's when I started to worry.

He could find out the real truth before I could.

Hell no. I couldn't wait. I had to get there. So I moved.

And I spent that whole summer searching for some damn thing I simply *could not put my finger on.* A mystery that refused to be solved until it was good and ready (which, I'll admit, was fairly admirable, if frustrating).

I remember talking to the house and the property and the trees, real polite. I'd say, "I respect your need for privacy, but these damn people are on their way with a bulldozer, so you better just SHOW ME WHAT YOU ARE HIDING!"

I needed to unearth their secrets before anyone else got the chance. Not to make excuses or clear their names. No sir. I promise.

I came to learn all I could about the evil, so I could control their legacy of terror. My family would walk hand in hand with the other great evils in the world, or they wouldn't walk at all. They deserved a seat at the head of the "most fascinating people of all time" table.

Which meant, of course, I would have a seat there, too.

I know . . . I know. But remember, I was fourteen years old, and fourteen-year-old girls tend to spend most of their time going off the deep end.

That reporter was going to ruin everything, no matter what he found. Exposing the raw underside of a thing drains all the interesting right out of it. And I don't think there's anything worse than being uninteresting.

To be honest, I was more worried they'd find out it was a normal, everyday family. Debunking urban legends should be criminal, I swear. I didn't want some plastic Ken doll from TV telling me my family was virtuous.

Great-grandma Anne summed up the whole thing best when she wrote, "Only foolish people believe in virtue. The imposition of virtue is a manipulative tactic used by those who run the world. If the masses are taught virtues, they don't fight back. Human beings are naturally evil."

That wonderfully wicked woman had a lifetime of journals right there in that trunk by the window. I read them all the week I arrived, and now I add my own to the collection year by year.

I suppose this will be my very last entry.

It's terribly sad.

So, anyway, I was only fourteen, and I was living on my own, in a haunted house, on a piece of haunted property, telling lies to my people back in Alabama so I could stay. And I searched. I hoped I'd find something. I was counting on it.

I worried it would be something boring, like an adulterous affair with a pious politician, or something typical like that. But I *dreamed* there would be some kind of murderous truth rotting at the bottom of a well.

What I didn't count on was a garden of human bones.

It was downright exciting.

I guess that's why I've decided to write the whole thing down today, a full ten years after those three days where the past and the present collided in one big glorious bang. Because, see . . . at the ripe old age of twenty-four, adventure has all but left my life.

I'm doomed, really. I've never, ever been a wallowing, sad type of person. But loss affects me now in a way that would have made my younger self ashamed. And it's *weak*. And that's why I can't continue to live.

Like, I never thought I would hear a song about young love and mourn that I won't ever fall in love for the first time again.

It's those last firsts that tear me up inside. They're the only things we can't really ever get back.

I'll never make love again for the first time. I'll never see Jack again for the first time.

I guess that's why I'm doing what I'm doing tonight. So I can have another "first."

Loss makes a person want vengeance against time. Sometimes I think that's what adulthood is all about. A war waged every day against time, and memories, and all the happy endings that didn't come.

That's how my cousin Eleanor Amore (the rightful owner of the Witch House) was when I first met her. Full of quiet vengeance against the lie of a happy ending. Her fairy-tale marriage was over. Her anchor, her one true friend, was dead. She was full of piss and vinegar and sold on the crazy idea that once free of everything she knew, she'd be fine. She'd be able to lay down her weapons and live a peaceful life. No one bothered to tell her there ain't no escape from love. It follows you, haunts you, terrorizes your sleep, ambushes you.

Love waits until you look for it, and then it hides.

2

Eleanor in the Brownstone
with a Wrench

THE BRONX, NEW YORK

WEDNESDAY, SEPTEMBER 2, 2015

6:00 P.M.

Seven-year-old Maj Amore lay under the kitchen table on the clean, worn floor, drawing the very best drawing she'd ever drawn. The two women she loved most, her mama and her Mimi, were talking about grown-up things in a hushed-loud way that made her draw even faster. It didn't matter, Maj already knew a whole lot about what was in store for them when they moved to Virginia. She was drawing it, after all.

She wasn't *too* scared, not really, because she was, at the moment, safe. Cocooned by the four stable legs of the table, her mama's bare paint-spattered feet, and Mimi's sensible shoes, nestled amidst scattered art supplies and crumpled discarded versions of the best drawing ever in the world, two barrettes that always pinched, three stuffed animals who were going to be the critics at her art show after dinner, and one sock. (It was the loose one, stretched from a puppet she'd made at church. She'd been bored, and thought it was a perfectly reasonable idea to remove one sock and have a little fun. But Mimi was angry and said she'd be punished for the sin of . . . she forgot, and now? She was being punished for whatever it was, because Maj hated when her socks weren't just right. Only, she wished she could take it back, because her toes were getting cold, and she should have listened to her Mimi when she had the chance, and hugged her more, too.)

Her red curls (the only thing most people noticed about her) bounced like tightly coiled springs each time she moved to choose a different color crayon. Her daddy, who was banging things around in their apartment upstairs, had brought a new box over, and it wasn't the ordinary pack of twenty-four that mama usually got at the dollar store down the street. This one was wider, more impressive. So impressive that Maj was being extra careful to put each one back exactly where it came from, turning the crisp paper wrappers so that she could read the names of the new colors. Each one like a drawing all its own. Cornflower Blue, Periwinkle, Burnt Sienna . . .

"You okay down there, Maj?" Her mama peeked in at her.

"Don't look! It's not finished. Did you know that there was a color named Permanent Geranium Lake. It's a pretty red color. It got retired in 1910."

"Crayons get retired?" Mama asked. "How do you know all this? Did you suddenly become a seven-year-old expert on crayon history?"

"No, but I was looking for it in this box, because I need it, and it wasn't here, and then I remembered that I used it from the toy box in the attic, and that they were really old, so I asked Daddy and he told me about the crayon graveyard."

"Daddy was nice, bringing you those new crayons, don't you think?"

"That's a question inside a question, Mama, and you told me I never had to answer those."

"Mimi, please tell me I'm not a terrible mother," she said, sitting back up.

But Mimi couldn't offer any comfort to Mama, because Mimi was dead. Besides, Maj's daddy had come back into the kitchen, filling it up with his anger and fear. Daddy couldn't see the ghosts. Mama could see them only when she was tired or sad, and then she always said things like, "I've lost my mind completely . . ." or "What good is a ghost if they can't wash a dish? I SWEAR."

But Maj could see them. And hear them, too.

Only, she knew she wasn't crazy, and neither was her mama. They were simply Amores.

Maj went back to work, because something was trying to tell her a secret. It would be hidden in her picture. All she needed was the right color for Crazy Anne's geraniums.

Eleanor and her almost ex-husband, Anthony, glared at each other across the kitchen table. She didn't want him to think the tears in her eyes were over him. He didn't want to believe they weren't.

Eleanor felt Mimi melt away into the air when he slammed

the back door. She couldn't get used to life without her grandmother. The only real mother, the only true support and friend
she'd ever had. Sometimes, when Mimi visited with her, she
thought her mind was concocting the whole haunting because
she couldn't bring herself to let go.

But she knew better. An Amore woman wasn't worth her
weight in salt if she didn't hang out for a while before dancing
into the afterlife. Eleanor was almost grateful for the argument
Anthony started, yet another tired continuation of all the others
they'd had over the years, because it helped her take her mind
off the lingering smell of Mimi and her lily of the valley perfume. And at the same time, it helped her become even more
resolved about her decision to leave the Bronx.

"I'm serious, Elly," he said. "It's dangerous."

"When are you not serious? You are a walking, talking warning sign."

"Stop, listen to me. All this stuff about that house . . . what
if the stories are true? It's irresponsible to up and move there
with the baby."

"She's *seven*."

"She's under the table," Maj sang out.

Eleanor and Anthony looked at each other, both ashamed for
arguing around her. Again.

"Time to take a bath, Princess," said Anthony.

"But why? I took one last night."

"Because your mother should make sure you have a bath
every night, that's why. It's proper."

"Why do you insist on doing that? If you have something to

say to me, say it. You don't have to filter it through her. It's borderline abusive, you know," said Eleanor.

"What are you talking about? You make this shit up in your mind. I was just answering her question."

"No you were *NOT*. You were implying that I don't bathe her! Which is untrue and mean-spirited and I can't even believe I'm arguing about this again! Don't you have a new home to go to?"

Maj emerged from under the table, scowling.

"I don't like it when you say bad things about each other. It's not right or fair. And you don't mean it. I can tell," she said.

Eleanor waited for Anthony to yell. He never liked it when Maj criticized their completely inept parenting skills. He didn't like to feel like he was making any mistakes, ever. But this time he didn't lose his patience, maybe because they were leaving the next day and he didn't want to waste any time.

Falling out of love should be easier, she thought. Instead of losing his patience, his damned handsome face broke into that wide open smile of his that broke her heart all over again.

"This one should be a lawyer," said Anthony.

"I will not be a lawyer," Maj said, her arms crossed in a huff.

"Oh, no? And what would you like to be, then? An actress, a vet?" asked Eleanor, deciding to follow his lead.

"Mama, let me ask you something. What is my name?" asked Maj, putting her hands on her hips and tilting her head.

Elly and Anthony look at each other, amused. Maj had just recently begun to flex her genetically inherited sarcasm.

"Your name," said Elly, pulling Maj onto her lap and squeezing her tight, "is Elizabeth Amore. You were named after the most wonderful great-aunt and friend in the world. And we call you Maj, because it's short for Your Majesty."

"Yes. That is my name. And that means I'd never want to be a lawyer. Or a doctor, or anything else like that. Ever."

"Why, do you fancy yourself a queen?"

"Of course I do. But I don't want to be a queen, either."

"Then what do you want to be?"

"Well, I used to want to be a piece of toast with butter and raspberry jam, but now I want to be the ocean. Is it time for the news yet?"

"Just about," said Eleanor.

Maj slid off her mother's lap, tucked the box of crayons under her arm, picked up her drawing, and left the kitchen.

Anthony and Eleanor listened for her to switch on the TV.

"I don't even know where to start," Anthony said. "That child is getting stranger by the day. You have to say something to her when she says things like that. People will think she's . . . she's . . . I mean, people already think she's an oddball."

"I know! Isn't it delicious?"

"Stop acting like it doesn't bother you. I'm not wrong about this, Elly. You can act like you're proud of it all you want, but at the end of the day, you wish she was—"

"What? What are you about to say? Because I know it wasn't normal. You wouldn't say that."

"I can't say anything."

"There's one thing you *can* say . . ."

"What?"

"Good-bye, farewell, see you next lifetime."

"Very grown-up of you. No wonder she is the way she is."

Eleanor tried (unsuccessfully) to hide the pain she was feeling as she fought with Anthony.

If she put all the events of the past two years in perspective, she'd have nothing to be upset about at all, except, of course, their impending divorce, and Maj's behavioral issues (which along with her move, was the current topic of debate, and which Eleanor believed weren't issues at all, because her daughter was simply stubborn. Not to mention born with a lot more of the Amore sight than anyone remembered any other member of the family ever having). Other than those two teeny tiny details, everything was, as Mimi would have said, dandy. Eleanor had found success as an artist, her paintings making a modest amount of money, and she'd repaired some damaged relationships (most notably with her mother, Carmen the Actress).

"Really, if I think about it, all emotions aside, I should thank you. I've come into my own, Anthony."

"Well, I'm glad you're not screaming at me, but I'm going to disagree. When you came to the Bronx eight years ago, you were a lost soul. And now? You're even worse off."

Eight years. Eight years since she'd come to the Bronx, pregnant and on the run. One year of falling madly in love, seven destroying that love bit by bit.

"Anthony, you've *got* to come to terms with the fact that you suffer from a hero complex. Think about it . . . you took care of your mother. Then when she died, you took care of Mimi and the rest of the old ones. And then I come back to the Bronx, all broken and pregnant and crazy. And you sweep me off my feet. Saving me. Only, I guess I didn't need you enough . . . was that it? Did you need me to stay weak and vacant?"

Is that why you left? she finished silently.

"It makes me crazy when you start talking all that mumbo jumbo. Complexes and shit. You were the one who started all this, Elly. Don't forget, you kissed that art dealer, and when I was still willing to forgive you, you kicked me out. Don't forget, you brought this whole situation on yourself."

Eleanor felt the anger and defensiveness rise.

"Yes. How could I forget? You won't let me forget. And you always leave out the part where you made living with you after that a complete misery. You wouldn't even look at me! You never even wanted to talk about *why* it happened. And look how it turned out. I'm lost again, packing up my life, and there you are living down the block happily with Josephine De'Fazio. Getting all hot and bothered over her perfect vacuum cleaner lines in her perfectly atrocious wall-to-wall carpet from *Sears*, no less, and probably chasing after her while she washes dishes in her apron, saying 'It's so sexy when you clean, JoJo!' But I didn't think we were discussing this again. I *thought* we were discussing the new renters moving in and what time you were picking up the U-Haul and Maj wanting to be toast!"

"The ocean, Mama!" Maj called from the other room.

"Calm down," Anthony said, glancing in Maj's direction. "You still look pretty when you're mad. . . . Is there any of Mimi's tea left? The one that calms you down? I'll look. Did you pack all the pots?"

Eleanor hated that he still had the ability to make her feel better. It was like her heart was betraying her head.

"I threw that tea away," she lied. "Besides, there's no magic strong enough to turn me into Josephine De'Fazio." She banged her fist down on the table. "And no magic I know of that can make this neighborhood, these schools, these other parents, *that priest* you like so much, accept Maj for who she is, not who everyone wants her to be. And that includes you, too. You and your idea of normal. Because if that woman is normal . . . I can't do this. Why don't you just leave, Anthony? I'm sure she misses you and is making you some new Jell-O mold as we speak."

"First of all, I'm staying in her guest room. Nothing more, nothing less. A man needs somewhere to lay his head, and when you threw me out on my rear end, Josephine was kind enough to offer."

I never thought you'd actually leave, she thought for the millionth time.

"And second," he continued, "I suppose this conversation is a good example of you . . . what was that you said a minute ago? Coming into your own?"

"Mama, come quick! They said the story is coming up next!" Maj yelled from the living room.

6:30 P.M.

Eleanor sat on the couch in apartment 1A at 1313 170th street in the Bronx and tried not to look at Mimi's lonely crochet basket at her feet. All the unfinished things that dead hands leave . . . She did her best to watch the screen instead of waiting for Anthony to put his arm around her, to tell her how sorry he was and how everything that happened since they were married was his fault.

Maj was stretched out on the floor, waiting for the news to resume.

In silence they watched two commercials for pharmaceuticals while staring straight at the television. No one could avoid eye contact the way Anthony could. It was the most aggravating thing.

"Who buys this stuff anyway," he mumbled.

"Daddy! *Shhh!*" shushed Maj as the interview began.

"We are speaking today with our very own Johnny Colder from *Sunday, Today, Tomorrow* about his much anticipated special airing right here on WBDM on . . . well, John, I don't want to steal your thunder, do you have an air date yet?"

"First, Brad, I want to thank you for having me today, I never get to mix with the weekday news crowd here at the station! And, as a matter of fact, we do have an air date. To be honest, the amount of interest the public has in watching my exposé of the Witch House—and the family that owned it—has taken me by surprise."

"Do you suppose that man knows how ridiculous he sounds?" asked Eleanor.

"Do you realize that everyone but *you* sounds ridiculous and stupid?" asked Anthony.

"*Shhhh!*" said Maj.

"So, don't keep us in suspense, John. When is the big reveal?"

"As you know, there's a lot of planning that goes into a live show like this. We all remember the fiasco with Al Capone's tomb, right?"

(Shared laughter.)

"So, in order to make sure we didn't have similar results, I've done extensive research on the house, the property, and the women. I've also enlisted the support of the team from the hit show *Present and Paranormal*. It took a lot of work, but we're finally ready to dive in. The air date is this Sunday, September sixth."

"Labor Day weekend. Fantastic! You heard it here first, folks. Tune in this Sunday and watch as Johnny Colder uncovers the Witch House of Persimmon Point. Ah, Persimmon Point—it sounds so sweet for a location with this dark history. Now, John, for those viewers who've been living under a rock the past year, what is it you are trying to find?"

"Well, besides investigating the myriad of urban legends associated, the main focus is whether or not these women were, perhaps, the most prominent uncaught serial killers in the history of the United States. We have at least a hundred disappearances from up and down the East Coast, spanning almost a hundred years, that can all be linked, in one way or another, to that area. To put it frankly, Brad, we're looking for bones."

"There you have it. It's a must-watch, that's for sure. Thanks for joining us, Johnny. And good luck."

"Sunday?" said Eleanor. That only gave her three full days to move into a house that hadn't been lived in since 1999 before it was on the national news.

"Do you want me to come down with you so you're not alone when all those people come? I could make sure everything is running good."

"No thank you, Mr. Hero. I can handle it. I'm sure I'll feel right at home with the chaos."

"I can't believe you signed the papers letting them go dig around there. Once that place is on TV, it'll bring all the crazies out," said Anthony, frowning.

"They paid me, Anthony. Real money. So I didn't have to sell this building. So instead, you could rent it out and I could try and get Maj out of here. I didn't know it would be a circus. Honestly, I'm sick to death of you making me feel bad. If you want me to stay, ask me to stay. But I'm the person you get. Messy me. Paint-in-the-hair me. No vacuum required. And this kid here? She's the one you get. The one your friend Sal down at the Sunoco called 'the Bad Seed.' Besides, Mimi willed it to me."

"That's unfair. Mimi left this building to you as well. You don't even know if she wanted you to go there. Wouldn't she have told you about it when she was alive if she was hot on the idea of leaving?"

"That's low. I mean it. Don't use my dead grandmother against me. She's been gone six months, but I'm still in shock, and you're using her to make me second-guess myself. I don't know why she didn't tell us. But I *do* know this family, and it could have been her simply hiding it from us because she didn't want me to leave *her*, not *here*."

"That's not it, Mama. She was hiding it from us because it scared her," Maj piped up.

"See, even the kid knows this is a stupid move."

"Mama, I—"

"Maj, go on upstairs to our apartment," Eleanor interrupted Maj. "I'll be up in a minute. I need to talk to Daddy. Alone."

She waited until the door was shut to say, "It's stupid? So, what's the smart move, then? I'm completely out of options. Anthony, I have to get Maj out of the city. We're on a first-name basis with the school guidance counselors at the public and parochial schools in a ten-mile radius. The way to make her life less about becoming who she isn't and more about being a wild redheaded impertinent child is to get her out of here. And you aren't helping. Because you agree with them. Because at the end of the day, she isn't yours. Not your blood. And you think she's like *him*."

For a second, Eleanor thought he was going to hit her. But then he bit his knuckles and took a breath.

"You are not out of options. You want to run. To put distance between me and you and whatever it is that's wrong with Maj. You don't want to face anything. So you deserve what you get. But Maj doesn't. Think about that, Elly. Maj deserves better."

"Maj deserves a mortgage-free estate on the Eastern Shore of Virginia with wild ponies and an art deco in-ground swimming pool. And a wraparound porch where her mother can paint. In a state that will let me homeschool her with far less restrictions than New York. That's what Maj deserves. And that's what she'll get. Now, did you fix the faucet upstairs yet or what? And when you're done, hide the wrench so I'm not tempted to kill you in your sleep and then take apart Josephine's Electrolux."

9:00 P.M.

"Mama, what were you and Mimi talking about when I was making my picture under the table?" Maj asked as Eleanor tucked her in. The nightlight glowed.

"Maj, sweetheart, remember what I said. I'm not absolutely sure that the energy we see is Mimi. It might just be my wanting so badly to see her. We can project things, you know. And even if it is some lingering bit of Mimi . . . it's still not her. Not really."

"I don't think that's very nice. It really, really is her. Really. Just because it makes you sad, it doesn't mean it isn't true."

"I'm not going to argue with you about this," said Eleanor.

Maj snuggled against her. "Tell me again, Mama. Tell me what you know about the house."

"Well, let's see. The documentation in the will said that my great-grandfather, Vincent Amore, was Nan Amore's brother. She was the woman who built the house that stands there now. And, my love, that was very unusual in those days."

"That's boring. Tell me about the photographs."

"I can go get them if you want to look at them again."

"No, I want you to tell me so I can imagine it. It's realer that way."

"We'll be there tomorrow."

"Mama . . ."

"Okay . . . The house sits on a little peninsula called Persimmon Point. Persimmons are a lovely orange fruit. Sour, I think. It has the bay on one side, and the wide Atlantic on the other."

"And the ponies?"

"Yes. Wild ponies on the beach, beautiful wild gardens, even a pool. Very fancy, with hand-painted tiles from long before it was ordinary for people to have swimming pools. I can't imagine it's the same, though. No one has lived there for a very long time."

"Why didn't Mimi and her family move there?"

"I don't really know, baby."

"Why doesn't she want us to go? She won't tell me. Or even show me in my drawings."

Eleanor considered the argument she'd decided not to have and instead asked a question she knew she was asking for both of them.

"Are you scared, Maj? Because it's not too late to call it all off."

"No. I'm not a bit scared. I'm just curious."

"I'm sure it won't be a bit like we expect. Will you miss Daddy very much?"

"Not as much as I miss Mimi."

"I miss her, too. With my whole heart."

"I'm going to get going soon," said Anthony from the doorway.

How much did you hear? wondered Eleanor. But decided it didn't really matter.

"Say good night to daddy, honey." Eleanor squeezed her tight before leaving so they could listen, one last time, to the far-off rattle of the trains.

9:30 P.M.

"Is she asleep?" asked Eleanor.

"Yes, finally. Elly, please do me a favor. Don't let yourself get all caught up down there. If there's anything at all that makes you uncomfortable, just come back. I won't judge you. I don't trust that place." Anthony looked around the packed-up apartment. "I remember getting this place ready for you. So you could paint here."

"Don't do that. Don't remind yourself that you were nice once upon a time."

"You cheated. I don't have to be nice."

"You weren't nice, and then I cheated. And it wasn't cheating. It was only a kiss."

"Elly, we're never going to agree on that."

"Or anything else. Like how you agree Maj is the Bad Seed spawn of Satan. I won't ever believe that."

"If I believed that, I'd have to believe that this whole family that I've loved and who took me in when I needed them was evil. And I don't. I just want her to be happy. These things she can do, the things all of you can do . . . they never made any of you very happy. I'm right. Admit it."

She didn't answer. She silently washed the already clean sink and waited for him to leave. When the door closed behind him, she sunk down on the floor.

Eleanor closed her eyes and sensed Mimi behind her. Very old, shaking fingers taking down her hair. One of Mimi's hands touching her face. It was rough, calloused. Mimi hadn't had one easy day in her life. But the roughness was warm, and with her grandmother's hand on her face, she felt like there wasn't any story too long, any adventure too scary, there wasn't any love too big, there wasn't any ache that couldn't heal. But Mimi was dead, and for one, excruciating moment, Eleanor wondered if she was making a terrible mistake.

3

Maj in the Witch House with a Crayon

THE BRONX

THURSDAY, SEPTEMBER 3, 2015

9:00 A.M.

On the morning they were leaving for Virginia, little Maj should have been upset about a lot of things, only she wasn't. She should have been bothered by the noise everyone was making around her, talking and yelling, bringing boxes up and down the stairs. She didn't like noise, it made her stomach hurt. When she was in school, she always spent lunch and music and recess at the nurse. She should have been upset at the way her daddy and her mama were growling and glaring and being mean to each other. But she wasn't. She should have been upset about leaving Mimi's spirit.

But she wasn't.

Mimi would be making her very own trip soon. Crazy Anne told her so.

Crazy Anne was the one true friend Maj ever had. Even though she was older, and a ghost, that didn't matter to Maj. All the other kids made fun of her red hair, her drawings, and anything else they could think of. It took a lot of willpower not to scare them. Maj could scare people with the things she knew, and the things she said. Most times, she didn't like herself very much when she gave in to those urges, but other times she was more than happy to see those that hurt her—or the ones she loved—squirm. Crazy Anne always showed up sitting beside her, graceful with long black hair and a secretive smile. She'd whisper all kinds of funny things to Maj to make her feel better.

Eleanor tried not to show how surprised and happy she was to see Maj waiting on the front stoop steps in the sunshine. It confirmed to her that moving was the right decision.

Anthony had successfully attached the U-Haul to the car without kicking it too many times, and before she knew it, it was time to go. He hadn't put up too much of a fight when Eleanor told him that she was leaving with Maj. *Now I know he doesn't love me*, she'd thought. She'd expected him to threaten her with legalities, and part of her was upset that he didn't, because then she couldn't respond with her planned attack.

"Just because you married me doesn't mean you are her real father. You have no parental rights. Maybe you should have been more aggressive in pursuing that stepparent adoption when I said it would be a good idea. But no, you had to be YOU and just accept everything for

what it is. How's this for accepting things? Try and stop us. I'll crucify you."

It was probably for the best, but still, she'd have loved to see his face when she spat out those words. She loved to see his face. She loved his face. She loved him. And she hated herself for it and knew she never would have said those lines to him, never in a million years.

"Is it time to leave yet?" asked Maj, skipping from one step to another.

"Not yet. You have to say good-bye to Daddy. Where did he go? Leave it to that man to help me all morning and then hold me up right when I need to leave. I don't want to hit traffic."

"He's right there, Mama. Bye, Daddy!" shouted Maj, who hopped running into his arms. He pulled her up and placed her, with one hand, onto his shoulders. Then walked her toward the car, put her in the backseat and strapped her in. He kissed her on the forehead, but spoke to Eleanor.

"Be safe," he said.

The only thing I've ever wanted is to be safe, and then you ripped that away from me.

"I'll do my best."

You never really loved me. You loved the idea of me.

"Tell Crazy Anne I send my regards," said Anthony to Maj.

"I will. I love you this much," said Maj, holding out her arms wide, stretching every bit of her little body.

"Who the hell is Crazy Anne again?" asked Anthony as he walked Eleanor to the driver's side.

"I don't know. Imaginary friend? Ghost? Ancient Egyptian demon? Remember, we still don't know what she can or cannot do. Why don't you read up on it and get back to me? Oh, that's right, you don't read."

"You can't let anything go." Anthony sighed.

"And you let everything go. See? Watch us go," she said, slamming the door.

Anthony banged on the hood of the car and waved. Eleanor looked at the brownstone through the rearview mirror as she drove away.

It was one of those beautiful, early September mornings with clear blue skies and a light breeze. Eleanor looked at Anthony and thought he looked sad standing there in the sunshine with the busy streets of the city moving past him so fast. *I will not cry.*

I'm on my way, she thought. *And I won't miss it here. I won't.*

"Look where you're going, Mama, not where you've been," said her wise, redheaded heathen child.

By the time they hit the New Jersey Turnpike, Maj was asleep, and Eleanor alternated between guilt and a free sort of airy hum of peace until the car and the road and the woman became one, and the peace won out. She was free for the first time in her entire life. Now she just had to figure out who she was without him.

2:00 P.M.

HAVEN PORT, VIRGINIA

Eleanor and Maj crossed the Virginia state line and then, after a ferry and some back roads full of a whole lot of nothing, passed the sign that read "Entering Haven Port." The drive had taken exactly five hours.

"Crazy Anne likes odd numbers," said Maj. "So that's a good thing."

"I'm glad she approves. Now, where do you suppose we find the actual house?"

Maj handed a drawing over the seat. "Here's a map," she said.

No matter how many times Maj exhibited her extra little talents, Eleanor always seemed taken by surprise.

"I can't look at it and keep driving, so how about you tell me where to go, my little GPS?"

"Go this way"—Maj pointed to the right—"when you get to the tree that looks like an old man's face. There's a stop sign."

Eleanor spotted the tree and turned right onto Grand Street, which wasn't so grand but still seemed like the main thoroughfare. It had seen better days. It could have been on one of those TV programs—*Abandoned America* or something. There were a few people going about their days, walking past mostly empty storefronts with large, dusty 'fifties-era signs.

"They're all looking at us," whispered Maj.

"When you're older, remind me to watch *Invasion of the Body Snatchers* with you. Maybe they're all looking at this amazing car. It isn't every day you see a 1965 honeymoon red Chevy Chavelle."

"Mama, are you blind?"

Eleanor looked around and noticed that the few cars parked in the local grocery store were all vintage. Not well maintained, but stuck in time.

"Maybe the place is just filled with people who appreciate a simpler time. That wouldn't be so bad. Actually, I think it would be great."

Maj was focused on her map. "We go until the street ends, and then the driveway to the house is sort of the street. Only narrow, I think," said Maj.

Eleanor wanted to ask her daughter if knowing these things scared her. She wanted to have her tested at some kind of ESP lab somewhere. She wanted to be able to understand Maj better. But she wouldn't. Eleanor had vowed to be the one person Maj could trust. The one person who would let her just *be* without question or compromise. But sometimes Eleanor longed to ask: "How do you know these things? Are they pictures in your head or are they voices? Does it hurt? Is it scary?"

Instead, she drove on, until the road narrowed and then ended at a tall, black iron gate.

"There are words on the gate, Mama, look. What do they say?"

Eleanor looked up and saw the decorative bronze plaque nearly obscured in green patina and moss. She took a deep breath.

"It says 'Memento Mori.'"

"What does that mean?"

"What, little miss seven-year-old genius in all things language and history can't read Latin? For shame!" teased Eleanor.

"Mama! Just tell me. I can read it, but I'm not old enough yet to understand the meaning. Some things you need years for."

"Okay then. It means to remember that we will die. Pretty

dreary. Maybe there's a good story behind it. Why don't you scoot out and push it open so we can get there before tomorrow?"

Maj didn't need to be told twice. She jumped out and pushed open the gate, and then climbed in the front seat.

The oyster shell driveway curved around, slowly revealing an open piece of land with one small house, a white bungalow with decorative Victorian trim, to the left, and what they both knew was the actual house straight ahead. The driveway circled the large grassy yard. It had a single willow tree and a poplar tree canopy, boughs arching and properly Southern. Oyster shell walkways led off to side gardens.

"It's like a fairy story, Mama."

"A Grimm version for sure," she answered.

As they pulled up, Eleanor examined the rambling house.

"Can we get out now? Please?" begged Maj.

"Let me have a second. It's the only time we get to see it for the first time. In person, I mean. We don't get another chance."

Maj rolled her eyes but smiled. There they were, pots and pots and pots of crowded, dense, beautiful red geraniums.

"It looks like a painting. But lonely, too. It looks lonely," Eleanor said, more to herself than to Maj. It resembled a Klimt, all golden and abstract without being confusing. All at once warm and imposing.

"Not really," said Maj, pointing to the young woman walking out onto the porch. A cleaning lady? No. Too young. A renter? The broker would have said.

Maj was waving.

"Stop waving. Is that Crazy Anne?" Eleanor whispered, unsettled.

"Mama, Crazy Anne is dead. That girl isn't."

Then, the girl, who seemed to be very impatient, yelled, "You gonna get on out of that car or what? I *SWEAR*, some folks can't help but waste time."

"Come on, Mama. It's safe."

Eleanor and Maj got out of the car and stood side by side looking at the girl on the front porch. She looked very much at home amidst its chaos. The odd angles of the house, the assortment of Oriental carpets hanging on the porch railings, mops and brooms and big bags of potting soil spilling out from the corners. There was a large German shepherd by her side.

The girl, who Eleanor realized was closer to a child than an adult, was wearing a blue kerchief in her hair, a vain attempt at controlling what would not be controlled, and an apron covered in vintage flowers blooming large in oranges and greens and blues.

"What on God's green Earth took you so long?" she said. "Now, come on inside. We got a *LOT* to do. I mean, damn. You can't count on *NO ONE* these days."

Maj started to walk toward the stairs, but Eleanor held fast to her arm. The dog tried to go down the stairs, and the girl held its collar.

They were at a stalemate.

"Now, wait just one minute. I don't know you. And it seems to me you're . . . what's that word?" asked Eleanor.

"Freeloading?" she offered.

"No, something else . . ."

"Squatting?"

"Yes! That's it."

The girl raised an eyebrow, folded her arms and looked amused. "My name is Byrd Amore Whalen and I come from Magnolia Creek, Alabama. I somehow managed to kill my mama, Stella Amore, while I was being born, and my daddy's trying hard not to be a drunk like my granddaddy. Yes . . . You heard right. *A. M. O. R. E*. Amore. This is my rightful house, but I knew you were coming. . . . Hell, I counted on it, so you can stay."

Eleanor didn't know how to respond. But then, Maj tugged on her hand.

"Mimi would call her a Pip, or a SassyPants!" said Maj, and Eleanor saw a smile. A real, true smile. A seven-year-old smile. So she smiled, too. And, unless the girl was lying, she was an Amore. Which meant, in no uncertain terms, family.

"Is your dog nice?" asked Maj.

"Depends."

"On what?"

"On her mood. But I can tell she likes you, because she's old and sick and I ain't seen her riled like this in a dog's age. Get it? If you want, I'll let her come on down and say hi. Her name is Delores. Now, if the interrogation is over, let's go inside and get this party started."

Eleanor hesitated.

"*OH, PLEASE*. Just ask yourself, what would Josephine De'Fazio do? And do the opposite," Byrd said.

Well, she's not lying about being an Amore, thought Eleanor. *A bona fide out-of-her-mind crazy mind-reading Amore, and I don't mind one bit.* She let go of Maj, who ran up the stairs and was licked all over by the dog, and followed Byrd into the house.

"So, you're the granddaughter of the old lady who went and died and stirred all this up?"

"Her name was Mimi, and she didn't do anything. I did it."

"Rushed me, is what you did. I was always planning on ending up here. *Eventually.* But I thought I'd be an adult first. I mean, I had to go to extreme lengths and had to keep track of way too many lies in order to get myself here. Mighty aggravating. But I guess I can't hold you responsible for that."

Upon entering the house, Eleanor felt as if everything around her was moving in slow motion.

She watched as Maj let her small hand linger on the ornate brass doorknob. Then held it up to catch the dancing flecks of dust in the large open foyer. Eleanor's gaze followed the light up the staircase, to a massive stained-glass window on the second-floor landing that bathed the stairs and foyer in multicolored light. She swept her own hand through their colorful rays as Byrd took them down a long velvety dim hallway, not dark or damp, just . . . soft. As her eyes adjusted, Eleanor noted that everything she saw was architecturally uncomplicated but filled completely with plants and books and artwork. Walking past the living room, she wanted to sink into the deep cushions of the sofa and sleep for days. Fans whirred in the windows, and the air smelled like ripening plums.

A clock was ticking like a heartbeat. *Tic tock tic tock tic tock. Tic.*

"I like it here," said Maj in a hushed voice. The one Mimi always asked for—but never got—in church.

"Also," Byrd said as she led, "you are welcome. I mean, I cleaned, planted, dusted, washed. . . . Lord, I don't think I've ever done a chore in my whole life. But see, that's just proof that you don't need to do chores, watchin' people can teach you everything you need to know. Stay lazy, Maj. Trust me. Now, take a seat, or wander. But we got to get to work. And what kind of name is Maj anyway?"

"It's Elizabeth, but there's a bunch of dead Elizabeths in our family, so they call me Maj. I like it sometimes."

"Sometimes?" asked Eleanor.

Both girls looked back over their shoulders at her, wearing the same expression. Maj was happy.

"Here we are, the heart of the house. Nan's kitchen," announced Byrd as they entered through a swinging door.

The kitchen was bathed in sun and was such a contrast to the hallway that Eleanor had to squint before she could get a good look.

It was an astounding size but still felt cozy for a room so big. There was a doorway onto the back porch on the left and a double set of glass-paned French doors on the right that led to a world of plants.

"You have a greenhouse inside your house?" asked Maj.

Byrd was gathering glasses and bottles and boxes of crackers from different built-in cabinets along the turquoise walls. "It's your house. Even if I can't stomach the notion. And that's a conservatory. Or atrium. Or whatever they are called. If you think that's something, wait till I take you out back tomorrow to see the ruins. Anyone want a drink? We have lemonade and coffee and whiskey. Water, too, only I haven't been able to get the well tested because I don't own the damn house. Which is plain wrong, as it is *MY* birthright."

"Aren't you much too young to drink?" asked Eleanor.

"Oh, I understand, you haven't had your come-to-Jesus moment." Byrd sat down with three glasses, a pitcher of lemonade, and a bottle of bourbon. She poured the lemonade. The first glass halfway, the second glass three quarters of the way, and the third almost full. She then topped them off with the bourbon, keeping the strongest for herself.

"I don't think this is a good idea, and if you're thinking that baby cocktail is for Maj, you really are crazy."

"Like I said, you haven't had your come-to-Jesus moment."

"Don't be angry with her, Byrd. She's worried," said Maj.

"Am I coming on too strong?" asked Byrd.

"Just a little."

"She's right here, and she isn't worried," said Eleanor, exasperated.

"Okay." Byrd got another glass. "Here you go, Maj. Plain old boring lemonade. Now, why don't you take a seat, and we can figure all this out. How about you ask the questions and I try to answer them. Good idea?"

Maj gave Byrd the thumbs-up.

"Let's start with: How old are you?" asked Eleanor.

"I am fourteen years old. And I can't stand it, because it's an even year. I prefer odd years."

"Okay, well, you are too young to live alone, so who lives here with you?"

"Alive or dead?"

"Alive, please." *Smart-ass.*

"No one, I'm on my own. And before you get your panties in a bunch over neglect or abandonment or what have you . . . wait, what time is it?" Byrd pointed at a large, round, industrial-looking clock. "Oh, look, you got to love good timing. You can ask questions for about thirty more seconds, then that phone over there is going to ring."

"I'd guessed you had the Amore sight, but if that phone rings I'm thinking yours is a stronger strain."

"Actually, I'm a GODDAMNED HYBRID . . . so, yes, it's a stronger strain. I got all kinds of witch blood colliding in me, and I bet young Maj here's a hybrid, too. Because until she got out of that car of yours, I thought I had the lion's share of those talents. But I'll tell you what, she's givin' me a run for my money. I'm not sure how I feel about that yet." She winked at Maj.

Eleanor opened her mouth to speak, and the phone rang.

"Got to love my aunt's propensity for punctuality. Sorry to burst your bubble, but she calls every single day at 2:45 p.m. Listen close and try to catch on, okay?"

Byrd went to the phone and picked up the heavy black receiver.

"Hello, Aunt Wyn. . . . Of course I knew it was you. Well who the hell else would be calling? No. She's right here. Yes. Well, I'll tell you what, it was a miracle! I can't quite get over it. We woke up this morning and I brought in her breakfast tray like I do every morning, I know, I'm a saint. . . . Yep, you got that right. She likes those awful raw eggs of hers. . . . And I said,

'Good morning, Miss Eleanor,' as usual. I said it really loud, though. Yes, I read the sign language books. But I had a *TRAY* in my hands, for god's sake, Aunt Wyn. I didn't grow another set of arms all of a sudden. . . ."

Eleanor sat at the kitchen table, staring in disbelief at the conversation she was hearing. Maj, wide-eyed with delight, held her hand up over her mouth to stifle her laughter.

Byrd held the phone out for a moment, and a child's tantrum echoed out. She placed it back at her ear, rolling her eyes conspiratorially at Maj and Eleanor. ". . . Oh, is the baby sick? Shut his damn mouth up, then. Look, do you want to hear about the miracle or what? That's what I thought. So, she just looks at me and says, 'You don't have to shout, I'm not deaf!' And I almost fainted, I swear . . . *Uh-huh.* . . . *Mmm* . . . *Hmmm* . . . How am I supposed to know? The doctor came straightaway and deemed it hysterical deafness or something like that. The long and short of it is, she's talking now. Would you like to talk to her? Thought so. Hold on."

Byrd held out the phone, and Eleanor took a large gulp of her laced lemonade. She glared at Byrd as she took the receiver.

"Hello? Yes . . . of course . . . I understand. . . . You know how those things go. I'm sure there will be tests. No, I'm not concerned, I had a stressful year, it seems. I'm glad you're relieved. . . . *Mmm hmmmm.* A handful. Yes, I'll have her call you tomorrow."

Eleanor hung up and sat back down across from Byrd.

"You didn't snitch. I think we're going to get along just fine," said Byrd, grinning.

"That was unfair, Byrd."

"It was funny, though. And it was also useful. I can't actually believe she fell for it. I've been here since May!"

"Look at me, Byrd. And listen very closely. I don't know who you think you are, or who you think I am. And I'm not going to make any waves here for you because you have, in fact, proved yourself fairly useful. I won't argue that this little ambush hasn't been successful, but don't think for one second that you will walk all over me. Seems like you have a little too much practice walking around on other people. Walking above them. That's not your fault, you've been spoiled. So I will let you stay here with us. But you will never tell a lie about me again without me agreeing first. You will help me take care of Maj. And you will be an equal partner in the upkeep of this house. Do we have an agreement?"

"You're awful pretty when you're mad," Byrd sighed.

"Do we have an agreement?"

"You'd let me stay here with you indefinitely?"

As Eleanor considered her question, she looked at Byrd's beautiful, strong, open face, allowing herself to acknowledge just how right it all felt. As if she'd been expecting to know this girl . . . to find shelter in this house. She felt safe. *How long has it been since I felt safe?* she wondered. When she finally replied, her words sounded far more stern than she felt. Because, like it or not, she'd have two powerful headstrong little wards on her hands before she knew it, and she had to lay the law down now.

"Yes. If you agree. And I suppose we have to get you registered for school, right?"

"You can't make me go to school. I'm already done with that mess. I'm a genius."

"I'll speak to your aunt about that. And if that's the case, you can help me teach Maj. I'm homeschooling her."

"Cursed, visionary children never do fare well with peers or teachers in traditional academic settings. Nor do their dogs. I speak from *experience*," said Byrd, petting Delores.

"Are you going to agree or not?"

"Agreed."

Maj clapped.

"Oh! I clean forgot! I have a little something I thought you might like, Maj." Byrd opened the doors to the conservatory, letting out the sweet, earthy scent of violet and sage. The floor was tiled in black-and-white squares, and a red velvet couch with throw pillows and blankets sat in the center of all the plant vines and pots. Byrd reentered the kitchen with a cigar box. "Here you go, kid. Have fun while your mama and I talk through this thing. Don't worry, Elly, I smoked all the cigars."

"Mama, look!" Maj cried, opening up the box.

It was full of red crayons. Permanent Geranium Lake, to be exact.

4

Byrd in the Kitchen with a Candlestick

A tour of the house revealed a wide first floor with the foyer front and center. A small living room and a library made up the left side of the house, and the right was a larger living room with a fireplace and a piano. Both sets of rooms had entrances to and from the hallway and the kitchen that ran the length of the back. The second floor was narrower than the first, with four equal-sized bedrooms and a large bathroom. The third floor of the house narrowed dramatically and had two bedrooms and a bath. There was also an attic. And, above that, like the topper on a cake, one lone cupola with windows all around.

Eleanor fell in love with each nook and cranny.

It had been a whirlwind tour. Byrd seemed to be on some

kind of schedule Eleanor didn't yet have the agenda for. Everything blurred together. Richly colored wallpapers and deep couches, sturdy four-post beds and white clawfoot bathtubs. Circular windows near doorways. Stained glass everywhere like the witch balls sold at fairs—round glass balls with strands of colored glass blown inside the centers, said to catch any evil and capture it in the web of color. (Byrd refused to linger in any of the rooms. "Seeing this house without the background information is a waste of time. It will look entirely different once you know its history.")

Only the necessary bags were removed from the car, and the U-Haul, still packed, stood lonely and alien against the darkening sky.

Back in the kitchen, Eleanor looked in the refrigerator. It was a very old model, one that closed with a metal vise.

"I kind of wish you'd taken care of the food situation as well as you seem to have taken care of the house. I see nothing in here I can make for dinner."

"I have the essentials. Bourbon and pie."

"Pie might do . . . for now," said Eleanor.

"What kind of pie?" asked Maj, pleased by the idea of dessert for dinner.

"Well, there's the usual, you know, apple, apple crumb, peach, cherry, you know. But my favorite is the lemon pawpaw. It's my very own creation."

"I think I'll stick with apple."

"Maj, I'm disappointed. I thought you'd be more adventurous," said Byrd.

Eleanor held her breath. Maj had a fine-tuned, dry, adult

sense of humor. But only with those she trusted and loved. She tended to get all balled up inside and defensive when anyone else criticized her about anything.

"No offense to the pawpaw," said Maj.

Eleanor exhaled.

"So, are you ready to explain all this mystery, Miss Byrd? What are we running out of time for?"

"That man, Johnny Colder, is coming here on Sunday. That leaves us two days, not counting the rest of today, to find whatever he might find . . . first."

"I'll admit, I could have waited to move here until after that 'circus' was gone," Eleanor said. "But every bone in my body ached to get here before he did. And I've learned it's futile to fight against the Amore instincts. Still, you've been here since May. With your strong Amore ways, and all your cleaning up and gardening, you haven't found anything. Have you considered maybe there's nothing to find? Maybe our mutual need to get here was more about what's going on right now between you and me and Maj. Maybe all this is a simple case of blood calling blood."

"*NO*. It's much more than that. I *SWEAR*, why do all my people have to flirt with ignorance before they accept who they are. Look here, there is some goddamn truth, some dark secret that is simply taunting me. I just haven't found it out yet. Anyway, that's why *I NEED YOU*. I figure if I tell you all the stories of the women who lived here, maybe you can help me put it all together. I'm convinced their lives are like a treasure map or something. Clues hidden inside their journals and documents and stories. And I'm so close to all of it I can't see the forest for the damn trees."

"Please help out your poor Yankee cousin. Why is it important that we find anything? It's going to be a pain in the ass to deal with those fools, but at the end of the day, they'll wrap up and we will know everything (or the nothing) that they find. Byrd, what am I missing here? You have to tell me everything."

Byrd sat down and started speaking slowly.

"There were rumors about this house and this land. Rumors that women were held captive and murdered in the wine cellar. Which isn't that interesting *AT ALL* if you ask me. It's been done before. And then there were rumors of dark magical curses. Stories about toxic plants and two-headed cats. None of that bothers me. It's humdrum yawn material. What bothers me is being *EXPOSED* without knowing how to control it. Like having your clothes yanked off when you never even got a good look at your own naked body. What if you had three boobies and a half a tail? See? Interesting if you got a chance to hint at the freak show before they exposed it, but if not . . . Elly, if we don't control the secrets Johnny might find, then we got to live all up inside *someone else's idea of who we are.*

"I ain't havin' that.

"It's one thing to announce we are the surviving members of the most terrifying family in these parts. It's another thing entirely to be told you come from a long line of psychotic women who deserved everything their sorry asses got. One notion is strong, the other is weak. And I can't abide weakness. I just can't."

Eleanor looked at Maj and then back at Byrd. "So . . . you want to make sure we have a say in our own narrative, is that right?"

"Exactly. It could be the difference between Maj and me growing up as the badasses of the Eastern Shore . . . or just two more women in a long line of forgettable sick-in-the-head nothings. It's the difference between 'the Witch House—I can't believe you're one of them! Tell me, can you really make it rain?' and 'Inbreeding. They say they have power, but all they have is sick, thin blood!'"

Eleanor was immediately reminded of the reasons she'd high-tailed it to the Witch House in the first place. She wanted Maj to be able to define her own reality. To be able to breathe inside who she was, versus who the world expected and wanted her to be. To find meaning in her differences instead of covering them up.

"Okay, okay, I get it, and I agree," she said. "You can stop now. Where do we start? We really need a historical society. Is there one in downtown Haven Port?"

"Haven Port has a thriving historical society. It's one of the only things this ghost town does right. Only it's not downtown."

"Where is it?"

"It's your lucky day. *I'm* the historical society."

Byrd walked over to the oven and pulled out a basket full of papers. "Me, and these. Man, do we have a night in front of us."

"You don't cook much, do you, Byrd?" asked Maj, with a giggle.

7:00 P.M.

Notes and photos and magazine clippings littered almost every surface in the kitchen.

"So this one is about how the house here now is built from the rubble of the house that was here first," Eleanor said, examining another *Virginia Is for Lovers* brochure.

Byrd read it aloud. "The original Haven House was thought to be charmed in some way. Everyone who went there said it was the most beautiful piece of land. One notable occasion was when Thomas Jefferson was said to have visited shortly before he died, where he exclaimed: 'If only I'd designed Monticello this way!'" Byrd and Eleanor both took a moment to question the verity of that statement.

"And Nan Amore, my great-great-aunt, who was also your great-great- . . . *great*-grandmother, she's the one who built this house, the Witch House," Eleanor said.

"A: that's a lot of 'greats,' and 2: you catch on quick. Maybe your sight isn't so backwards after all."

"Excuse me?"

"Well, I've been thinkin', and I guess there's all kinds of levels to these gifts we seem to share. You know, like in school when they take a kid out of regular classes and put 'em in special ones because they're not readin' on the same level or what have you."

"You mean special education classes?"

"Exactly. And just like those kids aren't upset about that reality, you don't have to be upset that you got a little gypped in the psychic department. Hell, if we were all like me . . . or Maj,

51

we'd figure out all the secrets of the universe and life as we know it would end. Or be plain boring. So, yeah. See? You saved the world!" teased Byrd.

"Shut it. You *need* me. Remember? Now, what else do we have about the house? I'm not finding anything that proves or disproves or even speaks to those rumors." Then she mumbled under her breath, "She just called me a learning disabled psychic."

"Well, there are spectacular reviews about the land. I've been thinking we should spend tomorrow digging beyond the gardens I already searched. But I don't know where to start."

"The deed says it's only five acres."

"The original acreage was over forty. Took up the whole peninsula, probably stretched into Maryland. That's a whole lot of digging."

"Can we dig now?" asked Maj. "I'd like to go outside and see the moo, moo, moo, moo, mooon. And Crazy Anne said I have to see the ponies." Maj had been patiently listening, eating too much pie (even the lemon pawpaw), and coloring, and she was plain old bored.

"Tomorrow. It's too dark anyhow," said Byrd.

"You see Crazy Anne, too," said Eleanor, with a deep sigh. "It feels a little strange. I don't remember deciding to be the older, wiser, silly, slow-on-the-uptake grown-up."

Byrd rolled her eyes. "She's my great-grandmother. And though it irks me to *no end*, I haven't seen her. And she won't talk to me. Or can't. You know, I gotta admit, it feels nice to have conversations about these things with people who understand. It's fun to see others react to things like ghost spotting, but even shock and awe can get boring after a spell."

"I think that's a good way to describe family. The ability to simply . . . be. And to know. And to not have to pretend," Eleanor said, giving a little half smile.

"Sounds great. Call me when you find one of those," said Byrd.

"But they're all here, Byrd," whispered Maj. "Nan and Anne and Lucy. Others, too. Like Ava. Anne's the loudest, but they're all here, and they are your family. They are *our* family."

"Well, they haven't haunted *ME* yet," said Byrd. "And trust me, I never met a spirit who didn't love to haunt me. And these are the ones I NEED TO TALK TO. Figures. And yes, sarcasm runs in this supposed family of ours. And a love of pie."

"They already told you all their stories. They're right up here," said Maj, tapping at her forehead. "Now you just got to tell Mama."

"I guess we could start with Nan. If you get a notebook from the library, we could start to draw up a chart or something," suggested Eleanor.

"We got a family tree right here," Byrd said, pouting.

"I know. And it's lovely. But if we write down dates and facts as you tell me her story, maybe we can make a connection you haven't made yet."

Byrd's face lit up. "Finally. You are useful! You are! No,

I mean it. That's perfect. I'll grab a pad. Sometimes it's the simplest things, I *SWEAR*." Byrd practically skipped out of the room.

"Maj, it looks like me and Byrd will be burning a little midnight oil. How about we get you all set up on the couch in the conservatory? We'll leave the doors open. That way you can hear us talking and you won't be scared."

"All right. But not because I'm scared. This house doesn't scare me one bit. But it can scare. It likes to scare. Sometimes it feels bad that it makes people sad. Sometimes it feels good to watch them run."

Byrd caught the last part of Maj's words as she reentered the kitchen, and she stopped short.

For the first time all day, it was Byrd and Eleanor who shared a look. One part worry, one part understanding, and one part alarm.

And the clock went *tic tock tic tock tic tock. Tic.*

9:00 P.M.

Maj burrowed deeply into a pillow nest on the couch in the conservatory as Delores curled up at her feet.

"Are you cozy, Maj?" Eleanor asked, covering her with a heavy crocheted blanket.

"Yes, very much. I like it here with this lamp, and I can see and hear you both at the table, like I'm watching a play, or TV. Don't worry, Mama. I won't stay up. Tomorrow I get to play outside. Thank you for bringing me here. Byrd, will you tell me a bedtime story?"

Byrd was lighting a candle. "A scary sort of bedtime story? Or a romantic one, because I don't like romantic stories. Not one bit." Byrd walked up, looking as though the word *romantic* had given off an awful smell.

"I don't like kissing stories. Aren't you going to tell Nan's story to Mama? The one with the girl covered in melted glass? Tell me that one."

"It's sad."

"I know."

"It's scary."

"I know."

"If it's sad and scary, I might just have to be a big party pooper, girls," Eleanor broke in. "I am the grown-up. This can't become some kind of free-for-all. Pie for dinner, sleeping on sofas, ghost playmates."

"I already know the story, Mama. I just want to hear it again."

Eleanor sat on the couch, and Maj rested her head on her mother's lap.

"I think I'm too tired to argue. But you promise to try and go to sleep. When we're done for the night, I'll bring you upstairs. I'll even carry you. Deal?"

"Deal."

"Okay, Byrd. Tell us about Nan."

"Okay, I guess here is just as good as the kitchen table. This story starts with a doorknob."

"That's not a very good start to a bedtime story," said Maj.

"You aren't even in a bed," Byrd retorted. "Oh, FINE. Once upon a time . . . does that work?" she asked. She had lit all the candles in the room. They flickered warmly. The one on the small side table reminded Eleanor of the doorknob.

"Yes."

"Once upon a time, at the very tip of the very coast of this very large nation (in an even vaster world) . . . there was a house. The people who lived there were rich, and those who saw the house thought there was no finer place in all the world. But even then, it had a sad history. Built on sour land, it soured the people who lived there. When Nan came across the ocean, she brought light into a dark place. Only, see, darkness always has a way of seeping in. A closet is left unclosed. A bed unmade. An argument. A lie. A secret. And when the dark came back, it came with a fury.

"Nan built this house knowing there had to be a place for both dark and light to live together.

"That's why it's blue and white. She painted the house as a warning. 'Can't be a good day without clouds. Can't trust a cloudless sky.'"

"Is that the same kind of thing that the words on the gate mean?" asked Maj.

"Yes. Kind of. Hold on . . . who's telling this story? Didn't you tell us you'd be going to sleep?"

"Carry on," said Maj in a fake grown-up voice.

Byrd cleared her throat. "Well, our Nan knew a little bit about life being untrustworthy. The world had taken too much from her. So much, that at one point, all she had left in the whole wide world was a pretty doorknob. But before that, she'd had so much love. Because the story . . . *our* story . . . yours, mine, and your mama's, all starts in Italy. Once upon a time in Italy. . . ."

The Book of

Nan

1900–1910

5

Nan Amore

As the sun rose over the rubble of the heaven she'd sought for so long, Nan Amore stood in the center of the destroyed foundation of Haven House, willing it all back. Something glistened from under a blackened piece of wood, and reaching down, and under, her fingers brushing against the sticking of dewy green grass (*fairies, Mama, that's fairy water, right?*), she picked the familiar object up without being able to identify it, so out of its context, yet so familiar it made her head spin. It made the sorrow and shock bloom into a nest of memories. It was the doorknob to Haven House. The one she'd touched with trepidation at the beginning, the one that grew into a symbol of comfort and safety as the years went by. She ran her fingers along its flower-etched surface until the heavy brass pulled her to the ground. It was all gone. "Give them back," she cried into the unforgiving morning. Her yelling didn't make it rain, didn't do anything but beat against the buzzing newly born sorrow nest, letting loose millions of stinging memories instead.

6

Nan in the Barn with a Boy

ITALY, 1900

Her beautiful mother sat in the sunshine and moved back and forth in her rocking chair. The creaking of it soothed Nan, though she didn't want to admit it. It was her birthday, she was turning sixteen, and what was she doing? Snapping the ends off green beans.

"I should be in Paris at a cafe, not here helping cook my own birthday meal," she said.

Her mother smiled, tilting her face toward the sun and closing her eyes. Nan loved the way her mama's hair collected all the light of the afternoon.

"But don't you agree, Mama?" she asked, putting the bowl of beans on the table. She then kneeled next to her mother, putting her head on her lap so that the rocking chair stilled. "I love you, you know I would never go far away. I'm just terribly bored. And I don't even like beans. Mama, are you listening to me?"

"This chair," said her mother, dreamily, "has rocked babies in our family for as long as anyone can remember. I rocked you right after you were born. The sunlight was just like this. I'd never seen anything more beautiful than you. We'd only just come to live here, and I was still trying to make a living selling the herbs and treatments. You are a wild soul, Anna. Much like I was. But you lack the fear I had. You've never taken any of my teaching seriously enough. You must start to learn the old ways, Anna. Without these skills, this community will not accept you when I am gone. I may have done you a disservice, allowing you so much freedom, so much safety."

Nan, not caring for the moment that she had just turned sixteen, curled up in her mother's lap like a little girl. Mama only called her Anna when she was serious. "I'll never have to worry about that, because you will never leave me," Nan said.

Her mother kissed the top of her head, and the two silently rocked back and forth together, looking out over the rolling hills and the dirt road that snaked its way to the horizon.

Nan's childhood had been like no other, at least not like that of the other children growing up in the small town of Stella di Perduto, where young girls were constrained by religion, the patriarchal culture, and violent crime attached to family pride.

The Amore family on the edge of the village was different.

Ava Amore was as feared as she was respected. Her curing, healing ways were known all throughout southern Italy and perhaps beyond. Ava tried to teach her children, Nan especially, the healing arts, but be it laziness on their part, or business on her own, not one of them knew enough to keep her little family safe.

When Nan was older, during those moments she dared to look back to that time and that place, the sun was always bright in the sky. The landscape was gentle. There were gentle rolling hills, gentle flowing rivers, gentle breezes. Nan often lamented not absorbing any of those qualities.

Maybe if she'd spent more time appreciating the world surrounding her, instead of daydreaming about distant shores, she would have been less reckless. Maybe if she'd paid attention to the way her mother's hands lingered on her hair, she would have noticed the impermanence of safety.

We never really know how much we'll miss people and places until they're gone.

No, Nan wasn't gentle or nostalgic. She was more like the colors surrounding her, brilliant and vivid. Green treetops against a blue sky with white fluffy clouds, the purple of the sage, the yellow of the squash and daisies and dandelions. The light, fresh green of white grapes and the deep blackish purple of the red grapes, the dark green grape vines and orange stucco on her home that faded pink in the sunlight. And then there were the blue-gray stone pathways that led through high yellow and green grasses on the paths into the village proper. The colors made Nan long for a brighter light inside herself.

And the air, ocean saltwater with hints of garlic, grapes, hardworking men, lavender, roses . . . Nan loved the smell of roses. Her mother would pour her a tub once a week, and when the roses were in bloom, she would add the petals.

"May I get Florencia to finish snapping these, Mama? I want to have my bath."

"I suppose so, but don't be mean when you ask her. You know she always feels I favor you."

"That's because you do," said Nan, kissing her mother on her cheek before flouncing outside and almost toppling the bowl full of beans.

See Nan in a metal washtub, her bare sun-kissed shoulders, her graceful legs. The tub is stationed just outside the kitchen, the door that overflows with herbs from pots and tangled window boxes. . . . See her floating just under the rose petal–dappled surface. Her eyes rest shut and she can smell the fragrance steeping, steaming, streaming out of each perfect petal. She dreams that she is in Paris, or any other fast city, and she is dancing, her hair wildly falling down against her back. She is the belle of the ball. The mysterious young woman from anywhere. See her sister, Florencia, and her brother, Vincent, spy on her from behind the sheets on the line. See her build a future that will never come.

Nan Amore had big plans. But she knew that to travel in the world, she'd have to pay her own way. She had no intention of marrying, so she was taking in sewing from those in the village. She didn't make much, but it was a start. As she sewed she thought of all the places she would go. First, France. Her father, before he died, always told stories about the coffee in France, how bitter . . . but what does coffee matter?

"Anna! Wash your hair!" her mother shouted through the window. To Nan she sounded a million miles away.

But Nan washed her hair dutifully, then called her mother to help her out of the tub. "Mama, you are the most beautiful of anyone I've ever seen." Ava Amore was petite, smaller than Nan or her sister. She had red hair, bright red with no signs of gray. Nan and her siblings looked like changeling . . . black hair, black eyes, round curves, high cheekbones, young, taut skin. Her mother showed her age on her face and her hands. Frowning was her resting face, and the frowns had created deep creases in her mother's skin. Nan loved them; she would trace them when they would lie together in the fields after picnics or at night when her mother snuggled with them, telling them stories of the magical world they supposedly came from. Nan's only fear about her wonderful plans was being away from her curious, warm-hearted, ever-frowning magical mother.

A month after her birthday, Giancarlo began calling on Nan Amore.

When he came to the house, Nan made fun of him. He was such a dandy. He wore a fancy suit—the same one every time— and had a silly little half-grown mustache that seemed more like a smudge of dirt than a symbol of his manhood. And his hair was slicked back with too much oil. He may have been handsome, Nan didn't know or care.

She'd been furious when Mama gave him permission to court her. But whatever anger Nan felt paled in comparison to the rage Ava unleashed on her when Giancarlo left.

"You will *not* destroy this opportunity. Do you know how difficult it was to find a suitable man who isn't scared of coming too close to us? Or who doesn't assume you and your sister have already had relations with the devil? Do not laugh, children. This is what is on the minds of everyone you see. Don't fool yourselves. Sometimes the only way to stay safe is to simply agree. And that works both ways. Understand?" Her children nodded. "Nan, be kind to that boy. He is your future."

"Mama, why are you entertaining this folly? Are you trying to marry me off, be rid of me?" asked Nan.

"Florencia, Vincent . . . go outside. Now," said Ava. Then she turned, placing both hands on Nan's shoulders, and roughly pushed her against the wall.

"As a matter of fact, I am. You are not a child any longer. And you are not protected by the ways of our people. This is not your fault . . . I thought we'd have more time. I thought I could teach you, and then you would apprentice, and once I was gone you would simply take my place and protect Florencia and Vincent. Listen to me, Nan, I am running out of time. You will have to marry."

"What do you mean, are you sick?"

"Not yet. I have some time. And I have some cures. But the chance, the real risk of it, helped me realize I will not be here forever. Just do as I say. I can't force you to marry him. But I *can* try to pave you a road. I did not raise children who are close-minded to ideas. Give this a chance."

Nan agreed.

So Nan and Giancarlo courted under the watchful eye of her siblings. But, after a few weeks, Vincent and Florencia grew bored tagging along. They didn't believe this sweaty, insecure Giancarlo would try anything improper with their Nan, so they let them walk alone.

Only, it wasn't Giancarlo they had to worry about. If she was supposed to consider marrying him, Nan needed to know if she could love him. She wanted to be touched, to feel the romance, to have her body explored. She led him to the barn and laid herself on the hay. He stood there, looking at her, sweating and dabbing his forehead with a handkerchief. "And what are you doing Nan? Taking a nap?" He laughed nervously.

"I want you to touch me." She said it unafraid of how he would react. No one thought she was innocent anyway. And besides, she didn't love him. She looked at him as the first adventure of her life. He was on her in but a moment, hurried and grunting, squeezing and groping. "Slow down . . ." she said. He tried, but when his fingers found their way inside her, he just shoved and shoved until her entire body began to shiver. She arched against his hand, never wanting him to slow down again, and then she shoved his hand away. She could see the bulge in his pants.

"Please . . ." he seemed to squeak out of his throat. She didn't know how she knew what to do, but she did. She undid his pants and took his swollen thing into her mouth. It didn't take long. When he left that day, she thought he would never come back, that she had shamed them both somehow, but she was wrong. He came back the next week. This time he led her to the barn.

They repeated their encounter, all fingers and mouths, but took more time. He played with her breasts and kissed them while his fingers worked, and she shuddered harder and faster. But they knew not to go further; they knew they could not sin all the way.

"We could do it if you marry me," he said.

"You don't want to marry me," she said.

Because she didn't want to marry him. She didn't even like him. She liked the way his hands and his mouth felt on her body (her body *loved* him), but other than that, the mere thought of Giancarlo made her want to vomit. She just didn't understand. How can you not love someone and still want to do all of those things with them? How could you not want to marry someone who you want to force into mortal sin? It just didn't make sense.

Their trysts in the barn went on for a month. And then, one evening, it was just too much. They had grown bored with fingers and mouths. "Can I?" he whispered.

She was wet between her legs, and there was a throbbing so intense she could not catch her breath; an emptiness that needed filling. Her breasts were bared, nipples erect, and his lips and mustache and teeth were on her like an animal and she wanted him to rip them right off of her. "Yes," she said, and it was done. It was glorious. He entered her and the fit was immediate, the whole world came into focus. They moved to-gether, frantic to finally feel each other from the inside out; they moved as one and came together in unison, holding each other's mouths to hush the moans. Immediately she knew she had made a horrible mistake. She'd unleashed some deep sorrow inside of her soul. A sadness that nothing, not the blue sky, the green grass, or even her mama's clean-smelling hands could erase.

She refused to see him the following week, and the week after that. She had Florencia and Vincent turn him away at the door.

By the time the morning sickness started, she hated even the thought of him.

Her mother knew. She didn't want to know, but she did. She didn't say much, simply, "Now you have no choice."

Nan stood in the small room above the butcher shop and surveyed herself in the mirror. Layers of lace could not hide the bulge at her waist. Her face looked older, her hair was brittle. "I don't make a good bride, Mama. I don't know why you would inflict this punishment on me. There were other ways."

"Do you think I want this for you? I have spent the past months writing letters to everyone I can think of. No one is willing to help us. We are alone, Nan. Tell me, what other ways do you see?"

"I could run away to Paris and say I was a widow."

"With what money? With what skills? You will end up in the streets selling your body and soul just to eat. And what about your brother and sister? Nan, be sensible. Once you are married and the baby comes, there are things we can do. But first we must make things right so these people will begin to accept you as one of them."

"I don't want to be one of them."

Ava stopped fussing with the dress. "You do not have to be. I would not want you to be. It is time you hear about our people. Not the fairy tales I've spun for you. The real truth. Most humans align themselves with blood. Chart their family tree through mothers and fathers. From as far back as we can recall, our people did not group ourselves by surname or lineage. We grouped ourselves by abilities. At the beginning of any society, people build upon commonality. Ours was not about land, or farming, or fishing, or war. Ours was simply safety. Each of those new societies had rules and beliefs, cultures that had no room for those who were able to do or see things no one understood. One seemed to be fine. A witch doctor, a healer, a soothsayer, a wise man . . . there was room for one such person, but not for any others. So, we were sent out, or we fled from the fires and the nooses and the stones. Slowly, over generations, we gathered in a stretch of land by the Black Sea. And we were safe. Can you imagine, Nan, a world where all the strengths of sight and alchemy and incantation were united? We were a powerful people, but we were smart, too. We stayed within the confines and waited for the world to catch up with us. Then, the plague. Word spread that there was a community where no one was dying. The irony is that there was nothing mystical in our survival, we simply understood how the virus worked. Many people came for help, and the elders of our clan chose, fatefully, not to share our knowledge. The price of pride, Nan, is death. Remember that. As more and more armies arrived, we were charged with the cause of the illness. And instead of waiting for our slaughter, we scattered. Used their own fear to create a mist that helped us escape to all corners of the world. And we stay that way all these many hundreds of years later. Alone and hiding amongst those that would kill us."

"Why didn't you find each other, band together to build again?"

"We saw what happened to those that refused to let go of their ways. Exiled, persecuted. No, better we scatter . . . find each other again in a peaceful world. This means we are all lost, on purpose, yes . . . but lost all the same. Still . . . when we meet those from our lost world, we know. It's not by name, or relation. There are many names that can be connected, it's true. But it's more of a glow. Or a tether. Yes, like that. The pull you feel that outweighs anything else. That is when we know we've found our home. And when enough of us find each other again, we will be free."

Vincent and Florencia came in bursting through the door. Vincent looked as if he'd been crying.

"Mama! Giancarlo is gone. The wedding is canceled. What will we do?"

"We will go home," said Ava, defeated. "Nan, take off the dress. I will be downstairs trying to repair what has happened. Come, Vincent."

After her mother left, Nan asked Florencia to help her undo the buttons. As they worked together, untying, unfastening, Florencia lectured Nan.

"All those silly hours daydreaming. You wanted romance . . . and you got it, on a grand scale, only it wasn't what you meant, was it? . . . It was romance between two bodies, not two people. You should have been more specific. I know that no one else is speaking of your sins, but I wanted you to know, as you stand before Christ and the Virgin Mother, that you are my sister no longer. I wanted to be the one to tell you that Giancarlo ran away to America without you. The only reason he agreed to marry you in the first place was that he thought Mama had money to send you both away. Are you surprised? Did you think he loved you? He does not. His father was so distressed by the thought of having you in his home, he went to the Don and begged for the money. And now the whole family is on their way to Palermo with pocketfuls of cash. This is how much they hate us, hate *you*. I wish you would die so I could restore some decency to our family name."

Nan held her tongue as Florencia raged on, but her heart was breaking. She hadn't meant to break the bonds of family. Never, not once, had she said she wanted to escape them—just see a bit of the world. Feel different air and wear fancy clothes. Dance.

When her sister finally stopped, Nan took a deep breath and said, "Our family name means love, Florencia. And I will always love you. You are my quiet, pretty, pious baby sister. But hear me when I say, I do not want to marry, I do not want a child, and I do not want to go to America. I am not a bit upset at this turn of events. Besides, isn't this child punishment enough?"

"It is not," Florencia hissed. She would not return home with Ava, Vincent, and Nan. The priest offered her salvation and a home with the nuns a town over. She would be redeemed, and then married. She would have a respectable life.

1901

"Nan! What are you doing!" cried her mother as Nan pounded her belly. She bathed inside now, in her tiny room, pouring water from the pitcher into the basin and washing herself roughly with a cloth. Rubbing her skin until it bled. It was no longer a life of roses.

"I do not want this baby! I do not want this life!" she cried.

"Hush now, it will all be fine. Please, Nan, I beg you, do not say such things. You will harm the child. And I know you want exactly that, to do harm. But we can not undo what is meant. It is a worse sin than any of the trivial things all these people worry about. You cannot alter fate. If you were fated to lose this child, you would. All you are doing now is summoning all the bad feelings. Do you want her to be a monster?"

"Her?"

"She will be a girl. A little girl. You will name her Ava, after me. That way, I can try to protect her. Neither death nor oceans can stop blood, my love. I will be with you, through her."

Ava opened up a towel, and Nan stepped out of the tub and into her mother's embrace the way she did when she was small. She allowed herself to be dried, dressed, and then she sat and rocked in the ancient chair.

"You will take Vincent to America," said her mother.

"What?"

"Nan, I have raised you with suggestions. I have tried to allow you the luxury of no boundaries and endless possibilities. That has been a mistake. I tried to shelter you from the reality of the world in which you've been born. I can not shelter you any longer. I am dying."

Nan rocked. She'd sensed for months that the light inside her mother was fading. "There is no cure? No magic?"

"No. As I said before, we do not argue with fate. An illness, a death, can feel right or wrong. When it is wrong, it can be altered. When it is right, it is our responsibility to let it become part of a bigger plan."

"You sound like that disgusting priest. God and plans."

"All religion comes from the same place, child. The same pool of knowledge at the edge of a connected understanding. But it does not matter what you think right now. Right now you must act. I have saved enough money to last you and your brother and sister a lifetime if you were to stay here. But it is only enough to secure passage for you and Vincent on a ship to America. Tomorrow we go to Palermo. The boat sails in one week."

"Mama! I will not go! I will stay here and take your place. I will take care of Vincent. And when he is older I will travel. Please, Mama. Don't make me leave you now. You still have time to teach me your ways. . . . The village will approve. How will they get by without a healer?"

"You are forgetting something, love. These people would have forgiven a widow. And, had my original plan worked out, that is exactly what you would have been, once everything had settled. But, no matter, we need a new plan. They will not forgive a whore who consorts with the devil. Don't look so shocked. I do not say that to be mean. And it is not something I believe. But once I'm dead, you will be marked, and they will blame each bad thing that happens on you. Each stillborn child. Each drought. Each flood. Each illness. This is a matter of life and death, Nan. You do not have a choice. Vincent deserves a future, and Florencia will be returning from her stay with the Catholics to take care of me. She's protected by her stupidity and the need for those who hate us to feel they've done their Christian duty. There's not an interesting bone in her body. There, I've said it. Now, go collect your things. We leave at first light. When you get to America there will be people waiting for you. A family who left years ago. They owe me a great debt. Vincent will find a home with them. And you must find Giancarlo."

"Why? I could simply tell everyone I'm widowed. Then I can be free. It's very American to be free."

"No woman is ever free, not even in America. You will have a baby who will need you. You have no true skills and no money. I don't care whether you stay with that man or not, all I care about is that you stay safe and you bring your child into a safe world. You must be with people who already know the truth. I thought I was free. Now look at this mess. You will be better than me. Smarter. I demand it."

Nan packed her things and got ready for her voyage across the sea.

Afraid people would notice her belly, Nan was forced to layer her clothes. Afraid that Vincent would be considered an orphan,

Nan was forced to become his mother. Afraid that her mother would haunt her forever, Nan was forced to love her unborn child. She would not look at her mother as they stood in line at the teeming docks in Palermo. Sweating hot with hormones and too many clothes, as she boarded the boat with her brother weeping at her side, a steamer trunk, and the rocking chair, everything seemed impossible. Be careful what you wish for, her mother always said. She'd wished for adventure, for a life away from everything she knew. But she never once thought to add her own joy into that incantation. The devil is in the details.

7

Lady Liberty on the Hudson with a Torch

1901–1902

The voyage wasn't colorful or full of interesting people. It was long, uncomfortable. She didn't make any friends or find any true kindred spirits. She'd had one fleeting moment of hope that maybe a handsome American returning from a European tour would see her on the lower decks and fall in love at first sight. Then she wouldn't have to find Giancarlo at all. She looked for him, this handsome fiction she'd created, for days. But all she found was loneliness, deep hunger, and physical pain. The hate grew. Vomiting and mad with a homesickness she never imagined she could feel, she began to starve herself, and the baby inside. "I don't care if we both die," she said. And then, hearing how some were sent back home if they arrived with illness, she ate everything in sight trying to gain back her strength. And then there was Vincent, who didn't speak a word. He stared silently out at sea. He slept. He ate. He hid in Nan's skirts.

"Get off of me you little sissy," growled Nan, trying to at least make him angry. All he did was move closer to her, and by the time the Statue of Liberty rose above Nan and Vincent Amore, she admitted defeat. When they arrived at Ellis Island (*Isola delle Lacrime*: the island of tears), she was in labor and flushed with a high fever. Waiting in line, her hands gripping documents and dragging her trunk, her stomach contracting, she thought she would die. She hoped she would die. As they disembarked they were herded, like cattle, up a wide pitched staircase that was dizzying.

"Vincent, the baby is coming," she said. "You'll need to talk. Not for me, but for you. There is no way I can help you if you don't stop this nonsense."

Nan held the rail and slid down onto a stair. She was sure she'd be trampled and Vincent would be lost. People were everywhere, a woman pushed her. A man pulled at Vincent. Someone's hard suitcase fell from their hands and the pitch of the stairs gave it momentum. It hit Nan's head.

"Nan!" Vincent cried, as he fought his way back to her and tried to shield her from the masses.

"Help!" he screamed in perfect English. "Help me, my mother is having a baby!"

Good boy, she thought as she lost consciousness. *Good boy.*

When Nan woke up, a nurse was standing over her, holding a swaddled baby in the crook of one arm and a clipboard in the other. "Where is your husband?" she asked, roughly tucking the infant into Nan's arms.

"Where is my br . . . my son? Where is Vincent?"

"He was sent along with the people who came to get you because he had papers that allowed it. You're very lucky. He made such a fuss about leaving you, he assaulted an officer. He could have been sent to jail. Not to mention your baby—she's an ugly thing, but she's alive. Now, where is your husband? The family . . . ? Yes. It states here that when they claimed your boy they said you would be claimed by your husband. We need this bed. Where is he? Do you have an address?"

"I don't know."

Nan looked at her baby. And looked away. She was skinny, and too small.

"We will contact the family. What will you name the child?"

"I will not name her."

"We'll just put Baby Girl on the paperwork. You and your people are backwards. Not even naming your children. Missing husbands. Sons you'd have to have been a child yourself to bear. I hope you find what you are looking for and then get out of this city. You drag us all to sin. You are a stain," said the nurse.

The baby, because she was born in America, helped her mother bypass the paperwork, and concessions were made that were not normally accepted.

She walked out of the gates with the baby in her arms, a baby for which she, barely an adult, would now be the sole caretaker for, and she scanned the skyline of the city. She was not impressed. There was no color here. No beauty. Everything was gray. Gray like her life had become, gray like the dingy blanket they gave her for her infant. Just gray.

The man sent to get her was named Marco. He was kind but also in a hurry. Everyone seemed to be in such a hurry. "Okay, ah! A baby! Nice. How will you work? Never mind. . . . But you will work, no?"

"I will figure it out. Is Vincent safe? Do you know?" she asked. Then she asked again, this time in Italian. *The language skills are strong, Mama*, she thought.

"You speak good both ways! English, Italian, Italian, English. Brava. That will help you. Yes, Vincent. He is good boy. He already found work. Two days. Very good boy."

Marco brought her to a section of New York that seemed just like the steerage on the boat. It was crammed tight with people, everyone seeking to satisfy their own comforts. She understood she would have to find a way out of this place, find Giancarlo and get money. Extort it, or whatever she had to do. At that moment she felt she could explode into one big scream that would take down the whole island of Manhattan.

"You will have to work for your living until you find the father of that child," said Marco, helping her out of the car. He grew serious, whispering in her ear. "You seem like a nice girl. You hold your head high. They do not want you here. They will try to make it hard. I will pray for you." Then, smiling again, he pointed at a building, a row house teeming with people.

"Right there, five flights up. They are waiting for you."

Nan looked around her at the world she was trying to become a part of. She walked up the stoop and into the building without saying a word. She walked up the stairs, peering into the open doorways. Everything was alien. She went to sleep listening to her mother sing, smelling sunshine and garlic, and woke up in hell with an ugly infant sucking on her breast. A nightmare, that's it. She looked at the life from above it. She saw the yellow-stained wife beaters on the men, the sweat, sweet cheap wine in jelly jars, and women smelling of sour breast milk waiting on the men hand and foot. Crowded rooms, sometimes ten people to a room. She looked down at her strange baby and wanted nothing more than to wake up. *How can I live here?* she thought. *I will not be afraid. I am weak to be afraid.*

Pausing before the landing that would lead her to the sixth floor. She took a deep breath. The tightness in her throat helped her identify this feeling. It was anger. It was not fear.

Her mother told her anger wouldn't help her. It was rage that led to making bad decisions almost impossible to undo.

But she was mad anyway. Furious. She turned and walked back down the stairs and into the city.

The anger seemed to keep her going. It was her sustenance, it fed her baby.

She strapped the baby onto her back and followed the crowds down on the pier. For a week, she watched and learned. She slept next to boxes, she ate from the garbage.

The next week she volunteered to help clean fish. She did it for free.

By the next week, she was offered money. It wasn't much, but it allowed her to rent a tiny room and eat less of other people's scraps.

She had not seen Vincent. She had not found Giancarlo. And she had to leave the baby alone in the cold room when she was on the docks. Each day Nan would ask the children on the stoop if they heard a baby cry. They always answered "no."

Nan started to believe the baby was stupid, born too early and ruined by Nan's hate. That's why she didn't cry.

But the baby wasn't stupid. She was very smart. She knew not to waste her breath. No one would come. The baby was alone all day, every day.

Nan came back to her baby each night stinking like fish and would carelessly pick her up and feed her a bottle of water with honey or sugar in it and try to feed her pieces of cooked fish. But the baby would refuse, which made Nan cry, "I hate you sometimes, baby."

But the baby knew it wasn't true. It wasn't hate at all, just fear. And the baby knew that Nan could only survive if she turned her fear into rage. So she stayed quiet.

It was Vincent who came and found her finally. He'd grown so tall. Nan didn't recognize him at first.

When she did, she immediately realized the price she would pay for her rage. She'd convinced herself he was safer there, in that tenement, working. But one look at his face, into his dulled eyes, spoke of a different reality.

"I heard you were here cleaning fish like a peasant. You know, everyone thinks you are crazy or dumb. I kept waiting for you to come get me, but now I don't want you to. I came to tell you."

"Vincent, I'm so sorry. That day, Marco brought me. . . . I had to leave. I couldn't live there."

"You don't know what it was like. I protected you. I got you help when the baby came. I defended you when they were going to let you rot on that island. I trusted you. And you left me there. I don't hate you, because you are my sister. But I will never forgive you either. Did the baby die?"

"No, she's . . . she's being cared for. Vincent, you can come live with me. We can save money and leave. How about that? You don't have to go back."

"Someday, Nan, I will own that building. I will own many buildings and have a family. I will provide for them. I will love them. And I will pay all these people back for the things they did to me. But I will do it alone, without you. I am finished counting on anyone but myself. Here." He slipped a piece of paper in her hand.

"What's this?"

"Giancarlo's address. One of us had to respect Mama's wishes. Do what you want." Then he handed her an apple and left her on the docks.

Nan had a decision to make.

Some time later, Nan came back to the rented room to find the baby had broken out in sores. Based on her mother's limited teaching, she knew it was due to a lack of fresh citrus fruit. It was time to find Giancarlo. For the baby, at least.

She put Vincent's note, now worn, into her pocket, strapped the baby on her back, and walked into the city night, talking to herself.

"He'll have to help us. It's the honorable thing to do. I can gather a little money and run away later. I can pretend to love him. A bath, maybe he has a bathtub. A dress. Some hot food. Yes, I'll love him."

By the time she arrived at the building, she'd convinced herself he was going to be happy to see them. That he'd fall in love with the baby at first glance and they would be safe. She bounded up the four flights of stairs and began to knock on a gray door.

"*Aspet, Aspet,*" (wait, wait) came a man's voice. Giancarlo, half dressed, skinny and tall with that same dark humorous mustache, opened the door. A woman lay naked on a mattress on the floor just behind him. The walls of the room looked too much like the walls she'd just left behind.

"Nan!" he said, surprised. He looked nervously at the baby. At his hestitation, Nan began to walk away. "Nan, wait! Stay."

"You? You want me to stay with you? Look at you with this whore. Living in filth."

She watched his expression change from curiosity to anger. She'd let her anger get the best of her again.

"Yes, I know she's a whore. Like you, isn't that right, Nan? I seem to like whores who spread their legs willingly."

He glanced at the baby again.

"Is she mine?"

"Yes."

He examined her more closely.

"Nan, what did you do to the child? Who cursed you? It's got sores all over it! Take it away from me before I get the curse, too."

"Me?! Who cursed *you*? You lying whore lover!" She got very close to his face and hissed, "I take it back. I curse you. You with your disgusting hands and sweaty fingers and your stink. Take the baby. I don't want her."

"Are you mad? You take her! This demon can't stay with me!" He slammed the door in her face.

Nan crumpled to the ground and wept. Her baby cried, too, and Nan pulled the makeshift sling around to the front of her body, cuddling her daughter close, then looked at her. She wasn't an infant anymore—and despite the sores, was rather cute.

"Don't cry. I wouldn't really have left you. Not forever."

The baby sucked her thumb.

"You need a name," she said, walking down the stairs. "Ava. That's what Mama wanted me to call you. So the oceans wouldn't be between us.

"I will figure something out, Ava," she whispered. "I will. But if you have any of your grandmother's talents, please help me. Guide me. A mother shouldn't lean on her child this way, I know, but you and I are all we have now. You've been so brave for me. It's my turn to be brave for you."

Wandering through the street market the following day, begging for oranges for Ava, she overheard women talking of a fishing port in a place called Virginia where there were many jobs and not enough people to fill them. She followed the chatty, plump, rosy-cheeked hens and boarded a ship that would sail her into a deep and startling unknown.

Standing on the deck, feeding orange slices to Ava, Nan thought she might be all right. She'd get healthy. And settled. And then she'd send for Vincent.

1902–1905

Nan thought Haven Port was paradise. The harbor was full of colorful boats and laughing people, and everyone seemed kind. She thought she would have to ask around to find out where to go for a decent job, but almost as soon as she stepped off the boat, a boy ran up to her with a flyer and said, "If you are look-ing for work, try the big house on the cliff, you can see it from here." He pointed. Nan saw a glass cupola balanced on top of the peaked rooftop in the distance. It would be easy to find. She adjusted the baby on her back and started to walk away.

"Wait!" he called out. "They won't hire you if you look and smell like that. You and your baby. Go the back way. Down on the beach you can clean up. Then there's a staircase built into the rocks that'll get you to the back property. Soon as you clear the juniper pines, you'll see the whole grand place. Some-times, when it's hotter than Hades in the summer, they let us kids swim in their pool."

"A pool?"

"Yeah, you'll see. Go on now, I got more recruiting to do. I get ten cents an hour. It's a fortune!"

"Let's go, Ava."

"To home?"

"Words? You said words! Oh, yes, home, my darling. Hopefully, home."

The boy had said juniper, and Nan knew what to do. She made her way along the beach, climbed the steps, masterfully carved, and once at the top, gathered some needles and cones. Then, she journeyed back down to the water's edge and used the juniper to wash with. It smelled clean. She even risked washing their clothes and Ava's sling, hiding between dunes of sand as they dried.

She'd not felt so good in a long time. Smiling, she made the climb back up the stairs and wended her way through the back gardens, trying to think of some lie to tell to get her employed.

As she made her way around the giant orangery and swimming pool (she'd thought, at first, that it was the actual house, it was so big) to the front of the estate, she saw a woman standing on the porch, like a ship's figurehead. Blond and tall. Graceful.

She smiled at Nan.

"Will you just stand there, then? Like a ninny in the garden? Well, do what you must, but come in for god's sake. It's probably 110 degrees out here."

Nan walked slowly up the elegant front steps. The wraparound porch was dizzying and seemed to go on for miles. As she walked into the foyer, she had to place her hand on the doorknob of the large front door for support. It was not an ordinary doorknob. Metal—gold, perhaps?—molded with whimsical vines and what Nan thought looked like little cherub faces (but could have just as easily been flowers).

I thought I'd miss home forever. Now I feel as if I'm alive again. I've never seen anything so beautiful, she thought.

"Are you thinking about how beautiful it is here? Don't worry, I don't read minds. I didn't seem to get those talents from my people, though Reginald is determined to recover them somehow or another.

"Before we talk business, let's have a tour, shall we? She's called Haven House. The Green family, who purchased the land when the community was new and still forming, built the house as a refuge. There was some kind of terrible falling out up north, and everyone scattered. Our half of the Green family, well, we are dangerously, famously wealthy, and we employ most of Haven Port's citizens. I assume that is why you've come. Did little Walter find you at the docks?"

"Yes, ma'am," said Nan.

"My name is Gwyneth Green. I am the lady of the house. Follow me, there's no reason to stand on propriety. You will learn we are not proper. Eccentricity is the privilege of wealth in this country."

Gwyneth walked into a large study ahead of Nan.

"I married my first cousin, which is perhaps the reason we haven't had any children. Or, at least, none that have survived infancy." Gwyneth glanced at Ava. "But the upside to inbreeding is that I didn't have to change the embroidery on any of my linens."

Nan probably should have felt uneasy at the immediate, intimate way Gwyneth had with her. Gwyneth was, perhaps, even crazy. But Nan liked her for it. There was an honesty there that reminded her of her mother. An authenticity of self. Besides, she'd spoken of talents. *Maybe I've found more lost witches, Mama,* thought Nan.

By the end of the tour of Haven House, Nan had become quite familiar with the more interesting details of the Green history. She knew Gwyneth and her husband, Reginald, led an aloof and estranged marriage, but because they understood the importance of family prestige and power, they feigned happiness. She learned of Gwyneth's intense need to have children. She heard the details about each of their six stillborn babies and how, after the last loss, Reginald moved into the east wing of the house with a view of the ocean from the top floor. The couple had very little contact after that.

"It breaks my heart each day," said Gwyneth as she walked through the house, "being so close and yet so far apart from the man I married. I grew up here, you know. My father and mother were estranged as well, and it's something I sought to avoid. Daddy spent all his time in the gatehouse doing god knows what. I thought we'd be different, Reggie and me. I really truly did. I know that if we'd had a child we'd still be close. I've prayed and prayed for a miracle, and here you are.

"Like the sunrise today! A pretty woman with a little tot of your own strapped on your back. I immediately liked you, which is a welcome surprise . . . as I like so few people. You're brave, and interesting. My goodness, how I do go on. . . . We've known each other for the better part of an hour now, and I don't even know your name. What is your name?"

"I am Anna Amore. But I am called Nan."

"Well then, Nan. Would you like a job?"

"I don't have many skills. I sew a bit, and I cleaned fish in New York. I can work on the docks."

"Nonsense! You can live here with us, and you will be my companion. How does that sound?"

"And Ava?"

"Is that her name? This delicious little thing. May I hold her?"

Nan gave Ava to Gwyneth, and Ava smiled. "Oh, she's lovely! Where is your husband?"

"I don't have one." Nan waited for the standard reprimand.

"Clever girl. They are more trouble then they're worth." Gwyneth laughed. "Let's get you settled. Then we can introduce you to Reggie. That is, if he ever decides to stop skulking about in the cellar or in his rooms. He used to be such fun. Now . . . well, anyway. I'll have to find you a dress for dinner tonight, but next week we'll go shopping in Richmond. You have the run of the house, so should we get a nanny for Ava? No. No, I think not."

Gwyneth chattered on and on, and at some point, Nan began to relax. She'd asked for Ava's help, and Ava had delivered them heaven.

Gwyneth and Reginald treated Nan well, and the two women became extremely close. Neither trusted anyone, but they both had great warmth: an abusive combination. Nan began as a companion to Gwyneth but soon became a real part of the household, with servants all her own. Ava was growing strong and beautiful, and she brought much joy to Gwyneth. Many times, Nan didn't see her daughter all day. Gwyneth, who was an avid collector of all things, insisted that Nan have a photograph taken of Ava as a child; Gwyneth would pay for it, as it was a new technology and very costly. Gwyneth had commissioned portraits of all her dead infants and kept them safe in the lovely round turret room made of stained-glass windows. It became a shrine. Nan agreed, to please her employer and friend, even though she believed all photographs were dangerous somehow. The idea of capturing a moment was too much for her to think about. But once the photograph was taken, she was glad to have it. Nan liked the photo so much she asked Gwyneth if she could keep it with her own things in her room. Gwyneth, who had grown to truly love Nan, could deny her nothing.

Ava loved Gwyneth and, as weeks turned into months, called both women "Mama," which made everyone happy. Even Reg inald was beginning to venture out from the east wing of the mansion. He would come out to the gardens and sit and watch Nan run around with the pretty, laughing Ava, and he watched as Gwyneth read or did needlepoint. He saw how she always seemed to have her eyes on Ava. The child brought out the best in her. They made an interesting, little family. But a family nonetheless.

For the first few years, all their joy and love was focused on Ava, who grew into a creative girl, and as she got older and was allowed to play on her own, she would hunt through the mansion for interesting nooks and crannies. She found hidden closets and trunks filled with old-fashioned clothing under the eaves in the many levels of the attic. She would climb up into the cupola and proclaim herself queen of the world. Her favorite spot became the turret room. It was cozy with Oriental carpets and the light of the stained-glass windows scattering designs all over. She loved to play in that room. It was where Gwen spent many hours as well. It was safe there. You could see all around you. There were no surprises.

8

The Fortune-Teller in the Library with a Revolver

1905

"Reggie, would you like to tell her or shall I?" asked Gwyneth at breakfast. Breakfast was always a big to-do at Haven House. Shining silverware, cold fresh juices, someone always there to refill your glass. Coffee in big, steaming pots.

"What is it, what is it, what is it?" cried out an excited little Ava.

"Don't be shocked, dear heart, but this news will not be so exciting for you. As a matter of fact, you may have to let Hetty put you to bed next Saturday night."

"Why on earth?" asked Nan.

"We are going to have a party. Our first soiree in more than four years. We used to have them all the time. Rollicking fun. In fact, Nan, thank you," said Reginald.

"For what?"

"For bringing the light back into our lives." He placed his hand on Nan's shoulder and squeezed. And unlike other times when he'd touched her, there was heat beneath his hand. And Nan did not try to move him away.

"Is it true there's to be a party, miss?" asked Walter. He assisted Nan whenever she went into Haven Port. Sometimes to pick up more lye for a new soap she was making. Sometimes to sell her medicinal preparations. In recent years she had gained quite a following as a local healer of sorts.

"Yes, it is. Very grand, so I hear."

"Be careful, miss."

"Walter, if you are concerned about any sort of—"

"There are stories, miss. Terrible ones. People used to go missing. Screams. Smells. Until a year or so before you came. Even the police thought it was fishy. It got so's none would go to those parties. It got so's no one that wasn't already working here would take a job. Until you."

"Rubbish. And don't spread that nonsense. No more, Walter. You hear? Or you might go missing as well."

Walter hadn't been wrong. That first party should have shocked Nan to her core with its lascivious nature and decadence. Velvets and absinthe, opium and wanton disregard for moral proprieties. Only it didn't. When the morning after elicited no reproach or embarrassment, Nan found herself eagerly waiting for the next party. Which led to another, and then another. Nan was introduced to yet another way of life. Costumes and champagne. Lavishly produced stage plays and themes like "Exploring the Amazon" and "Taming Cleopatra."

"Smoke this," said Reginald. And she did.

"Kiss me," said Gwyneth. And she did.

Wear this, take this off, be this, be that. Dance. Dance.

"Touch me," growled Reginald. And she did, happily.

"I should be disgusted. I should be running from this den of iniquity," Nan commented one morning after another debauched evening. She stretched lazily between Reginald and Gwyneth on the overstuffed pillows strewn across the back lawn. All three were trying to watch Ava get ready to see the ponies.

"The sun! I'm like a demon. It's burning me. There was far too much absinthe in that punch, Reginald."

Nan laughed and then let Gwyneth and Reginald lead her inside so they could play with each other until the hangover wore off. Nan never felt as if what they did was sex, though it pleased her. It all felt like a delicious haze. But as time went on, she ached for Reginald. To be alone with him. To be one with him. And she thought he wanted that, too. Which scared her.

1907

Nothing mattered.

The intensity of physical pleasure mixed with the use of

mind-altering substances allowed Nan to forget about the things she'd promised. Like sending for Vincent and writing to her mother. And then it was too late.

A package came from Florencia. Nan's mother had died, and Florencia was immigrating to America. She'd sent Nan the only thing her mother had of value. Her book of magic. A big black book filled with drawings and scribbled notes.

She found Reginald in the library (where he was going over the ticker for the stock exchange), and told him. He poured her a drink and held her as she cried.

"Would you like to travel to Europe for the funeral? I can make the arrangements."

"Oh, Reggie, you're so generous, but whatever rites were to be performed would have been done already. If there was any sort of concern it would be for my brother, Vincent."

"And where is he living again?"

"In the Bronx."

"Ah. Well, how about if we make a visit? Greens from up and down the East Coast gather and summer at Far Rockaway beach each year. We've successfully avoided those trips, but perhaps it would do us all a bit of good to get another view of the world. And it would do me good to see my family."

"You didn't grow up here?"

"No, no. I grew up on a tiny island off the coast of Fairview, Massachusetts, called Fortunes Cove. I miss it there. I long for it, and for my family as well. I understand how you feel about your mother and your brother, my dear."

"Then why don't you go back?"

Reginald sighed. "Do you believe in magic, Nan?"

"I do," Nan said, quietly, hoping she'd been right. Hoping he was one of her "people." Those that her mother had spoke of back in Italy.

"I know you do. Well, I lost my faith, or my way. . . . Hell, I don't know. I was asked to leave Fortunes Cove. And I can never go back." Reginald made a fist and banged it against the wall. Books fell from shelves all around.

Nan wanted to ask more, wanted to know more . . . but Reggie seemed so angry and sad, so instead, she changed tack.

"I see. . . . Well, it would be good to see Vincent. And to meet your family. But what about Gwen?"

"I've never made her go, so she should not object. Contact Vincent. Have him meet us there. Tell him I'll pay any wages he loses for a few days of vacation by the sea. It should prove to be great fun. What do you say, Nan?"

"I say yes."

"Marvelous. But you must do something for me in return."

"Anything."

"Do not ask my family about me. Do not pry into that which is dead."

FAR ROCKAWAY, NEW YORK

Not two weeks later, they were amidst a strange subset of Greens frolicking on the beaches of Far Rockaway. Nan had thought she would be tempted to break her promise and ask questions about Reggie. But she didn't feel the need. His inter- actions with them were warm and held no ominous feelings.

Besides, the air was sweet with victory for Nan. She'd left New York in rags, and returned in riches.

"Didn't your brother say he'd come today? The sooner you see him, the sooner we can leave this hovel," huffed Gwyneth. Reggie'd been right, she hadn't objected to the trip, until they arrived. But she'd been moody from the moment she'd seen his younger, beautiful cousin Margaret.

And then, as if Gwen had conjured him out of sea foam, Vincent, all grown-up, emerged from the blinding sunlight.

"Nan, what's happened to you?" he asked, frowning. "You look like a harlot. Do all women wear their hair down and paint their faces in Virginia Society?"

"It's nice to see you, too, Vincent. Look there to the waves, do you see Ava? She's getting bigger day by day. Come, take my hand, let's go to her."

Vincent's face softened. He took her hand.

Nan and Vincent talked for hours. They argued about loyalty and trust and family ties. They laughed over old memories and cried about the loss of their mother. And in the end, they quietly agreed that their lives were very different from one another.

Nan would never give up hope that she could right the wrongs she'd committed against him.

Vincent would later marry Reginald's cousin Margaret and live out his own somewhat tragic life. He would visit Nan once or twice after the destruction of her own world, but, much to Nan's dismay, they would never be close. To Nan, Vincent would always be the little boy who saved her on the steps at Ellis Island. And to Vincent, Nan would always be the one who let her body ruin his happy life in Italy. There was no in between.

1908

The party that was planned for their homecoming from Far Rockaway would prove to be Nan's last. That night, Gwyneth and Reginald introduced Nan to the famous fortune-teller Evelyn Pratt, whom Reginald had known growing up.

"It's impossible to book her for events, but Reggie pleaded with his Aunt Faith at Far Rockaway. Now she's here, so that barbaric trip was not a waste of two perfectly good days after all." Gwyneth said. (She'd been rendered to frequent, insecure bouts of anger since seeing Reggie with the clan of strange Greens).

As if on cue, a stunning woman wearing a deep-sapphire satin gown glided into the parlor on Reggie's arm.

"Come, Nan. Meet Evelyn."

"My dear Nan. It is delightful to meet you. I've felt you in this house from the moment I arrived. You are like a beacon here, staving off the more destructive forces. Is your child asleep?"

Nan looked toward Reginald and Gwyneth, but they were gone again, swept up in the dancing dancing dancing.

Evelyn Pratt took Nan roughly by the arm and pulled her into the library. She closed the doors.

"I don't know why I'm doing this. It usually does no good once I've cast the bones. But you are different, Nan. You have real talents. Reggie was right. Magic flows through you, does it not?"

Nan shrugged. "So my mother said, but I have seen no instances of it."

"It is a muscle, like everything else. You should practice and see what you can do. Did you learn English quickly? Do you feel yourself drawn to immoral behavior, guided more by your own set of values rather than those of the society? Of course. Those are two very important telltale signs of one who has great magical potential. Now, more important, you must leave this house, Nan. As soon as possible."

Nan walked to a small bar and poured herself a drink.

"Think of it. When was the last time you thought of anything beyond this property? Your brother, growing up alone in New York City. Your mother, in the ground in Italy. Your sister, what has become of her? And Ava . . . is this the mother you wanted to be?" She knocked the glass out of Nan's hand. "You must not drink any more of this. These people, this place is soiled. They are using you, Nan. Nothing good can come of this. Reggie told me he's been honest with you about the fact that he cannot return home. But do you know why?"

"I don't want to hear any more of this."

"Your mother tried to teach you and you didn't listen. You suffer for that obstinance now. Reginald grew selfish and wanted more than the magic he was born with. He broke rules that ought not be broken."

"I will not leave him."

"Do as you wish, but my assistant, Albert, will stay for a few days after I go. I've instructed him to watch you. And when you have cleaned yourself out, he has been instructed to make sure you can escape. Do this for Ava. She does not deserve the future I see, Nan. It is a terrible future that will cast a net of sorrow and imprison generations. Please alter it."

Before Evelyn left, she gave Nan a cryptic note.

When fire destroys all you hold dear
and sorrow plagues you year by year
and one that wasn't meant to be
falls down the steps of devilry
send her dying soul to me
send her dying soul to me.

She didn't leave. She couldn't. She wouldn't. But she didn't go to the parties after that. And she stayed clear of the absinthe punch and opium pipes.

Without the strange goings-on in her mind, one fact was clear. Nan was desperately in love. She sent Albert away. She did not need to escape and found it silly Evelyn had been so insistent. Nan would heed the warning, and remain vigilant.

At first Gwyneth and Reginald were amused by Nan's new austerity. Then Gwyneth became annoyed. But Reggie seemed to understand, and soon, the parties ceased entirely. Nan took that as proof that she was in fact, a beacon of light in their lives. A savior of sorts.

She forgot to remember that most saviors must eventually sacrifice everything for their flock.

9

Gwyneth in the Turret Room with a Lighter

1910

Nan pushed open the door to the stone gardener's cottage, and petals fell from a low-hanging fruit tree branch.

"You should always have petals in your hair," said Reginald.

Lifting her skirt from behind, his hands caressed her, full of wanting. She turned, and they locked in a kiss that released far too many hours of being apart.

He rested her on the ground, and as she opened herself wide to him, he groaned as he drove himself inside her.

"Closer . . ." she breathed.

"I can not get enough of you. Only you. Forever you," he said. Each word punctuating his movement inside of her.

After, she rested her head on his chest and listened to his heartbeat. She'd never felt more safe.

"It's as if I didn't know the entire you for all those years. I adored you. I adored Ava. And I certainly enjoyed the company we all, shall we say, kept. But here you are, in a completely different light. A purity lingers over you in your sex. I want to devour it."

"Then by all means, do. . . ."

"You know. . . . you and I have never really spoken about the magic," he said, as they finally gathered their things.

"I don't know what you mean."

"Enough of this. You must start talking to me! I was forced from Fortunes Cove because I made a mistake. I've known magic. I've lost it, and spent my whole life trying to regain it. I came here and married Gwen because there was speculation that her father, Archibald, had the talents. Whether he did or not is up for debate, but Gwen did not. Does not. So please, if you love me, tell me what you know. Evelyn saw so much power in you. I see you with your big black book and working with your medicinal herbs—the garden is lovely, by the way. What else can you do? What else does that book hold? Will you teach me? I want to go home, Nan. How I long to go home! I can't even cross that body of water. Can you imagine being so far from home?"

Nan nodded.

"I'm sorry. So sorry, my love. That was terribly insensitive of me. I spoke before I thought. Of course you know. Please, please help me."

"What I know are simply stories," said Nan. "My mother knew so much more. But feel free to ask questions. I'll answer what I can."

Reginald held out his arm companionably, and Nan took it, squeezing her body close to his as they walked.

"Can you raise people from the dead?"

"No."

"Can you cast love spells?"

"Reggie, you are speaking of dark magic. You cannot do dark magic. It is too dangerous. What do you need? You know I will give you anything you need. We can start there. Tell me something you desire, and I'll try to make it happen. That way I can practice the arts, and then, if I do have any of my mother's true gifts, I will learn them and teach them to you. I swear it."

"I want a child."

"Is that all? Well, no magic is necessary."

"Are you?"

"I am.'"

Nan had expected Reginald to be upset, or even happy, or silly. She'd expected a long conversation about logistics and planning and how to tell Gwyneth. What she didn't expect was for his face to lose all hubris, as if a mask had come off. There was love in his true face. And fear. So much fear.

"Reggie, what is it? Are you ill?"

"We must leave here, Nan. I'll take you back across the ocean and we will live together, the four of us. You and me, Ava and the new baby. But we must go. Quickly."

"Why?"

"There are things you do not know. I was not expecting . . . never expecting . . . damn it!"

"What about Gwen?"

"It isn't safe. She will take this new child's life. As she took the others. It is not her fault, I will do what I should have done years ago. There is a doctor, in Fairview—he will take her in. Our family has had one too many residents at the asylum there, sadly. Something in the blood. Now go, find her. Make her calm. Give her some of that tea that helps her sleep. I'll make the call from town."

Neither of them saw Gwyneth standing just outside the garden gate, hidden by the willow. Neither of them saw her face grow slack and her eyes grow dull with madness.

Nan could feel the tension in the house, and she worried that somehow Gwyneth knew. So she searched her out to smooth over whatever oddness her dear friend was feeling.

Nan couldn't find her at first, but then she found her in the turret room with Ava.

"I've made you some tea, Gwen. Let me brush your hair."

Later that night, Nan couldn't sleep. Evelyn Pratt's warning was pounding in her head. Something was very wrong in the house. She checked on Ava. Ava was not in her room.

"Don't fret, dear," said Gwyneth from the hallway. "She wanted to sleep with me in the turret room tonight. It so hot outside, and the windows let in such a fine breeze. Three hundred sixty degrees of breeze and all that. You should come as well."

"Where is Reggie?"

"In his bedchamber, I suppose. Why don't you go check?"

Anyone would have been able to hear the animosity in Gwyneth's voice, but Nan heard it in her heart.

"Gwen, I love you. I love this house. If I have hurt you, please know I did not intend to do so."

"Hurt me? Because you laid with Reggie? That is silly. . . . We have all had ways. This way, that way, up ways, down ways . . . I've had all the ways. Is there anything we did not do? And if you think there might be, were you always awake? Sex means nothing. It is a pleasure to be had and taken and given away. And, in your case, borrowed."

Nan wanted to shout about the baby growing inside her. Proof of love. But she held back. Gwyneth was going mad. Reginald must have known how close she was to the edge, which was why he wanted them to leave before she found out. Her eyes were wide, almost unseeing. And Ava was in the turret room, with only one door and one staircase that led to it. Gwyneth blocked the way, only shifting to walk slowly up the stairs.

Nan went downstairs to the kitchen, to think, to make tea, to calm herself. And to find Reggie. A tapping at the kitchen door startled her. A woman had come to fetch her for a difficult birth happening in town. Reggie came in just as Nan was going to send her away. She quickly told him about Gwyneth and Ava and the conversation.

"I will take care of this, you go get some air. Help this woman. It will be good for all of us."

"I must get my watch. Timing is necessary for healthy births."

"Take mine," said Reggie, handing her his pocket watch.

And with that Nan left Haven House to deliver a baby.

But no sooner had she arrived at the small beachside cape full of moaning, she felt—no, heard—what her mother had called "red waves of warning," of finally knowing the awful truth of actually *knowing.*

Nan rushed back out into the street and broke into a run as the lights behind her eyes glowed stronger.

Nan sees her from the long winding drive. Gwyneth stands in the turret room. The house is too dark, but Gwyneth is illuminated. A silhouette against the pale moonlight. Why weren't the gas lamps lit? Nan wonders. And then believes she can hear a voice clearly say: This is why. Watch closely. Gwyneth lifts her arm and makes a motion with her hand. She's striking Reginald's lighter. The right side of the house explodes.

The mansion rested in piles of rubble and sharp edges that looked almost normal. A table standing in a kitchen with no walls, a window held up by a single slab support beam.

People must have followed. She couldn't remember them, but there were arms blocking her from running into the flames. There was a blanket placed around her as the damp night became morning and the bodies were pulled from the rubble. Nan was held back from the destruction. But before the many hands of the community could reach in to shield her eyes, she saw Ava. Her tiny body was burned beyond recognition and her limbs twisted by the force of the blast, yet somehow, like a dark fairy tale, she was encased in blown out and melted shards of stained glass, that, defying nature, sparkled in the brilliant and unyielding morning.

"Come away from there," they said. The firemen and the

canners and the mothers who still had their daughters. The wives that had their husbands. The women who had their men. Nan shook her head and spent the days and weeks that stretched forward silently picking through the rubble. Sifting up bits and pieces of her sins. Finding the doorknob.

All was gone except the one sin she couldn't undo. And it would become her redemption. She would name her daughter Lucia Amore. Lucy. She would raise her right. Nan would be the woman she should have been all along. A God-fearing, simple, and hardworking woman.

Nan needed to sleep the sleep of the just.

The Book of

Lucy

1910–1940

10

A Spirit in the Parlor
with a Slice of Toast

Maj woke up next to her mama in the big bed. Mama said not to be scared if she woke up first and didn't know where she was. Mama worried a lot about all kinds of things she didn't need to worry about, which wouldn't be so bad if she also worried about the really big things. Grown-ups, Maj had decided, don't pay attention to any of the right things. She'd be different when she grew up. In any case, Maj knew exactly where she was as she blinked her eyes against the sun of the brand-new day. She was in the Witch House, in Nan's bedroom. The one that her new friend Ava talked about. (Crazy Anne had introduced them in her dreams.) The pretty room with the blue-and-white flowered wallpaper. There were saints, the ones like Mimi had, on low shelves next to the deep-red reading chair near one of the almost floor-to-ceiling windows. There was a dresser with a mirror on it that Maj could see her reflection in when she sat up.

She sat up and down a few times, playing peek-a-boo, until she woke her mama.

"Why are you bouncing?"

"That's a silly question. I bounce, that's what I do. It's one of the things I do best."

Mama pulled a pillow over her messy bun and groaned.

"Wake up wake up wake up!" laughed Maj, pulling the pillow off. Mama reached for her and drew her down under the blanket, holding her tight.

"Go back to sleep for a little bit. Let me hold you."

Mama loved to cuddle with Maj. She didn't like to cuddle with anyone else. Maj thought that was kind of sad because Mama was a really good cuddler and should share it with other people, too.

"No no no noooo! It's already getting hot outside. And you should have your coffee."

"I should. Crap. There probably isn't any coffee."

"There's all kinds of things. Let's go look." Maj pulled her by the arm and dragged her out of bed.

"It's nice in here," she said. "I really wasn't expecting it to be so clean. That Byrd did us a huge favor. You okay?" Mama leaned down with her face all scrunched up.

"I'm fine, Mama. Really fine. I'm not homesick. Now, let's go! I want to play outside."

She dragged her down the hall past the bathroom.

"Beep beep. We have to stop here, Mr. Conductor," said

Mama. "Go find your toothbrush. I think it's in the duffle bag by the front door. Get it and come back. Do not pass go, do not collect two hundred dollars. I mean it. Do not explore. Do not go outside."

The bathroom glistened white in the morning sun. Mama leaned into the mirror in her white tank top and white underwear, staring at her eyebrows.

"Do you want me to find your pants?"

"Go get your toothbrush, smarty."

Maj skipped off down the hall toward the stairs and thought . . . Mama is happy. She doesn't know it yet, but she is happy here already.

Eleanor woke up thinking about Nan. About the terrible loss that occurred on the property right under their feet. And that strange urgency to discover the secrets the land held motivated her to get some coffee. She was also feeling a sense of overprotection. She wanted to hold Maj closer to her than ever. Byrd would tell her the next installment of the family saga, and then they'd sit down and figure it out. Together.

The house looked different in the morning. Not as lonesome or dim as it had the night before. And yet, the clock. *Tic tock tic tock tic tock. Tic.*

No matter where she went, she heard it. Felt it. Her head was pounding. A genealogy headache.

She glanced out the bathroom window and saw Byrd sipping from a mug on the side porch. The screen door opened, and

Maj started to go outside. Eleanor quickly opened the window, fear shooting through her.

Strange thoughts zipped through her mind. . . .

Don't let her out of your sight, you're being a lazy mother. You'll pay and lose everything.

"Young lady, I swear to God if you take one more step—"

Byrd looked up at Eleanor. "Good morning to you, too, Elly. I'll make Maj some toast. Would you like a valium with your coffee?"

As she made her way downstairs, Eleanor examined the paintings hanging in the hallway. Nan, Lucy, Anne, Opal, Stella. Names she hadn't known until the day before, a whole part of her history she'd never heard. The portrait of Stella looked so much like Byrd would when she was older. Byrd, who seemed so very alone, who'd lived alone for months accomplishing things a fourteen-year-old shouldn't have been able to accomplish. But she was no ordinary teenager. *You weren't either. None of them were. Maj won't be*, she thought.

Reaching the foyer, she turned to walk through the great room, but stopped short.

There was someone in the parlor. Eleanor knew this feeling, the one you get when you are in the presence of the dead. There is sound where there ought not be sound. A shape where there ought not be shape. An extra layer to the air. She knew, somehow, that if she faced forward, the spirit would disappear. And part of her, magic or not, was scared it wouldn't. She'd convinced herself ghosts didn't really exist. Echoes, surely, but not spirits. But even more, she knew that was just something she told herself.

The sheer curtains danced in the breeze. Except it was a flat, windless morning.

Here we go, she thought, bracing for an actual encounter. She tried to recall what Mimi had told her about spirits. But right when she turned to greet the ghost, there was nothing. Just an emptiness in the air that was worse than anything she could have imagined. A cold sadness that wasn't her own.

"It's different, isn't it? The way the world looks from these windows," said Byrd, holding out a coffee cup.

"Thank you."

"You're welcome."

"No, Byrd . . . really. Thank you. I think Crazy Anne was about to bite me."

"Must you haunt everyone but me?!" yelled Byrd at the ceiling. Then she stomped out.

Eleanor leaned against the window and drank her coffee. She didn't know if it was the fact that the glass had been repurposed from an older, damaged home, or if it was some kind of message, but Byrd was right. Everything was stretched and rounded. The road, the walkway, the trees. Like being inside a snow globe.

As they went into the kitchen, Maj ran over to Eleanor and started bouncing again.

"Whoa!" said Eleanor, holding her cup high. "I don't want to spill any, there's no more to make. We'll have to hit the market in a little while."

"I want to explore. Can I go, can I go?"

"I suppose. Hold on, I have to find my shoes. Can you wait ten minutes or so, honey? I want to finish my coffee."

"I don't want you to come. I want to be shipwrecked on an island and starving for food. I have to draw a map of the whole yard because it is the island. And the house is the wrecked ship. And I have to find a good fort. And scavenge for food. And hide things."

"Absolutely not. I haven't explored all the child hazards yet. Old wells, snakes. Cliffs. Strangers with guns."

"Whole lotta imagination flyin' around this room," said Byrd.

"I'll stay by the house. Right in the garden. Please, Mama? Pleeeeeeease?"

"How about we walk her out there together and we can set up some rules, and then you and I can keep an eye on her from the porch. The porch is the best place to tell Lucy's story anyway," Byrd said.

Eleanor sighed. "Okay, kid. But don't leave my line of sight. I mean it."

"Some of the plants are bigger than me. I may be in and out."

"Just stay in one place and come when I call you."

"Yes, Mama," called Maj, already skipping down the steps and disappearing into the garden.

"Nan's story really got to you, didn't it? Good. Now let's talk about Lucy," said Byrd.

"I saw her portrait on the stairs. She was beautiful. Like a movie star."

"And crazy like a shit house rat."

"My branch of the family likes to use the term batshit crazy thank you very much. Now, go get some paper, our notes will be important."

Eleanor sat back and watched Maj dart in and out of the hedges surrounding the kitchen garden. She heard the phone ring, listened while Byrd chatted.

Leaning back into the porch swing, holding her coffee cup, Eleanor noticed her breathing was easy. Breathe in, exhale, inhale, breathe out . . . all her own air, all her own little molecules of sorrow and joy dispersing into the air around her. Not Anthony's or Nan's. Not Byrd's or Ava's. Just her own. And in that moment, she saw her own truth. Nan's story hadn't just "got to her" as Byrd said. It was changing her.

I will love him forever. And I will grieve, but what a gift it is, this pain.

She'd never before faced a day ready to enjoy all the pain and peace of life.

The house was unwinding her, she could feel it.

"You ready for Lucy? Because the world wasn't," Byrd said, sitting back in her chair.

"Hit me," said Eleanor.

9:30 A.M.

Maj walked through the side gardens, winding her way through a poplar grove, and tried to think of good things so she wouldn't cry. She didn't know why she felt like crying—she was brave and happy. But she knew that feeling, the heart-beating-fast, almost-throwing-up kind of feeling. She knew it well. She'd have no choice in the matter.

"Why are you sad?" piped up a little girl who emerged from behind one of the poplars.

"Ava!"

It had to be Ava. Anne had promised she'd play today. But to be sure, Maj closed her eyes and counted to ten the way Mimi taught her. That way you could tell if the person was alive or dead. You do that when someone seems to appear out of thin air.

Ava was still there.

"Do you want to play sardines?" the ghost asked.

"What's sardines?"

"Backwards hide-and-seek."

"I don't really like hide-and-seek."

"Me either. Backward or forward."

"When I came over here, I felt so sad, was that you, Ava? Are you sad?"

"And scared, Maj. I'm so scared."

"What are you scared of?"

"I think I'm supposed to be somewhere else. But I'm scared I'll stop being me. I know I'm dead. But I don't want to be dead. And I don't want to disappear. I want my mother to come get me. I thought she was coming once, only she wasn't. She was scared of me. And I used to have Gwen, but then she left, too. I'm lonesome. But maybe you're just sad on your own. Could that be it?"

"Maybe. But I don't think so. Why are you lonely? Doesn't Anne stay with you?"

"She's bossy. And she's not here all the time."

"Did she ever tell you where the secrets were hidden here? She won't tell me. All she wants to do is color. We have to find them all out by tomorrow and we aren't getting very far."

"Anne's like that. Always playing tricks. I can ask her about the secrets, though."

"Want to play pirates?"

"I thought you'd never ask!"

11

Nan in the Witch House with a Bible

1910–1940

The Witch House did not earn its name, it learned it.

Gossip-worthy from its birth, the Witch House teased its neighbors with its oddness, hinting at horrors that people began to talk about without fear. With Reginald and Gwyneth dead, rumors that had only ever bubbled below the surface broke wide. Missing people and devil worship. Poppy fields and infanticide. Gwyneth most certainly killed all her babies. Reginald must have had rows and rows of cages in the cellar for the people he experimented on. The monsters he made. Then killed. Then fed to all those who came to their soirees.

Any doubts Nan might have had about changing her life completely no longer mattered: now she had no choice. These were the types of verbal weapons she left Italy to avoid. Her baby would not grow up unsafe.

When word spread that she'd been left the deed to the property, the talk was about her affair with Reggie, and the baby she carried. She cried. And then she went to church and fed their fears.

"I will not speak of it. It was terrible," she'd sniff.

"You were taken prisoner by them?"

"I will not speak of it!"

"They took advantage of you."

"I will not speak of it."

"You poor dear."

She'd wanted to hex them all. But she wouldn't. She would accept the church. She would pay for her sins. She would speak her native language and shun the magic. She would raise her daughter right.

And as she'd been robbed of the time and space and luxury to mourn those she loved the most, she threw herself completely into creating a new home, a new value system, and to sharpening her hatred for the world. She'd make that house safe. She'd make certain she never lost anyone she loved ever again. First, she would avoid love. And second, if love happened, by accident or nature, she'd destroy anyone who tried to take it from her.

Her last act of magic from the book her mother sent was a dark spell of protection, cast under the full moon as she buried Reginald's pocket watch in the earth turned over for the foundation.

Tic tock tic tock tic tock. Tic.

———

Born from the rubble and remains of Haven House, the Witch House was constructed with aid from neighbors and other generous volunteers, as well as church groups who wanted to help. It was a mixture of styles but beautiful all the same. The foundation came from stones salvaged from the ruined east wing. Most of the lumber was new, but the porch columns and serpentine scrolling in the corners and eaves were taken and fixed and placed on the newer home as decoration.

Somehow one lone cupola from Haven House survived all damage. It was secured to the top of Nan's new home. Slightly off-center, like a paper party hat on a restless child.

It was a crazy quilt of architecture and design. The house had windows mismatched in both color and shape, strange ornamental flourishes used as foundational parts of the structure, and a majestic carved wood double door beneath the roof of the wraparound porch. It seemed unlikely that the house would end up beautiful, but it did.

If one were to think about the inside strictly in terms of number of rooms, the house would become very confusing indeed. Its internal structure was a mishmash. Odd, yet useful.

The kitchen had a large cooking fireplace, a deep porcelain sink, and hardwood floors, which were the easiest to keep clean.

And, there was, of course, a multitude of windows. A surprising amount of glass remained intact from Haven House, and the builders used every bit. There was a vast assortment to choose from: plain glass, stained, etched, leaded, milky . . . all sorts of panes to play with while building the new house.

In the kitchen, there was a rounded breakfast nook where a long narrow oak table began and then extended into the middle of the room. The nook itself had a bay window with stained glass along the upper portions, which bathed the room in dancing colors on sunny mornings and then again in the afternoon. And a conservatory was added, because even though there would be no more dabbling, there would be healing ways. It was income, after all. So Nan needed a potion kitchen, and a potion kitchen she received.

The two halls off the kitchen ran parallel to a front hall that was never used much. Nan understood its importance but found it a waste of space. The stairs curved down, the banister gently swooping to allow for wide bottom steps. The front door was carved with mermaids and mermen and flanked on both sides by stained-glass windows of every color, leaded in the shape of flowers and gardens.

And there was the doorknob in case she forgot her penance. And in the library, the grandfather clock.

Nan hung up a picture of the pope in each room. Each exactly the same size.

Upstairs in the bedrooms, the beds all shared crisp white linens and heavy drapes to keep things warm in winter and cool in summer.

There were deep-red velvet drapes on the windows of her own bedroom, creating an almost theatrical backdrop for the altar adorned with statues of Catholic saints and little colored glass candleholders that flickered with candlelight prayers.

There was a suite of rooms on the third floor that Nan wanted arranged for Vincent. But when she wrote to him, he refused to come.

"I have a life all my own now. I don't need your charity," he'd said.

Nan knew what he meant. It was too little, too late. He was punishing her for leaving him to fend for himself all those years ago.

She would pray for him.

She loved the kitchen the most. It was full of light and warmth and space to practice her own sort of magic—her cooking. She didn't need much else. There was a pantry that was eventually turned into a wash closet and then a full bathroom as the years passed, and she was always quick to upgrade the house for ease.

The living room housed a beautiful piano, though. The centerpiece was the fireplace and on the mantel Nan kept mementos taken from her life at Haven House. Scavenged treasures. Colorful bottles and pretty glass vases to catch the sunlight. And charred photographs in fancy frames.

The house's extremities, the attic and basement, were opposing spaces, not just because one was at the very top and the other at the very bottom, but because the basement was damp and dark whereas the attic was dry and bright. The basement was gloomy, as most basements are, and it would flood every spring, bringing panic and chaos. Finally Nan gave up putting anything at all on the floor and chose instead to use the cellar of the gatehouse.

She bottled wine. She went to church. She made fresh pasta. She worked her fingers raw.

And she never forgot, not one time, that she was already dead.

12

Lucy in the Gatehouse with a Gun

1911

After the house was completed Nan gave birth to Lucia, who would grow up beautiful and wild and would demand to be called the Americanized version of her name, "Lucy." Nan tried not to compare Lucy to Ava, but it was impossible. Each breath Lucy took invoked a river of regret in Nan.

Nan fell swiftly and deeply in love with her new baby, and the more her love grew, the more the guilt grew. This guilt tempered her outward affection toward Lucy. She would find herself wanting to fawn over her darling girl, but instead, Nan was full of discipline, and when Lucy was grown, she would tell stories about her childhood. "That woman has *ice* in her blood," she would say. Lucy would never know the love Nan had for her, the love that lived on the inside of Nan's skin, the love that came out in the food she cooked, in the gardens she kept, in the priests she served at church. Everything she did was for Lucy, simply everything.

Lucy was irresistible. And she was naughty. She learned early to lie, often and well, and if caught . . . to smile and be charming.

"You think too much about the past," Nan's priest told her. "Lead a simple life in both thought and action. Each day, make a list of tasks, and follow it. Do not color outside the lines. Sorrow lives there."

Nan listened, and she listened well. One of her tasks was to find tenants for the gatehouse in order to make ends meet. So as she left the church she went straight to the newspaper office to post an ad, and though many prospective renters came to view the gatehouse, no one rented it.

She went from looking ten years younger to ten years older in the course of a few months. Nan was happy with the effect. She didn't need to be young and attractive; she wanted to be left alone to her house and her garden.

In her dreams she was young, and she was still dancing with Reginald. Little Ava watching from the stairs. Her true family.

In reality, she was far away from home, and she had no one, and no one had her. And though she loved Lucy, she hated herself.

1918

Lucy had a sickness in her brain. From the time she was small, she suffered from chronic, random fits of terror, but the flu that hit Haven Port and the country at large pushed the little girl into a clear frenzy.

From all the corners of her mind, like shadows, "the crazies" (that was what she called them as she grew older) would come and the world would get dark. A low *hummmm* of anxiety existed inside her mind. When it was low, she could function. But when the *hummmm* grew loud, piercing, as it did late at night or when she was alone or when she cared too much about anything, the sound became deafening and even her screaming couldn't quiet it.

Lucy's first "attack" had terrified Nan. But Nan dealt with it as she dealt with everything else . . . stoically and with God. She dragged her raving daughter, past bodies waiting for caskets in the streets, to a priest and insisted Lucy had a demon inside of her.

But Nan was wrong. Lucy's soul remained chained in the dark recesses of her own mind even as she tried to live life, as she pretended to be just fine. And she never quite forgave Nan for not being able to take it all away.

"I want to know about my father. If he is alive, I want to live with him. I can't stay here with you. You are too cold. I think I need more love. If you loved me, I wouldn't have my fits." said Lucy.

Nan started mumbling in Italian.

"Speak English, Mama, please. I understand it better."

"Lucia, you do not need to know your father's name. He is gone. There is no family. There is no point in discussing it. And of course I love you."

"Who is the little girl on the mantel, Mama—they say she was yours."

"Who says that?"

"The nuns, the neighbors, just everyone, Mama."

"Lucia, they are all fools! Just a little something pretty I took from Haven House."

"I don't believe you!"

"You don't have to. But understand me, Lucia, this is nothing but a shadow. . . . Nothing but a shadow in a pretty frame."

Nan wanted to tell her daughter that the terror and pain Nan herself had suffered at the very start of Lucy's life was the root cause (she was certain) of Lucy's fits. That the hidden things in the dark were her own memories and longings. Lucy could feel the secrets. A sorrow that never belonged to her was suffocating her.

But Nan wouldn't tell Lucy. She'd woven too many lies to turn back. Besides, she'd kept her safe from the flu. What more did the girl want?

1920

Two years later, a man arrived.

At first, Nan couldn't make out his face, but something made her go out onto the porch. Something in his posture that reminded her of pulling hay from her hair and the taste of disgust on her tongue.

"It can't be," she whispered.

"What is it, Mama? Are you okay?" asked Lucy, alarmed by the look in Nan's eyes.

"I will never be okay again."

"Why? Who is that man?"

"He is my penance. Go to your room and don't come down until I say. Go now."

"You look well, Nan," said Giancarlo, sitting in her sunny kitchen as if he had all the time in the world. "And this house is magnificent."

"It is."

"How many years has it been? Seventeen? You've made quite a life for yourself, no?"

"I have no time for small talk, Carlo. What is it you want from me? You want money? I have no money. You want to see your daughter? She is dead. There is nothing for you here. I was kind, letting you sit at my table and drink from my cup. When you finish your coffee, you will leave."

"How is it you don't have any money? This is a fine piece of land. This is a fine house. I saw a smaller one at the end of the drive."

"What do you intend to do, Carlo?"

"I intend to stay here."

Nan thought it over. He was a virus. He needed to be contained. And she needed a renter.

"You will not live *here*. You will live in the gatehouse. And you will pay rent. And you will speak no words of our daughter again. I have another one to raise."

"And if I refuse? I can take this from you, Nan. I can rip it away."

"How? You have no idea who I am or what I can do. Maybe I can illuminate it for you. When I got here, I grew into my mother's ways. You remember her, I'm sure. How the town feared her. You were so afraid of her you almost married me." Nan laughed but all Carlo heard was a cackle.

He pushed back from the table and agreed to Nan's terms. She didn't seem as formidable as Ava Amore had been back in Italy, but he didn't want to take the chance.

Giancarlo hadn't really intended to stay. He'd run into Vincent, that little shit brother of Nan's, and he was bragging about Nan this and Nan that. So when he lost his job (for drunk and disorderly conduct), he thought it would be a good time to investigate.

But, when he got there. . . . the house called to him. It wanted him for something. He didn't care what it was, just knew he had to stay. In the end, it didn't matter what the house wanted—what mattered most to Carlo was *Lucy*.

She wasn't his daughter, and he was glad of it. Child or not, Lucy kept him awake at night in his room, watching her window from his own. He'd never wanted a body more than he wanted hers. He'd never been attracted to children like the perverts in the papers. Still, he ached for her. And it disgusted him, and it fascinated him.

———

He hired a boy named Vito from town to help Nan with the grounds.

"I'm too old to work like a mule. The boy is good, from a good family." he'd said.

Lucy knew Vito from school, and as he spent all his after-school hours on the Witch House property, the two children became quite close.

Giancarlo tried to use their friendship to manipulate Lucy. To have her over to the gatehouse for lemonade. To play games of cards on the porch, but she refused.

When Vito asked why, she answered.

"I can't stand the way it smells in that house."

She hated the gatehouse more than any other place on earth. She hated it even more than she hated the Witch House.

Lucy began her obsession with France right around the same time that Vito mistakenly told her Giancarlo might be her father. Instead of asking anyone if it was true, she decided she was going to run away to France. Of course, Vito would have to come.

When they were fifteen Vito had to quit his job to work with his family business.

"I want you to stay away from Carlo. I don't like how he looks at you. I don't care if he married your mother, or if he may be your father. He's not to be trusted."

My father? Mon dieu! thought Lucy.

———

"Are you my father?"

"Of course I'm not." said Carlo from the doorway.

"I'm not sure if I believe you. Have you ever been to France?"

Carlo saw his opportunity. "I have, in fact. I also have a set of very rare books on France. That I bought . . . guess where?"

"In France?"

"Yes. Come inside. I'll show you."

"I shouldn't."

"Don't be silly. You were just convinced I was your father. We are family. I watched you grow up! The bookshelf is right over there." Carlo opened the screen door and she walked inside.

Lucy found the bookshelf and honed in on the books she needed. How to speak French, how to cook French food, all about French plays, French history, French music.

She began to read.

He grabbed her from behind.

"Let me go."

"I will set the books on fire. You won't have them anymore."

"What do you want?"

"Just keep reading."

And as she read, he touched her in *almost* all the ways he'd dreamt of. She was older now, it wasn't such a sin. Soon, he'd own her like he'd owned her mother all those years before.

He told her she had to come back or he'd tell Vito and Nan she was a whore.

No one noticed she was being abused.

They noticed other things.

Vito noticed her sudden interest in all things French.

Nan noticed her night terrors that had subsided, returned, and brought her to the priest.

The priest said her change in personality could be the result of yet another demon. "So many demons you have, Lucia!" declared Nan, dragging her home.

Could someone scream themselves to death? Lucy wondered. So she had to concentrate on other things. Lucy was concentrating very hard on becoming French.

The nuns at school noticed her sudden interest in literacy—oh, but the books they would catch her reading! There were books on French fashion (couture!) and culture, and food, and the music; books on sexuality and love; books on French gardening and temperament.

One night, while Nan was cleaning the living room as Lucy sat on the couch, ferociously reading a book on the history of the French Revolution, she decided to confront her daughter about this obsession.

"Lucia, it is like there is a fire in you. . . . You are not French, you are Italian. Please don't do this to me! It embarrasses me. I don't understand it. Don't be like this!" Nan begged her.

Lucy stood up, immediately furious; she always had trouble containing rage. "How would I know that? I could be half French. . . . Maybe you don't even know. You never talk about my father!" Nan slapped her across her face. Lucy stared hard at the floor and whispered, "Mama, there is so much I don't know. Can't we talk? Can't you tell me who he is? Who he was? Alive or dead? Rich or poor? Italian? *French?* Just tell me it isn't Carlo, Mama. Because he is a bad man. The way he touches me. . . ."

Nan froze. She didn't want to believe Lucy. And she wanted to believe her. She wanted to hold her close and love her. She wanted to push her away. She just didn't know how to love Lucy. It had been too long. Nan was in a panic, so she pretended to be in control. She chose the easiest path.

"You lie."

"Please, Mama, what I tell you is true," Lucy cried, running upstairs to her room to fetch a ripped nightgown. She held it to Nan's face, but Nan pulled away.

"Get a hold of yourself, Lucia, and go wash your face. Tears will make the skin bad. I will make some tea."

Lucy grew very calm. She got up and said good night to her mother, kissing her softly on the cheek. Nan felt better and assumed she had been right about Lucia lying, once again, for attention. "I won't take tea tonight. Thank you, Mama." Lucy walked out of the kitchen, and Nan turned to put water on to boil anyway. But Lucy did not go to bed. Instead, she walked right into the front room, took off her clothes, every single stitch, and out through the front hall. She opened the front door quietly and stepped out into the night. She did not look back. She did not run. She just held her torn nightgown against her nakedness and watched her bare feet walk down the hill. Down the hill and over the bridge to Vito. She would be reborn.

When Nan went to check on her and found her gone, she was relieved. Lucy wouldn't be her problem anymore. And yet she sat on her bed and cried, cried for many reasons, reasons she did and didn't understand. But as always, the next day came, full of chaos and all things good and bad. Time doesn't stop for runaway children. Time doesn't stop for tragedy or elation; it plods onward, always onward, for the living and sometimes even for the dead.

As Nan expected, it was Vito that Lucy went to for her rescue. They were married the following weekend. Nan had to sign papers that came from the court, because Lucy was so young.

Lucy did not go back home. She did not talk to Nan. It is surprisingly easy to avoid people, even in a small town. Nan missed Lucy. Lucy missed Nan. But they didn't understand that the empty pit in both their stomachs belonged to that very missing. If they noticed, then it would be a nuisance to their lives. And Nan, at least, had no time for nuisance. And Lucy did not miss the house.

Giancarlo kept to himself after Lucy left.

It was the smell that told Nan something was terribly wrong. She knew what she would find when she entered. She was expecting a mess, but not quite the mess she found. Carlo was hanging, had hung himself from the broad sturdy beam that went across the kitchen ceiling.

She gave him a little push with her hand, and he swung for a moment. The noxious odor that came out of him made her feel faint, so she stepped back to catch her breath. She leaned her head on the Hoover hutch in the kitchen that served as a desk for Giancarlo. Her eyes caught on her name, and then Lucy's, on a piece of writing paper.

His confession.

"I can't go on without her."

Nan fell to the floor and cried up at heaven. "Oh, my dear sweet God, what have I done? What have I done? I knew he was a sick man. I chose not to believe her!" She steeled herself. "You did what you needed to do . . . now go clean this up."

She washed the floor. She put down an old sheet, cut him down, and then called the constable.

"Fuck you," she whispered when she was done.

As the constable asked her questions, she pretended not to know anything and was believed. She thought she could, should, would, apologize for not believing her. But it was over now. And she had a gatehouse to scour and rent. She'd go tomorrow.

Lucy would love her again. Tomorrow.

13

Vito in the Alley with a Machine Gun

Eventually, if one tries hard enough, it becomes the little things, the accidental things, that make a home: an apron hanging on a nail in the cellar stairs, a stack of books, the chair that becomes dedicated to a carelessly thrown wrap, a key hook. These things become nostalgia. Lucy crafted nostalgia well.

Vito painted their house bright yellow with a green door and green shutters; it had a brick basement like all of the oyster homes on the bay side of Haven Port. Oystermen needed tall basements for storing the oysters. Vincent's family didn't only oyster, they fished, and they thrived.

The house was very small but cozy. The architecture was the same as every other house on the river, but this one felt special . . . kinder. The first thing Lucy did as mistress was paint the door a bright raspberry red. She found the paint in the basement. Vito bought it thinking she would like it for inside. But he was wrong, and amused, and he loved her more for it. She had him create little wooden window boxes and in the spring and summer filled them with vining flowers and greenery. She knew to put impatiens on the shady side of the house and petunias on the sunny side. She asked him to make the kitchen window box bigger so she could grow herbs to put in her "one-pot wonders." Lucy was always making magic with her cast-iron soup pot. Whatever she threw in would simmer all day, fill the house with tantalizing smells, and then taste even better.

Lucy liked to walk to the docks and mingle with the Persian women. She would visit their shop stalls and buy wonderful, vibrant fabrics with which she created pillows, bedding, skirts, aprons, and her favorite: large patchwork satchel-type bags that she would take with her to market. The Persian women began to buy the bags from her, and then the women in town were soon to follow, knocking on her door, asking to purchase her creations. Lucy colored the town. Everyone loved her. She was a rainbow. Lucy's life was sweet and safe.

The baby came a few years after they were married. No gossip necessary. They named him Dominic, meaning "for our Lord," because both Vito and Lucy wanted to protect him from all the evil they believed surrounded them. To cast a godly light onto their lives and remove the stains Giancarlo had left all over them. They made love all the time. And they loved madly. Lucy still had fits, but Vito knew all about them.

He knew Lucy. Inside out. He felt her blood running through his veins.

One time, before Dominic was born, he was out on *Forever Lucy* taking in a great haul with his brother, when suddenly, he was overcome with crippling nausea. "Frankie!" he called out. "Frankie, we need to go in! I need to get to Lucy!" And sure enough, when he ran into Oyster House, he found her naked in an empty tub, shivering and rocking back and forth. Her protruding stomach made her arms and legs look stick thin and vulnerable. She was having a fit. He took off his shirt and got right in the tub with her. He held her so she could feel his breath, hear his heartbeat. He held her until their heartbeats became one and she stopped shaking. Then he picked her up and carried her to their bed. He pulled back all the bright bed-covers she had made them and tucked her in. He locked up the house—she liked it locked up when she felt like this. He made sure she heard all the latches clicking and windows closing, and then he climbed into bed with her and held her close once again. He could feel his unborn child kick on his belly, almost as if the baby were inside of him. It wouldn't take long . . . a few hours maybe, and she would be right as rain. This is how it went with them. This is how he took care of her. This is what people do when they love from all the right places and for all the right reasons.

She would always whisper, "I am so sorry, Vito . . . ," and he would always reply, "You have nothing to be sorry for—if you changed a bit, I would leave you forever. . . ."

And so Dominic was welcomed with love, security, and a

sense of humor. Life was easy for Lucy and Vito until the fishing began to dry up.

When the money got tight, Vito took a chance. He had to provide, and there was only one option left. He had family in New York City, and there was money to be made during Prohibition. Good money, the kind that was dangerous to make. He knew she would put up a fight, so he agreed without telling her. He knew best.

"You can't go there. You will die! How dare you? *How dare you?!*"

"I won't die."

"You will, Vito. You will."

"I won't."

"And what if you do?"

"I won't. Hey! Think of it this way: with all the money I'll make, we can all go to France. Me, you, Dom . . ."

"France?"

"Yes! Oh, my sweet Lucy, I can send you presents from Fifth Avenue. And I promise, I will not die."

"But what if you do?"

"Babe, if I die . . . then I will be on that other side, that side that makes you so afraid, and I will send you signs, great big signs, that everything is okay over there . . . and then you won't be afraid anymore. And I'll just wait for you, and one day, when you are an old lady, when it's your time to pass, you can bet I'll be there to collect you."

She didn't have a choice; she had to let him go. She had to trust him. She sent him off with love. They held each other very tight. And then, handsome in his new suit and shiny shoes, he was gone.

Deep in the middle of a moonless night on the river, Lucy woke up sweating and crying and knew. She knew he was dead. Saw guns, and cement, felt the lead in his gut. It wasn't the sort of panicky anxiety she was so used to: this was knowledge, it was plain unadulterated knowing. Dominic woke up as well and climbed into her bed. They were silent. They cried a little, and in an effort to "keep it together," as Vito would have wanted her to at least try to do, she hushed him: "It's going to be fine . . . hush, he is with us . . . hush now, we will be fine. . . ."

Lucy waited for his sign. She waited for a very long time. She waited and she waited and she waited.

To her credit, she tried, successfully for a while, to keep it together. But then a potent strain of the flu, reminiscent of the one that haunted her as a child, came like the boogeyman, like the nightmare that just wouldn't end. Everyone would die around her; there would be bodies in the streets.

Lucy began to lose her mind. Better to lose her mind than her son. When Nan came by, she tried to talk to Lucy through the door. Nan begged her to come home.

"The Witch House? That's what everyone calls it, you know. That's the kind of place you created. You want me to come to the Witch House!?"

"Lucia, what are you going to do? You have to come. If you don't come, I will get the constable and tell him you are unwell. I can have them take you away. Don't forget, Lucia, your Vito is dead now. You are alone! You hear me, Lucia?"

she spat. She turned around in a huff, and Lucy watched her old lady of a mother walk away, knowing she meant what she said.

Dominic was scared of his mother. She wouldn't let him go outside, and she was washing them in basins every hour. She locked him in the house and went outside so she could burn all the clothing. He finally escaped through a front window and went first to find his Uncle Frank, but when he wasn't at the bridge, he knew he only had time to run to one other person, no matter how afraid he was. And by now, he was more afraid of Lucy than Nan.

Nan marched down the hill and straight to Oyster House. She flew up the walkway and banged her fist on the raspberry door. Lucy was busy scrubbing every surface yet again. "Lucia! I have your boy! Come here right now!" Lucy opened the door. Nan had Dominic by his collar. "Get dressed and come home." Nan turned around and dragged Dominic back down the walk with her. She didn't turn around. She knew Lucy would follow. There was nothing else to do.

Frank, Vito's brother, came after Lucy and Dominic moved back to the Witch House. He stood in the middle of Lucy and Vito's enchanted and now abandoned life. He packed up their essentials and left the rest. They wouldn't sell or rent this house. Dominic would need it, probably sooner rather than later, and as Frank locked the raspberry door, he had a heavy heart, knowing that whatever magic had once lived there was lost, that Lucy died with Vito in the streets of New York. What would become of them?

Lucy was full of terror those first few weeks back home. It

was surreal. Her mother had taken dictatorlike control over the grandson she barely knew, and though Lucy felt bad for him, there was a certain relief that came from letting someone else handle everything.

But then, one afternoon, Lucy heard weeping from the front hall. Dominic stood, positioned in a corner, by the door. His posture said it all; he needed to escape but was unable to make himself leave the house, so he compressed himself as hard as he could into the corner by the nearest exit. Lucy knew this feeling, this need to flee. Her boy was down there, her baby boy, her beautiful strong wonderful miniature Vito. She flew down the stairs and grabbed him fiercely by the shoulders and pried him from the wall. He turned to her but would not take his hands from in front of his eyes. He did not want her to see him weak. He was a good boy, a noble boy, a strong boy. He was his father's boy.

"Baby, Mama is sorry." Her voice took on a forced strength. "Mama is so, so sorry. I am going to try, baby. I am going to be good. I swear . . . Mama is going to be good. Don't cry!"

And he believed her, because he had nothing else to believe in, and she *was* good. For a few years she tried her best. She put her unruly hair back up and wore a red kerchief on her head as she cleaned. Lucy sang songs Vito had taught her. They made her want to break down, to spiral uncontrollably into a dark abyss, but she knew they comforted Dominic. So she sang them.

She went up to the attic and brought down the Haven House possessions that Nan put away. Lucy took her time looking through trunks of clothes.

The black silk shawl with the black fringe and the multicolored embroidered flowers all over it. She wrapped it around herself in the attic that day, and afterward, was rarely seen without it.

She tried to get along with Nan. She made friends with the ladies at the church even though she still refused to go, and she would make trips to the farmers market to sell her colorful bags. She didn't have to cook anymore; that was Nan's magic. This made her sad, but she had her son and his love, and she tried her best to wait patiently for a sign from Vito, the sign he promised to send.

And then Nan rented the gatehouse to a mousy, tall woman named Lavinia Masters. She had a young son, Jude, and an angry, handsome, rich older brother who was setting her up in Virginia to avoid some kind of a scandal that Nan said was "None of our business." His name was Gavin, and what a man he was. There had never been, it seemed, anyone more handsome, so utterly damaged and in need of repair. Gavin was born looking for the road back home. And he could never find it. But he thought he'd found it when he met Lucy. Gavin Masters would be the final undoing of Lucy, but he would be the beginning of Anne.

14

Gavin on the Docks
with a Bastard

1939

We all bring our pasts with us into a new relationship. Memories haunt every single reaction we have. And when people like Gavin and Lucy try to make a go of things, things go south real fast.

Gavin's memories were far worse than Lucy's. They were even worse than Nan's.

Gavin and Lavinia's father, Early Masters, was very bad man. But that was Early's magic, being bad. He could ruin everything just by breathing. Sometimes Gavin thought even the plants would roll up and die when they saw him coming. For some reason, Gavin's mama saw him as a sick man, a wounded man, a man she could save . . . but Gavin knew, was born know-ing, that he would be lucky if he saw grammar school.

There was a bit of a respite when Early left to go preach in an Alabama parish for a few years. But he came back after his granddaddy died on the saw, and things got especially bad.

When Early returned, he was bona-fide crazy. He told everyone Jesus was talking through him, and he started charm-ing snakes.

A few years later, Early told Lavinia to watch their baby brother Junior who'd just learned to walk.

Somehow or another Junior got ahold of one of those snakes . . . and after the fuss and the funeral Early took Lavinia into the music room and locked the door, screaming about di-vine justice.

But instead of killing Lavinia, he killed himself.

He just shot himself in front of Lavinia, some kind of sick witness.

Gavin ran far away . . . fast. His mind went first, and then his body followed.

Three years after Early shot himself, Gavin went home.

His sister met him at the door toting a toddler that was the spitting image of Junior and told him her secret. Their crazy father had raped her in that music room before he killed him-self.

That's when Gavin knew there was no God.

He'd been to Haven Port once with his mama. She'd loved it so much, she'd said that little town, with its ocean music and ponies running wild, could heal anyone's soul. So that's where he brought Lavinia and her boy.

He came to Haven Port a broken man. He saw Lucy from the decks of his boat as they anchored. She was walking with a young boy on the piers, looking at all the fresh catch. Her skirt was bright red and her blouse was white and it fell off of her shoulder. She had a flowered black shawl wrapped carelessly (yet with great care) around, through, and under her arms. He had to follow her.

She was joking with the boy, teasing him, making him laugh.

Gavin pretended to trip on a piling and he fell gently into her. She turned to see who had been so rude, and that was that.

"Excuse me, beautiful lady, which way to Persimmon Point? We're expected at the gatehouse."

She smiled, he fell in love. Her hair, those black curls, took an extra three seconds to follow her face, and he felt he was in the presence of a great lioness, a gypsy, a witch, a real honest-to-goodness woman.

"You seem to have stumbled right onto your welcome wagon. I've been sent to fetch you, Mr. Masters. Would you like to come home with me?" she said.

She wasn't shy. Once Lavinia and that boy of hers were set up, Lucy took him into her bed. He knew there was something not right about her, not right about the house and the land it was built on. But he didn't care. It was good. Until it wasn't. Nan didn't like him. Dominic, Lucy's son, couldn't stand him. Lucy started to get distant.

He wanted to take her and Lavinia and the kids back down south but she wouldn't hear of it. . . . She mumbled something about waiting for signs. His drinking increased as his patience decreased.

And then Lucy dropped the news that she was pregnant. And she refused to marry him . . . she just wanted him in her bed.

He started going on more and more fishing expeditions. The next few years were spotty for Gavin, hazy with sea spray and bourbon. He recalled trips back to the Witch House. His daughter was a beautiful little birdlike thing. She was quiet, though, and it seemed everyone liked her just about as much as they liked him. He felt sorry for her . . . but in the end, he felt Lucy would be a good mother to the girl. He could still see Lucy on the dock where he first met her, playing with Dominic: that mothering part of her was half the attraction. Each time he came back, Lucy was a little crazier, a little drunker, and an ocean grew between them.

When it was clear she didn't want him anymore, he left. When he asked her one final time to come, she sent him word that he was no longer a part of her story. He was washed from her memory.

He should have tried harder. Because he left his little bird daughter in terrible danger.

This danger had a name, and it was Jude. Gavin's bastard nephew and half brother. Evil was in the lineage. A toxic mix afoot.

15

Maj in the Backseat with the "What If" Game

FRIDAY, SEPTEMBER 4, 2015
12:00 P.M.

"This seems as good a place as any to take a break," said Byrd. "Anne's story comes next, and hers is the longest," said Byrd.

"I finally get to learn more about Crazy Anne?" asked Eleanor, putting down her notes.

"Yep, Crazy Anne. My great-grandmother."

"It's astounding to think how much hate and loss was suffered here. I've always thought that houses were like sponges, soaking up everything. But I don't feel the sorrow here. This house still feels like a hug."

"I agree with you there," said Byrd. "But maybe it isn't the house at all. Later, if we take Maj to see them ponies she keeps yammering on about, we could take some time feelin' out that old foundation."

"Good idea, but for now, let's go grocery shopping. We cannot live off coffee grounds and whiskey."

"You just lack imagination, but FINE. I'll get Maj. Do you see her? I don't see her."

"She's right there—see the hair bouncing over the topiary?"

"I love that hair." said Byrd. "I love that kid. She's just my kind of weird."

Elly smiled. Someone else was noticing the amazing parts of Maj. Someone else was loving Maj for who she really was. It was lovely to no longer be alone in the adoration of her child.

12:30 P.M.

Driving away from the house, Eleanor looked at the gatehouse, overgrown with weeds and boarded up. Like a bruised face. She wondered if she should clean it out and try to rent it, as Nan had. Or maybe use it as a painting studio. Then she shivered. It was as if two parts of her were arguing. One pragmatic, one visceral. She put all of it on hold. Too much was happening already.

Once on the main road they played the "What If" game in the car. Byrd fit right in.

"If you were an ice cream flavor, what would you be?" asked Maj.

"Vanilla," said Byrd.

"Me too," said Eleanor.

"I'm cherry," said Maj.

"Cherry ice cream or cherry ice, baby girl?"

"JUST CHERRY."

"Fine," said Eleanor.

"If you were a punctuation mark, what punctuation mark would you be, Mama? I'm an exclamation point," said Maj.

"That's a good one. You stumped me. And I think you're an exclamation point, too," Eleanor smiled.

"I'm a question mark," said Byrd.

"Yes you are!" laughed Eleanor.

"Mama, you have to answer. What would you be?"

"Baby, I don't know."

"You'd be an exclamation point, too. It's . . . what was that word Dr. B used, Mama?" asked Maj.

Eleanor thought back to their last psychotherapy appointment. Then she remembered. "*Genetic*, is that the word you're thinking of?"

"Yes! See, if I'm an exclamation point, so are you."

Eleanor parked the car in the half-empty lot.

"I wish I were. But . . . I'm a. . . ." Eleanor felt the tears come before she could fight them back. The sorrow came on so quickly when she stopped focusing on the Witch House and its mysteries. She missed Mimi. And she missed Anthony and hated him and loved him and now she was trapped in the car with her baby girl and her odd young question mark of a distant cousin, about to lose her mind because of a game.

"What's the matter?" asked Byrd. "Question mark?"

"I'm just sad. Sometimes people just get sad, and there's nothing much they can do. I don't like to be sad. Don't people in Alabama get sad? How about you take Maj in the store, and I'll get my act together."

"Maj is right here," said Maj.

"Sad means regret, did you know that? Seems to me you're angry, not sad. And there are plenty of angry folks in Alabama, believe you me. There's an emergency cigarette in the glove compartment. You know, for times like these," said Byrd.

"It's my car. My glove compartment, and my emergency . . . oh, can it, kid. Go inside. Leave this almost-middle-aged woman with her crisis."

Eleanor watched them walk inside and defiantly lit her cigarette. She thought about all the things Anthony used to say to her. And it didn't really matter that she knew he was only lashing out because he'd been hurt.

"I hate it when you smoke. I don't understand you. You seem so much smarter."

Yes, she thought, because this is the real truth:

I am not an exclamation point.

He is a long story. I am an ellipsis. . . .

Or maybe, on a rainy day, a comma,

A fucking pause,

Yes. I'm a pause.

Onward to the groceries.

2:30 P.M.

After the groceries were unloaded, Byrd wanted to resume the stories. But Eleanor needed a break.

"I'd like to rummage around a bit myself. I know you've found all there is to find, but two sets of Amore eyes can't hurt. Can you watch Maj?"

"Sure. But yell if you find something. The clock is ticking, you know. . . ."

Eleanor knew. *Tic tock tic tock tic tock. Tic.*

She wandered the house alone, listening to the two girls running and shrieking as they played outside. Then she focused on the library. The door was stuck. Typical. She turned the knob and forced it open with her shoulder. Then she tumbled forward and fell sideways into the room, knocking over a humidor cabinet, which broke, splintering in front of her.

"Nice one. Graceful," Eleanor grunted.

A thick white envelope had fallen out of the cabinet. It had a proper label on it, addressed to Byrd at "The Witch House," but in the corner, where there would have been a postmark with a date, it simply said, *"There is no such thing as time."*

"Byrd! I think I found something!" Eleanor called. She got up, placed the envelope on the desk, and looked around while she waited.

There were boxes of books next to half full bookcases. They seemed to be organized by name.

Nan, Lucy, Anne, Opal, and Stella.

Nan's were lives of the saints. Lucy had plays. Anne had all the dark magic books. Opal's box was full of romances and adventures. And Stella's books were about families.

"What is taking you so long, Byrd!?"

"I'm right here! What happened?" asked Byrd, looking at the broken cabinet.

"I'll never be a dancer is what happened. I'll clean that up. This is for you, honey."

Byrd hesitated, then carefully took the envelope and left the room.

And even though she was curious, Eleanor let her open her letter alone.

And past the juniper, on the edge of a cliff, Maj began to sing.

3:00 P.M.

One, two, three, four, five,
Once I caught a soul alive,
Six, seven, eight, nine, ten,
Then I let it go again.
Why did you let it go?
Because its sorrow hurt me so.
Which soul did cause this fright?
This little one who likes to bite.

Maj sat on the cliff watching the ponies with Ava and Crazy Anne.

"So, Byrd will tell your mother my story next, love," said Anne.

"Yes." Maj tried not to be shy around spirits—they could walk all over you. But Anne was different—stronger, angrier. Maj automatically became a polite, well-mannered child in her presence.

"I don't want you to listen. I've shown you all the important parts, but there are some things you cannot unhear or unsee.

There are things that will be told that could follow you, haunt you. And I do not want that for you."

"Aren't *you* already haunting her?" asked Ava, giggling. Maj braced herself. Anne exploded into a swarm of blackbirds and flew away.

"Why did you do that? I don't like when she's angry."

"Because I want to watch the ponies. I don't care about the stories. I always think those ponies will lead me home to my mama."

"You're brave, Ava."

"I'm not really. Anne says all I have to do is call for mama and she'll come. But I don't do it. I don't know why. Oh, and I have news. Anne said she'd tell you the secret!"

"When?"

"Tomorrow. But right now, I think you might be in very big trouble."

Maj turned around to see her Mama and Byrd running toward the cliff.

4:00 P.M.

"*Dear God, Maj!* What were you thinking!" yelled Eleanor, shaking her daughter.

"LET GO OF ME!"

"Are Anne and Ava still here, Maj? Because I can't see them. Why won't you let me see you?" cried Byrd.

"You never took me to see the ponies and you promised and *I wanted to!*" Maj started crying.

Eleanor shook with anger and fear. She looked to the bottom of the cliff, and thought, *It would be easier to jump.*

Then, she took a breath and pulled both girls into a tight embrace safely away from the edge.

"Wait, this is what it does. This house . . . it hits a panic button. We need to calm down and think things through."

All three stood still in a sort of shock, and then . . . calmed.

4:15 P.M.

"That was intense." said Elly, walking back from seeing the ponies.

"It just wants us safe." said Maj.

"What does?"

"The house. The land. It loves us, and I got too close to the edge, and it lost its temper inside you. Because it doesn't have a body."

"Of course," said Byrd.

Eleanor, Maj, and Byrd continued to talk, as stars twinkled in the darker half of the sky and the house stood up straighter, with a sly smile, its angles, spires, and shadows reaching inward to embrace its new darlings.

9:00 P.M.

"She's asleep," said Eleanor to Byrd, who was sitting in the library under a glowing green stained-glass reading lamp. "Good.

I don't care what Maj think she knows, this isn't a story for her. This is horror. The real kind. You ready?"

"Byrd?"

"No time to waste here. Is this question you're about to ask me pertinent?"

"Everything is pertinent. I'm hearing all this for the first time. But you aren't. And it's all much closer to you, honey. We are talking about things . . . genetics . . . I don't know. I hope you're okay with all this."

"The way I figure it, everyone's family has hidden shame. I'd be a piss poor witch if mine weren't downright horrible. And as bad as you think it is, it gets worse. The sooner I tell you about Anne, the sooner we find out the secrets this place hides. And about that . . . well, uh, see . . . we're going to have a guest tomorrow."

"And who would that be?" Eleanor raised an eyebrow.

"Well . . ."

"Spit it out, Byrd!"

"I may have called a psychic. You know, like a medium."

"You called a psychic? Byrd . . . technically speaking, *we* are psychics! That's the last thing we need. What if this person . . ."

"Amazing Andy."

"Oh, God. What if *Amazing Andy* hooks up with Johnny Colder and they—never mind. What's done is done." Eleanor sighed. "Tell me about Anne."

"Well, Anne's story is my favorite, even if it's the worst of the bunch. She was the one woman who loved the Witch House the way it wanted to be loved."

The Book of

Anne

1940–1999

16

Intermezzo

Look at them, the women of this house. It is night and they are sleep-ing soundly. The moon is full, so we can get a good look. It is midsum-mer and the windows are open and the ocean breeze is making for perfect sleeping weather. Salty air floats through this house with the moonlight. The women . . . their hair fades gray to black and black to gray. They are old and young, and young and old. . . . They are crazy and sane. They belong to each other, and they belong to no one.

Look at Lucy, how she sleeps. She looks like a young girl, her curly hair sweeping out onto the pillow beside her, her graceful hand, palm open, next to her cheek. Lucy is dreaming, dreaming of a life before this one, one with the sticky sounds of a happy baby, boats coming in from the harbor, and her Vito coming in from a long day of work. "Dance with me, my Lucy, dance with me, Forever Lucy. . . ." Lucy's lips turn up in her sleep. She always wants to be dreaming, longs never to wake up. There are wind chimes in her dreams, and mourning doves. She smiles; she is happy.

See Anne; see her tucked into her grandmother's bed. See the ghosts on either side of her. Anne does not dream. She sleeps balled up like an infant in the womb, yet she is all angles and tense lines. . . . See how she curls her thin body around Ava protectively. How she holds her tight. Ava is snuggled with her face buried in Anne's chest (she need not breathe), her little ghost hand entwined in Anne's hair. Gwyneth spoons them both, absorbing Anne's dreams, and watching over Ava in a continuous act of redemption.

See Nan; her sleep is orderly, everything just so. See the blanket tucked in neatly, hardly disturbed. A cup and saucer are on the nightstand, out of place. Nan was tired this evening. Nan dreams. It is always the same one. Nan dreams of playing with her sister outside their farmhouse in the Italian countryside. She dreams in Italian. She can smell the grass and the dirt baking in the sun. Her mother is cooking inside; Vincent is singing in the fields. She is laughing and spinning and teasing her sister and her brother. . . . There is nothing but comfort here. Nan dreams of home. When she wakes up, she will carry that dream with her all day, like she does every day, and she will resent everything around her, because she will never be home again.

It is coming on morning now, andiamo . . .

17

Lucy in the Bedroom
with the Crucifix

1940

Lucy was screaming and God wasn't listening. She'd labored in her mother's bedroom because that's what Nan said she should do. Something about God and Sin and being unmarried. The window was open, letting the winter in. She needed the air. The first snow collected in delicate layers on the wide, wooden sill.

Earlier, when the pains were coming farther apart, Lucy went to the bedroom window and held her hands against its icy glass to cool them off. The cold beneath her palms was lovely, it calmed her. She watched the dancing snow and wished she could be standing in it, letting it glitter in her hair, letting it clear the antiseptic, old-woman smell of the midwife from her nose. She wanted the snow whirling all around her, in her, through her. She knew that if she could just get out into the snowy night, all would be well.

When the pains came on stronger, with no relief or pause, she began to panic. She opened the window, struggling to unstick it from its frame. She felt a fleeting sense of victory when it lurched open, and she breathed in the night. The snow cooled her face. The feeling of respite lingered, and she rolled her body to lean against the wall, pressing her face against the wallpaper. It was covered in blue flowers blooming in a constant spring. Lucy traced the leaves with her finger before doubling over in pain. This aching was urgent and tore at her fragile mind. She kneeled on the wooden floor.

She was naked. Her suffocating nightgown had been tossed aside. Damp curls clung to her face and spilled over her shoulders.

Lucy closed her eyes, clutching a set of garnet rosary beads to her with clenched, white knuckles, and she prayed. She prayed to the statue of the Virgin Mary on the dresser, she prayed to the crucifix above the attached mirror, she prayed to the house.

"Holy Mary, mother of God, pray for us sinners now and at the hour of our death." Another pain ripped through her. "Oh, damn it!" Her eyelids flew open and she jerked her head up, staring with bright, lunatic eyes at the statue. "I can't do this! I don't even remember the whole prayer. . . . Please, sweet lady, please make this child come out and I swear . . . I swear to God I will name her after you!"

"Lucia!" Nan shushed her, entering the room with the midwife, Zindonetta, to see her there, crazy on the floor, arms outstretched to the statue, her body shaking with sobs. They brought her, scratching and kicking, back to the bed and held her down. Her struggle against them, coupled with her scream-ing, forced the baby swiftly out.

"Let me see her, let me see her," begged Lucy, only the baby did not make a sound. She was absolutely blue. The room was silent and heavy with worry. It was as if the house were heaving . . . pushing now that Lucy's turn was over. The floor-boards, the doors, windows, and even the walls bloated from strain. Lucy knew the house was trying to give birth to some-thing of its own.

Finally, the midwife broke the frightened paralysis and put her mouth over the infant's nose and blue-tinged lips, sucking out the mucus and spitting it on the floor. The baby's eyes snapped open and she turned pink, but she did not cry. The house went straight again.

In the attic of the house, snow fell in through a cracked win-dow onto the small square floor of the cupola and arranged it-self in the form of a marble Madonna and child, just as a phantom woman held a phantom child in the attic and twirled away the snowflakes, dancing in wide circles, soundlessly. *Chaînés, chaînés* . . .

Later, after Lucy slept off the haze of pain, she held and ex-amined her new baby. She had a strange fluttering feeling, like a life leaving her. And even as she cradled the baby, ready to love her, ready to coo and coddle like she had with Dominic, she noticed that the feeling would not leave. It was still there, a strange . . . *grayness*. And the child! She just stared. Was she broken?'

"Have you decided on a name? The child could die any moment. Zindonetta, go get the priest. Just in case." Turning back to Lucy, she said, "I know you liked the name Peach, but how about Plum or Strawberry? Maybe Pineapple?" Lucy was too tired to play Nan's game. When Nan predicted a baby girl, Lucy had thought that Peach would be suitable, something bright and vibrant to help ward off the evil in the house. But there had been no end of recrimination from her mother.

"Well, I suppose you win again, Mama." Lucy pointed half-heartedly to the statue she had prayed to. "I promised the virgin over there I would name this baby after her, so I guess she will be Mary."

"Lucia," the old woman said, "that isn't the Virgin Mother, that's a statue of Saint Anne. Notice the hair and the color of her robes? As that good-for-nothing excuse for a man is gone now, we don't have to name her after his mother. What kind of Anglo name is Ivy anyway?"

"Of course," whispered Lucy. "I guess she will have to be Anne. Like you, Mama. And like the little orphan in the funny papers."

Lucy began to fall asleep. Though she loved dreaming, she didn't like falling into sleep. It was suffocating. Usually she eased it along with a drink, but this tired wouldn't wait.

"Mama?" Lucy called out despite herself. Nan was quickly by her side. She took baby Anne and handed her to the midwife.

"Yes, Lucia? Are you all right?"

"Mama?" Lucy's face was damp with sweat and tears. Nan resisted the urge to crawl into bed with her and instead took her hands. "Mama, I don't want to fall asleep."

"How come, my Lucia? You worked so hard. How come you don't want to sleep?"

"I am afraid . . . I am afraid of the dark behind my eyes."

"Ahhh, yes. . . ." Nan released one of Lucy's hands and began to push her daughter's curly locks back from her face. "Do you remember when you were just a little girl, and you were so afraid of the night? How I would take you in your nightgown to walk down the hill to the river? Remember how beautiful the moon was, how the whole world was quiet? I told you to not be afraid of the night. God is in the night, Lucia. He created the night for us. It is like a dark blue velvet blanket, made to comfort us, not to frighten us. Do you remember, Lucia?"

Lucy let go of Nan's hands and rolled away from her.

"I remember being dragged to the priest." Then she brought her arms up to embrace herself.

Nan sighed and glanced over at the baby. The child was fine, cooing in the Moses basket, reaching out already, pulling her arms free of the swaddling and grasping at invisible fingers in the air.

"Zindonetta, come with me out of the room."

The two women conferred in the doorway, speaking fast with their hands, using their native language.

"What is it, Nan? She can't sleep?"

"It is not just that, Zindonetta. You know very well she has never been right in the head. Now I have another child to raise."

Zindonetta knew. Everyone knew Lucy was damaged. It was so sad. And now this new shame brought upon the family, this child with no father. Nan was a saint to put up with it all. Nan, a respected member of the parish, was looked on as a wise woman or *strega*, the curer of the evil eye—so why would God give her so much evil to deal with? Zindonetta once sent for her in the night when her son was having fits. Nan took the curse right off him. It was the reason she agreed to help with this birth. She owed a favor.

"Why can't you get rid of these demons, Nan?"

"I don't know. I have tried. I pray all the time, nothing works."

Zindonetta went to her bag and brought out a few bottles. "Here. She must take these. They will make her manageable."

Nan grasped the bottles close.

The midwife gathered her things and left. She was happy to leave. The house had a stink about it that made her sick to her stomach.

Days later, Lucy lay in bed, nursing her strange baby. And something happened. Anne looked right at her mother, not into space as she normally did. She locked eyes with Lucy and moved her lips around Lucy's nipple into a milky smile.

Lucy was caught off guard. Love, deep and full, washed through her. A greedy love, a love she had not known with her first baby. She wanted to devour her. She could tell Anne would grow up to be striking—her eyes were bright green like the sea before a squall. It was too much, this love. She could not do it. She could not be this child's mother. She could not betray her true family this way. She would not love this child at all if she could not love her just a little bit.

And why was she always staring into space? What could she

be seeing? The old Italian women always said that when babies stared like that, they were looking into the afterlife. Could Anne be seeing Vito? Taunting him with her existence? No. This would not do. She popped her nipple out of Anne's mouth and brought her downstairs to the kitchen.

Lucy plunked the wailing baby into Nan's arms and ran back upstairs. When safely back in her bedroom, she yelled, "I'm weaning her, you take her. Bring her to your church, give her to your God, make her a nun for all I care. I'm *done*!" And with that, Anne lost her mother.

18

Nan in the Kitchen with a Wooden Spoon

1940–1950

Anne was a good baby, by Italian standards anyway. She slept. She ate. She did not cry. Anne happily amused herself, even when there was nothing amusing around her. But when she turned three and could talk, things began to change.

One day, Anne was running through the rooms in delight, squealing as if someone was chasing her. This unnerved Nan so much that she pulled Anne to an abrupt stop by the neck of her dress.

"What do you run from, Anna? Who do you see?"

Anne, trying to get away from Nan and back to playing, answered, "Gwen and the little girl! Lemme go!"

"Gwen?" An icy shiver ran through Nan. "What little girl? Who do you speak of?"

"The little girl on the mantel! Lemme go!" Anne kicked her feet.

Nan picked up her granddaughter and sat her on the kitchen counter while she pumped cold water into the sink. Then she dunked Anne, fully clothed and screaming with fury, under the icy water.

"There are no such things as ghosts, Anna."

It didn't take long for Anne to learn her lesson. Every time Nan thought Anne was playing with "her ghosts," she punished her. A slap on the hand with a wooden spoon, a pinch to her arm, and sometimes just a cold stare. Anne learned to hide her joy.

She grew into a small little girl, thin and short for her age. Her hair was black like Lucy's, but straighter. Thick and unruly, as soon as it grew long enough it was braided, harshly, and braided it stayed. Her face was sweet and delicate, but no one noticed because her eyes were so large they took up most of her small face and, if caught in the right light, tended to disappear altogether. She had pale, freckled skin, unlike her mother's, or her Nan's, or her big brother Dominic's. Anne didn't look like she belonged to any of them. She was a quiet child in an unquiet house, who wandered around sneaking up on everyone by accident.

She preferred to be alone in the attic with her ghosts.

"No one believes me," Anne said to an ever-twirling Gwyneth.

"It will be all right. You have *us*." She could always make Anne feel better. Gwyneth even took away Anne's dreams. Anne never knew a nightmare. "Dreams can be bad," she told Anne, "so I steal them away from you."

Gwyneth wore the most beautiful old-fashioned white gown Anne had ever seen, even in storybooks. It was a dress perfect for dancing. *Chaînés, chaînés.* Anne loved the way it moved.

And ghosts move fast. And when they are angry, their eyes go black.

When Anne wasn't with her ghosts, she was with Nan.

Anne respected Nan because the house loved her. And Anne loved the house. Sometimes she thought she loved it more than her ghosts or her family or anything there ever was or ever would be. It belonged to her. The Witch House only existed because Nan created it. Anne understood this. And Anne understood Nan. Even when she spoke her native language.

Time went by. Nan watched little Anne grow, and she loved the child well. Sometimes she looked in the mirror and didn't recognize the old woman staring back at her. The world had gone to war twice, and she'd kept those she loved safe—though they didn't know or appreciate it. Nan spent her days mostly happy. Or at least satisfied. Yet there were deep sorrows that haunted her. Lucy slowly slipped away from her. She would play solitaire on the kitchen porch and smoke cigarette after cigarette. Lavinia still lived in the gatehouse, but her strange son, the reason that man had invaded their lives (Anne's father or not), was sent away to boarding school. He'd grown stranger year by year. Gavin, who was still in and out of their lives, did his one good deed sending the boy away. And Dominic had grown older and more distant still.

She wondered if there wasn't room for a little magic now that everything had calmed down. And maybe she could help Lucy, or figure out what was at the core of her worry over Jude. And finally reach out to Vincent and his family. To bring them all to the Witch House, where they belonged.

But Fate, she was a cruel bitch. Because just as Nan began to lower her guard and trust the world around her again, a letter came from her sister Florencia in New York, giving her the news that her brother, Vincent, and most of his family had died.

Full of grief, Nan was more sure than ever that her decision to turn to piety and prayer, to the protection it could offer her family, was the right decision.

Which made her frightened.

"I know something is wrong with her," Nan told Zindonetta in hushed tones during a visit to the market after she told Nan of her own troubles. "I have reason to believe she has supernatural talents, that they may run in our blood. Tell me, Zindonetta, is there a way to block her from these talents?"

Zindonetta told Nan to pray.

"What is wrong with me?" Anne asked in perfect Italian. The women stared. Zindonetta turned in a huff and walked away: having unintentionally aired her own dirty laundry in front of Anne was discomfiting.

"What is wrong with me?" Anne asked again as Nan dragged her back home.

"You have no father," Nan said. "Someone in this family should have a proper father."

And a part of Nan believed that. That maybe a father would have been the best thing for all of them. The Amore women were in need of balance.

Zindonetta was right. God would have to suffice.

Gavin came back when Anne was four, bearing a gift for the house.

The sculpture was actually a chimney flue. A big piece of metal capping with a fanlike top that he found at a secondhand shop and decided to bring home. It never made it inside.

"What is that thing?" Dominic asked.

"Get it off my grass," Nan said, before she went back to shelling peas.

Lucy said nothing. She walked back into the house and shut the door.

He was gone the next day, but the new "lawn ornament" stayed.

Anne, on the other hand, little though she was, was convinced it would be how he found his way home again, a beacon of sorts. She was the one with the candle in the window, the one left behind, the prisoner in a strange place with strange eyes and a strange complexion to go with her strange outlook on the world. The sculpture would stay as some kind of stand-in for Gavin, becoming almost beautiful in its rusted imperfection.

Anne began her education at the Our Lady of Sorrows Parochial School when she was in the first grade. Anne was so quiet and strange that her family forgot to register her for kindergarten.

Once enrolled, she caught right up and was, in fact, a stellar student. She even became the teacher's favorite because she did all of her work perfectly and on time and never made a sound or even got dirty. The nuns were convinced she had the calling, and this endeared her to her grandmother.

When Anne wasn't with her ghosts, she was with Nan.

Nan who kept the peace. Nan who kept tradition. Nan who anchored them to the daily ins and outs of their lives.

Monday: Catechism.

Tuesday: Trash day.

Wednesday: Ladies' Guild.

Thursday: Canning (or off-season harvest).

Friday: No meat.

Saturday: Bread baking.

Sunday: Mass.

Sunday supper was always an affair rife with tension.

Nan would sit at the head of the long oak table, while Dominic, now a man of eighteen, would shovel food in his mouth in an effort to escape the house sooner. Lucy sat with her chair at an angle, wishing she were back in bed. Her beautiful awfulness took up too much air in the room. She didn't eat. She had a glass of bourbon, and she smoked a cigarette.

"Lucia, put that out! Please!"

Lucy took a long drag of her cigarette and gave her mother a sideways stare.

"You're the one who makes me come down here." She exhaled the words and smoke at the same time.

"You can't live in your room," said Nan.

Dominic cleared his throat and in an effort to be done with this meal dumped his salad onto his pasta in silent protest.

"Why do you disrespect the pasta? It didn't do anything to you," said Nan.

Anne raised her hand.

"Damn it, Anne," Lucy growled, "put down your hand. You're not in school." Lucy mumbled under her breath, "Slow. I don't care what those nuns say. She's *slow*."

Nan had enough.

"Lucia, why not ask her if she has something to say? Would it kill you?" She turned to Anne. "What is it, Anne?'"

Anne stood up on her chair. It looked as if she were in a spelling bee and it was her turn at the podium. They looked up at her curiously. She had their attention. It was time. She froze for a moment, and then spoke.

"Listen to me. We have ghosts here. There are two of them . . . *two*." She held out two fingers.

Nan, Lucy, and Dominic all began talking at once.

". . . get down."

". . . Crazy Anne!"

". . . foolish girl."

"We heard you the first decade!"

Anne got down off her chair and stared at her plate. She

twirled a braid with her finger. And then felt a hand on her arm. She turned to face her mother.

"Anne," said Lucy. She trembled, tears pricking the corners of her eyes. "You listen to me. It isn't ghosts . . . no, not ghosts and ghoulies . . . it is this gobbler house. You better run, little Anne, run far away!" Lucy had both of Anne's arms now and began to shake her.

"It ate me, Anne. It eats me every day." Lucy pulled Anne into her chest. Anne drew in a deep breath of her mother. It was so rare that she had the chance. "It is the house, it is the house, it is the house . . ." Lucy whispered, her wet lips pressed against Anne's forehead.

Then, as if possessed, Lucy began to say it louder, her voice strangled as she gripped Anne's braids, pulling them until Anne was forced to stand on tippy toes so her braids would not be pulled right out her head.

Instantly Dominic was prying Lucy's hands off Anne's hair. Lucy fell back into her seat, deflated. Dominic returned to his spot and continued eating.

"Anna," said Nan in Italian—her attempt to soothe the child with something they alone shared—"there are no such things as ghosts. And this house is a miracle for us. It is the best and finest house. Why not go outside and play, okay? Let your mother rest, she is unwell." Nan turned to Lucy. "Lucia, did you take your medicine? You have to take your medicine!"

Lucy laughed. "Is it an illness or is it demons? Make up your mind, old woman."

"How can we make them see us, love?" asked Gwyneth later, in the attic.

Ava was cuddled up in Anne's lap, her wheezing chest pressed to Anne's own. The sound of Anne's own strong heartbeat, made Ava's seem more real. Anne shrugged her shoulders. She didn't know either.

"How am I supposed to know? I am not a ghost . . . or at least, I don't think I am. . . ." Anne trailed off.

Gwyneth danced across the attic, her dress skimming the wide floorboards. Anne sighed. "You are so pretty, Gwen. I wish I looked more like you."

In a flash of white, Gwyneth was in front of Anne, cupping her face in her ghost hands. "My Anne, you are by far the loveliest little thing I ever did see. Someday you will notice."

She danced away again, saying, "About the scaring . . . we will do our best. But you need to help, too."

"What do you mean?" Anne was confused.

Gwen answered her in a singsong voice.

"Little Anne, you are us and we are you. We are the house and the house is you."

Anne, still puzzled, tilted her head at Gwen.

"What I mean, Anne, is it is all connected. Why not do some of the scaring, too? Come on! Join us in the fun!"

Suddenly Anne was full of ideas, and in no time at all, the Witch House was full of screaming.

19

Anne in the Bedroom with a Jar of Spiders

It began with the spiders. Anne liked spiders, but her brother didn't. She kept a collection of them in jars in the attic nestled amidst the empty bottles Nan used when she made her famous homemade dandelion wine.

Wolf spiders were the best. They were not big like tarantulas, but big enough. It was so easy to unscrew the metal tops off the mason jars and dump them out on top of Dominic while he slept. She knew she should just dump them and run, but the temptation to watch the chaos happen between her pets and her pests was too good to pass up.

At first, she had to nudge the straggler spiders out of the jars to join the confused fuzzies already trying to figure out their new environment. They scurried about, feeling their way across his forehead and into his deep thick hair. Dominic didn't wake up right away. He squirmed and flicked his hands in his sleep. But as the spiders found nostrils and eyelids and a mouth, he woke up fast, jumping to his feet, slapping them away.

"What the hell, you little freak!?" he asked.

"It's a going-away present. I didn't want you to forget me," said Anne.

If it wasn't spiders, it was knives.

"Mama, come get her before I kill her!" Dominic would yell, holding a pillow against his chest and warding his little sister off. And Lucy would run in quick and heroic, to hold Anne's hand, the one with the carving knife, up over her head. This effectively made the scene look even more dramatic than intended, and Anne silently thanked her mother for the embellishment.

If it wasn't knives, it was hanging herself.

Anne had invented a harness of sorts that allowed her to hang herself from beams and light fixtures without *really* hanging herself.

Dominic woke to the beam creaking.

"Anne! Oh, sweet Anne!" He scrambled to hold her little body up and save her.

This made Anne give a nervous giggle. Her eyes opened, seeming to glow and wobble in the moonlight. This sent Dominic jumping back with even higher-pitched nervous screams.

There she was, hanging and dead, yet not dead.

"You are really crazy," he cried.

Anne, still hanging, shrugged her shoulders with her palms up as if to say, "And?"

She released the clasp between her legs and was on the ground before Lucy could even enter the room.

Anne crept away into the shadows and drew her knees up to her chest. She put her hands over her ears and rocked back and forth. This episode frightened her as well. She never would have thought her brother cared so much. Anne was confused.

Anne watched as Lucy sat with him. She looked like some sort of mother goddess in the moonlight. Or like the saints and icons Anne studied in school.

"I hate you," she whispered as she rocked. "I hate you. I hate you. I hate you."

The next day, Lucy and Nan put a lock on the inside of Dominic's bedroom door. Anne, though she was disappointed, wondered why they hadn't thought of it sooner. Stupid. They really are so stupid, she thought.

Late one night, after being banned from terrifying her older brother, Anne and her ghosts were at Nan's kitchen table. Anne sat cross-legged on top, and Ava stood just behind her. She was playing with Anne's braids, bringing them up, and letting them fall. Gwyneth relaxed in one chair and had her legs up on another, her hem dragging the floor. She was telling Anne wild stories about when she was little: her strange father, quiet mother, and silly boys at balls.

Gwyneth made Anne laugh. It felt good to laugh.

"Tell me again about the watermelon! Tell me again how you threw it off the roof and everyone thought you fell and were dead! That one is so funny, Gwen! Maybe we should try that one here tomorrow?"

They all giggled.

Waking to the sound of a child's laugh, Lucy, curious, came down the back hall steps and entered the kitchen the same moment that Nan entered from another doorway.

They saw Anne, sitting on the table, surrounded by candles. She was laughing. And impossibly, her braids were looped upward, as if there were an invisible string suspending them.

Nan looked at Lucy's horrified face, but said nothing as she turned around and left the kitchen.

Anne, startled, stopped laughing, and the braids immediately dropped.

"Mama?"

Lucy went to turn away as well. But she hesitated. She wanted to invite that lonely girl, that lonely haunted girl, right into her arms and fold her up and take her away. She wanted to smell the top of her head and tell her, I'm sorry. But, no. It was too late for all that.

"I have to get out of here!" Lucy cried instead.

But where could she go? Lately the doors, front and back, would not even open for her. How . . . ? It was too much, again. And so she tied her robe tight, did not answer Anne, and took the path she had ten years earlier, the path leading away from Anne.

She locked herself in her bedroom. Like Dominic, who slept better because of the lock.

The night before he graduated high school and left the Witch House for good, Dominic packed, excited about moving to a new city. Lucy was helping him. She'd quietly slid the bolt across the door. Dominic didn't want to know that his mother, his beautiful broken mother, was scared of Anne, too. He didn't want to leave her alone with all the crazy.

"Maybe you should send Anne away."

"Why?"

"Don't do that, Mama, don't act like you don't know."

Lucy thought for a moment and went to her son, her best friend since Vito died, and held both of his hands.

"Dominic, my sweet boy . . . maybe you don't see this, and I am sorry to be the one to tell it to you. Anne belongs here. You are the one who has to go." She looked at his trunk and half-packed things and continued, "I'm not right in the head. Nan isn't either, even if she hides it better. We may kill each other. And what about the house? It never liked you, never liked me either . . . but it likes Anne."

Just then, there was a chafing, squealing sound of metal against metal. The lock on the inside of the door was slowly jimmying itself back through the metal loops securing it to the door.

Dominic and Lucy stood there and watched. They didn't scream. The time for screaming was over. It was time for him to leave. The house was spitting him out. The metal slowly clicked completely away from itself and the door cracked open. The house had spoken. Here's your hat, what's your hurry?

Meanwhile, Nan sat on the edge of her bed holding the black book. She couldn't deny it any longer. Anne was seeing spirits, and her other talents were growing.

If left unguided, very dark things could be unleashed. Besides, Nan was beginning to ask herself some very important questions.

What if turning her back on the magic was a mistake? Not for her—that was her sacrifice—but what if one of her future loved ones needed to understand their talents? That was the day she began to allow herself to believe—no, to accept her magic. The next day she gave Anne the black book.

"What is it?"

"Read it. Add to it. You're a smart girl. Use it to help you. Start by seeing what makes those that hurt you afraid. When you know their fears, you can stop them from hurting you. Or at least you can try."

20

Anne in the Closet
with a Rope

1951

Anne walked home from school up Grand Street Hill and rounded the corner onto her own block. The spire of the cupola seemed to smile at her, welcoming her home. She picked up the pace, swinging her books by their belt, enjoying the crisp fall day. She'd heard that the further north you went, the better the foliage, but she didn't care. Anne thought the most glorious natural show God created on the planet was right here in Haven Port at Persimmon Point.

There would be a lot of work waiting for her at home today. Fall was always a transitional time for the Witch House gardens. There was the pruning back of perennials and the removal of annuals. There was the winterizing of sod and the fertilizing of the vegetable plots. The ivy turned bright red, and the berry bushes gave one last burst of fruit that seemed out of place on the tongue.

The deciduous trees along the street and on the property took on jeweled tones that resembled large, half-ripe nectarines or lemons or pears. Anne thought that nature always mirrored itself and wondered if human nature did that, too.

In the fall she would often leave the schoolyard before the bell rang to run down instead of up the hill in order to sit on the bridge for a while with her feet dangling through the iron guardrail bars. She would sit there and think about all sorts of things, but mostly she would watch the people. Her seat on the bridge had a sweeping view of the riverbanks where people would gather at the late-fall farmers' markets and all the way up Grand Street to the downtown as well. This was a particularly brilliant and sunny afternoon, so Anne had lingered a little longer than planned. And now she was rushing a bit. She did have chores waiting and homework and daily news reports to give her ghosts, after all.

She stopped to pick up an oddly formed stick that she thought would make a nice ax when she played Anne Boleyn with Jude in the ruins later on. Things had been way more interesting since he'd been kicked out of boarding school. They were just starting to get to know each other again . . . being cousins and all that. Walking with the stick, she even tried it out as a cane, pretending to be an old crone.

She heard them before she saw them. The neighborhood children were not a kind bunch. And Anne, for her oddness, was an easy target. They were chanting that stupid rhyme they had made up about her.

Crazy Anne is in your cellar
Crazy Anne under your bed
Crazy Anne is creeping slowly
Just one look and you'll be dead!

Anne felt the first pebble hit the back of her head and began to run. When she reached the fence in front of her house, she ran dragging the stick against the bars . . . thunk, thunk, thunk, wanting to wake up the house, her ghosts, anything that might keep her safe. Anne had to think fast. She slowed, never letting go of the stick. Thunk . . . thunk . . . thunk . . . and arrived at the gate and faced her enemies. She pointed the crooked stick at them.

"All of you, all of you gathered here! I put a curse on you! See these words above this gate? It's Latin. The language of witches and priests. It says, MOMENTO MORI! Remember you will DIE!"

She dropped her books and with her free hand pointed her first and ring finger at them.

"Malocchio!" she cried. The call of the evil eye. It made the group nervous, because if anyone could curse them, it was Anne. They stood stunned for a moment and Anne took the opportunity to run through the gates and up the drive. She ran so fast she fell.

"You okay?" asked a red-headed girl who Anne didn't know.

"Fine," Anne said, getting up.

"Why didn't you go with them? And why did you come through the gate. No one does that. This is the Witch House. Aren't you afraid?"

"Should I be? I'm new here. And for the record, I wasn't with them in the first place; they were chasing *me* before they found you."

"Why?"

"My hair."

"They're crazy, it's lovely," Anne said, feeling generous.

"Thanks!" The girl smiled shyly. "So, you are Anne, right?"

"Yep, that's me. Crazy Anne. And who are you? I don't have the benefit of a poem."

"Fiona. A pleasure to meet you, Anne."

"Well, Fiona, would you like to come over for a while?"

Fiona hesitated. She was new to the neighborhood and had heard the stories. But she was ever so curious. She could make a friend, or at least come away with classified information that could perhaps be used as a bartering tool for a few days of peace.

"That would be lovely."

Anne closed the iron gate behind them and the two girls walked up the poplar canopied drive arm in arm.

"What a cute garden!" Fiona exclaimed as Anne steered her toward the back of the house. "Like elves or fairies live there!"

"That is the vegetable garden. We grow a lot of vegetables. And it would be too big for fairies. Fairies are small, like fireflies. Maybe elves though," Anne said, her voice serious.

Suddenly, Fiona felt a little silly. "What kind of vegetables do you grow?" she asked, trying to change the subject.

As they walked through the garden, Anne gave a verbal tour.

"There are lettuces and sweet peas in the early spring; pole beans and tomatoes, cucumbers and squash, beets, radishes, onions, garlic, carrots, cabbages and even rhubarb." Abruptly, she stopped talking. "Fiona, are you ready? For the real secret?" she whispered to her new friend.

Fiona nodded her head.

Behind the vegetable garden was the meadow that was the footprint of the old house. In the middle stood the ruins. The gardener's cottage still stood, a thriving, though overgrown, herb and perennial flower garden next to it. And the property line was marked by a small juniper and pine tree forest and incredible amounts of overgrown wild raspberry bushes that would, magically, bear fruit from June through the first fall frost.

Anne ran into the meadow. "Come on!" Fiona ran after her, fascinated by all she saw. The cottage, the ruins, the sheer expanse of it. The girls ran in circles until they fell together into a dizzy, laughing heap.

"Do you like it?"

"Oh, Anne! It's wonderful!"

And Fiona *did* like it. She felt warm on the inside, fuzzy with delight. She never wanted to leave. She sat up on her elbows and looked around again.

But then, a strange feeling came over her, a badness. Fiona began to sweat. Anne noticed the change.

"Want to come in the house?" she asked

Fiona was now sick to her stomach and shaky.

"May I have a glass of water, Anne?"

"That would mean you would have to come in the house,

so is that a yes?" Anne felt giddy. She was very, very close to having a real friend. A girl. Her own age! She liked Fiona. And it seemed as if Fiona liked her back.

Anne grabbed Fiona's hand and dragged her across the meadow, through the backyard, and up the back porch steps into the kitchen. Anne reached up before opening the screen door and pulled on the clothesline that was attached; she rocked the rope back and forth to hear the squeaking. Fiona looked at her funny.

"I do it for luck. I have a lot of habits."

Fiona shrugged it off. It seemed a fine explanation. And she wanted water.

There was an old woman in the kitchen. Her gray hair was tied in a severe bun and parted in the center. The part seemed to mirror the small space between her top teeth. She was peeling and rinsing a sink full of beets. She turned to the girls and wiped her red-stained hands on her apron.

"Well, Anna, what do we have here? A guest? Oh, my, you are a pretty girl."

"Yes. A guest. A new . . . friend. Fiona, this is my grand-mother, Nan. Everyone calls her that—even her daughter, Lucy, my mama. Even the ladies in the Ladies' Guild. Even the priest! Her real name is Anna, but you should call her Nan, too. I am named for her, so it avoids confusion anyway." Anne liked sound-ing like the authority on her family.

"Nan, please get Fiona a glass of water." The two girls sat down at the large oak table, and Fiona drank her glass of water while Nan tried to clean Anne's scratches and pulled the pine needles out of her braids.

"Come on, Fi," said Anne, trying out a pet name already. "Let me show you around!"

"Anna, don't bother your mother," Nan warned in Italian.

"It's my house and I'll do what I want," said Anne.

"What did you say to her? You speak . . . what was that, Italian?"

"Yes, fluently," said Anne, tossing her braids vainly. "Let's go." She hooked her arm inside of Fiona's, and off they went.

"Don't you just love all the windows? The volunteer glass-makers gave what they had, so we have all these different types of glass. I think it is brilliant."

Everywhere Fiona looked there was something to see. The rooms on the first floor were enormous and danced with light.

"My Nan can't help it," said Anne as they looked upon the bright, warm color combinations: orange glass canisters, plum drapes, and red velvet fabric. "She is drawn to the warm colors of the Italian countryside." Anne liked feeling exotic.

The air in the house had a peculiar smell. There were drying herbs hanging from the large wooden beam that ran the length of the kitchen. They perfumed the whole house with a bitter earthiness. Fiona couldn't help feeling like she had walked into a fairy tale. Like Hansel and Gretel. Anne saw Fiona looking up at the beams and molding.

"The builders took every bit they could from Haven House to build this one, so sometimes there are odd things about. There is always something new to find!"

As they crossed the foyer into the great room, Fiona caught a glimpse of a life-size statue of a saint and hundreds of flickering candles in red glass jars, like at church. Fiona looked away, back into the light of the great room. It glinted off bottles of all shapes and sizes. Glass of all kinds, everywhere she looked. Her eyes fell on a photograph on the mantel.

Fiona was blinded for a moment by Anne's hands covering her eyes. "Don't look at that picture, Fiona, it is a picture of a dead little girl, and she might eat you up!"

"No, you're teasing me, that's not a dead girl."

"It is! I own her ghost. She lives here with me. I have two of them, actually." And then Anne took a chance. It was now or never. "Want to meet them?"

And then Fiona, woefully unskilled at crazy, made a very bad mistake. She laughed. She was cursed with the disease of laughing when nervous, and Anne's harsh look only served to make her laugh louder and more hysterically.

Anne was confused. And hurt. And mad. She cocked her head to one side and stared hard at Fiona. Anne didn't think that this girl belonged in her house after all.

"Stop laughing," Anne demanded.

But Fiona couldn't stop.

"Stop laughing!" Anne shouted with a stomp. "I was going to show you the heart of the house."

Fiona laughed a little harder.

The shift in mood was palpable. The light seemed to have shifted, too. It was darker now.

Anne ran out of the room and back into the foyer.

Fiona heard a door close upstairs.

"Anne?"

She walked upstairs and down the hall. No Anne, and it was

dark. Fiona ran back down the stairs, heading for the double front doors. The carvings on them of the mermaids and mermen seemed to be glaring at her, their eyes fixed on Fiona. She let out a little yelp and tried twisting the doorknobs. The doors were locked.

Afraid to go back into the living room, she had no other choice but to go back up. Fiona ran up the sweeping staircase, no longer shy. She took her two little fists and pounded on the first door she saw.

It seemed like a lifetime, but the door opened, and Fiona couldn't quite believe her eyes. It was Lucy. It had to be! All the kids would be amazed that she'd even met the elusive legend Lucy Amore! And though she was terrified, there was a part of her yelling *"Bonus!"* deep inside.

Lucy was as stunning as the stories, but her eyes were wild. She wore a silky white bathrobe and a fancy black shawl strewn across her shoulders. One armed was cocked out with a lit cigarette, and she smelled like alcohol. Fiona knew the smell too well. Her father owned a pub.

"Well, well, well. What do we have here?" asked Lucy, blowing out a cloud of smoke as she spoke.

"I . . . I lost Anne. I lost Anne and I can't find her and I can't get out!"

Lucy, remembering that she had been a nurturer once upon a time, decided to practice the art of kindness again. She beckoned the girl toward her. Lucy stubbed her cigarette out in an ashtray. There were ashtrays everywhere.

She leaned down to face Fiona and said, "I know. This house can be difficult. It won't let me out either."

Lucy stood up and put her hand on Fiona's shoulder. "Okay, Red, let's look for her together. How about that?"

"Yes, thank you," whispered Fiona.

Lucy put pressure on Fiona's shoulder and guided her through the house.

"Let's see. She isn't in here. And she wouldn't be in my room." The room made Fiona afraid. The door was ajar, and everything looked somehow rotted. The vines on the wallpaper seemed to shift and writhe. *No, don't be silly, Fiona, they can't be.*

Lucy took the girl downstairs.

"Nope, not here either . . ." Now they were back across the dining room in the kitchen. "Hold on," said Lucy, holding up a finger to her lips in an amused hush. "Let's go back upstairs. We need to check the bathroom. Sometimes she hides in the tub and waits for me. She just stands there for hours. She wants to kill me. The house. Nan. Anne. They are trying to kill me. *Shhhhhh . . .* Don't tell her I know."

"Nope," she said, pushing past Fiona. "I need a drink."

"Miss Lucy?" asked Fiona.

"Ahhh . . . she knows my name. Do they all know my name? Still . . . I suppose it is a good thing. . . . Still fancy after all these years. . . ."

"Miss Lucy," Fiona persisted.

"Yes?"

"I need to find Anne . . . or to leave. Can you show me?"

"Oh, right. Look, Red, see that door? That door leads to the attic. Try there. I don't go up there. No one goes up there. But be my guest, sweetheart."

Fiona went into the attic. She didn't want to, but she had nowhere else to go. It was huge, running the length of the house. It was set up like a bedroom with colorful quilts and pillows everywhere. It seemed a comfortable place, and yet, there was a dryness to the air that hurt her throat.

Something moved in the corner under the eave. She heard a muffled laugh.

"Anne? Come on, Anne, this isn't funny."

The tightness in her throat increased. She started coughing. She couldn't breathe. Choking, Fiona ran from the attic and back to the hall. Lucy leaned against her bedroom door swirling a glass of whiskey.

"Do you want a sip? It is imported. From France," she said, taking a drink. She didn't seem to notice Fiona's hands clawing at her little, pale throat . . . or the silent *ackkk* coming from her open mouth.

Fiona fell to the floor. She thought she was dying. And then it stopped. The strangling feeling was gone as fast as it came.

She got up from the floor, shaky.

"Please?" she pleaded. "Please let me go home. . . ."

Lucy stared at her. The emptiness Fiona saw in her eyes was something she never wanted to see again.

"I know where she is," Lucy said, flatly. "Follow me."

Lucy, very drunk now, staggered and swayed down the hallway, then stopped. She pointed at a closet door in front of them.

"You open it. I won't."

Fiona opened the door.

She began her screaming on the up arc. It was immediate and relentless. She turned in a circle, unsure of which way to go. She ran and slid down the front hall stairs to the front doors.

She yanked on them with all her strength, and they opened with an unexpected and oily ease that threw her whole body backward. She scrambled back up and ran out the door, still screaming, all the way under the poplar canopy to the main road.

Lucy stood looking at her daughter. Anne was in her special place. A linen closet turned into a clubhouse of sorts. The shelves were removed, and the walls were a collage of all things dead. Magazine pictures of awfulness clipped from *National Geographic* and vile photos ripped from newspapers overlapping with prayer cards and religious pictures. The pope peeked out from under a lion eating the inside of a zebra. Hanging from the slanted ceiling were dolls' heads whose lips were smeared with lipstick, creating jagged grins across porcelain faces.

Anne was hanging, too. Swaying back and forth.

"Really, Anne, come on now. That is *no* way to make a friend."

Anne opened her eyes. She unhung herself and felt warm inside. Her mother had said something motherly. Then she got mad at herself. Why did she care?

Anne retreated to the attic. The ghosts were not there. They were supposed to be there when she needed them. This has to stop, she told herself. She would have to write some rules. If the ghosts were all she had, the ghosts must listen to her. That was that. She went to an old book of nursery rhymes Gwyneth used to read to her and tore out a blank page. She found a pen and called her ghosts. They didn't come. She called again, and still she was alone. She waited, and eventually they floated up the stairs.

"I am making rules," Anne stated. "Everyone needs rules. It is *very* important. You will both follow them."

"Anne, where did you get that paper?" Gwyneth asked.

"I tore it from a book."

"That isn't the way we treat books is it?"

"*See?* Rules are *very* important. But these are for you, not for *me*," Anne continued.

Anne knelt on the attic floorboards. She liked being close to the floor. It smelled like toast.

She read the rules aloud as she wrote them.

"Ghost Rules: by Anne," she began. Her old-fashioned pen scratched across the paper.

"Rule number one: Ghosts cannot go through an unopened door. If a door is closed, they cannot open it.

"Rule number two: Ghosts will never travel outside of the parameters of Witch House property." She stopped.

"Gwen? Is it perimeters or parameters?"

Gwyneth was annoyed. "In this context? In this context I would say either," she grumbled.

"Okay . . . and rule number three: Ghosts will always come when I call, so I know where they are."

"Little Anne?" asked Gwyneth.

"What?"

"How can we come when you call if you shut the door when you leave?"

Anne tapped her pen on her chin, thinking.

"Well, I won't need to call you if I know where you are."

"I see," Gwen said quietly.

"I don't want to be locked up anywhere, Anne. It's not fair," whined Ava.

"Fine. I'll cross out number one. But if I need you and I call you and you don't come, I get to re-in . . . re-in . . ."

"Reinstate," said Gwen.

"Reinstate, yes . . . I get to reinstate it."

"Agreed."

Anne sealed the document with a dramatic flair. She took a pin from a nearby dress form and pricked her finger, blotting each rule with her blood.

Finally satisfied, a tired Anne climbed into the cupola to survey her kingdom as the sun set. It had been a busy day. She had gained and lost a friend, created a set of rules that would contain the friends who remained, and even heard kind words from Lucy.

From the cupola, she had a 360-degree view of everything. She spread out her arms and spun slowly, taking in the view. Persimmon Point, the ocean, the Haven House ruins, the ponies. All of it bathed in sun shadows as the night caught up with the day and tried to keep it hostage in pink clouds. But the sunshine slipped away, as it always does, and Anne remembered that the night was lovely, too.

Fall would slip by, winter wouldn't last long, and summer would come early as it always seemed to do. Then the fireflies . . . To Anne, they were stars that fell from the sky. She would go outside at night and run with them. Jumping and chasing, but never truly trying to catch them. Gwyneth once suggested she put them in a jar. Anne was horrified. *Cage them? They were stars! Magic from the sky.* She could never do such a thing. That realization was like a message: Gwyneth and Ava shouldn't be caged either. They were her stars in her very own sky. She'd have to apologize for even thinking of it.

Summer was Anne's magic time. She felt her strongest, and yet her most fragile, during the summer. She felt human. She especially loved late summer and always would, even when the smells of the high grasses and overripe fruit, bursting tomatoes, and overgrown herbs made her remember the day she began to hate the world.

21

Jude in the Ruins
with Himself

1952

It happened slowly, the love she fell into. She hadn't paid much attention to Jude. He'd played with her a little bit when he first came home, but then got new friends. It didn't matter that he was her cousin. She tried not to think of Aunt Lavinia or that bungalow at all, because then she thought of her father—she didn't like to do that. It hurt something inside her, made her throat tight.

Besides, he was older, after all. Which is why she was surprised when he called out to her from his window in the spring following what Anne now called "The Fiona Fiasco."

"Anyone ever tell you you're pretty, Anne?" he asked.

Then he started walking her back and forth to school.

When school let out for the summer, he'd walk her to and from town.'

"Don't want any more of that 'Crazy Anne' nonsense."

There wasn't any taunting when Jude was with her, because he scared people. And she liked that.

She felt something deep and visceral when he looked at her. No one else paid any attention to her. Dominic had left for school, Lucy was in a constant state of oblivion, and Nan, well, Nan was just plain busy. Busy with the garden, busy with cooking and cleaning and church functions and never forgetting her all-encompassing worry over Lucy. She spent hours saying novenas for her mentally ill and godless child. So Anne felt privileged that Jude—a teenage boy!—would single her out. And his face! Everyone agreed he was beautiful. All the girls in Haven Port had crushes on him until they realized he had no interest in them whatsoever, which could have, *should* have, been the first warning sign.

He'd hang on the kitchen garden gate looking like some kind of Roman god, chiseled and illuminated from within. So light and fair, with blond hair, blue eyes, freckles. So easy to look at. Easy like the sun. Anne forgave him for being related to Gavin.

Jude began to sit behind her at church, saying funny things just to make her laugh. He left her presents, little trinkets of affection, things he noticed she liked. And once again, Anne couldn't believe that someone had noticed her in that way. She had suddenly become visible.

One day in late summer he walked by the wall while she was reading up in her pine tree. He startled her, which startled her all the more because she was always the one sneaking up on people. "Can I come up there?" he asked.

"Do what you want," said Anne. He came in through the gate and was perched next to her in no time at all. "What are you, a monkey?" she laughed.

He grinned. "No. Last time I looked, I was a Jude. You want some of my apple?"

"No, thanks," said Anne.

"Suit yourself. . . . Anyway, I know we're cousins, Anne. But, I want you to know, I like you. And I'd like to spend more time with you. Like, go on adventures and things like that. Friends. Good friends."

"You like me?"

"Does that surprise you?" Jude asked.

Anne put her book in her lap and looked at this teenage boy sitting across from her. She squinted her eyes; she was suspicious, but intrigued. "Well, I am younger than you. I'm sure there are a lot of older girls who'd like to be your friend."

"Well, I *did* think of that, but I have done a lot of watching, Anne, and I have decided that you are more interesting than any other girl in the whole wide world."

"You are watching me?"

"I watch people." He shrugged.

"Me, too."

"So, do you want to spend more time together?" He very gently looped his finger between her turned-down ankle sock and her skin. Anne was again startled.

"I guess?"

"Well then . . ." He paused, pulling on one of her braids and then curling the end in his fingers. "You have to do me a favor." He threw the apple core on the ground. Anne wondered if he would pick it up or leave it there. Maybe a tree would grow and she could call it Jude.

"Hey, you!" He pulled her braid again. "You dreamin'? I said you have to do me a favor."

"Okay . . . what?"

"Well, this might sound strange, but I think you'll know what I am talking about. I feel something around you, Annie, something fearful. It scares me. You might say I have a special gift . . . the gift of sight . . . and I see you are in great danger." He looked deeply at her. His pretended seriousness made her want to laugh, but in case he really was serious, she didn't.

"Anyway, I don't know what it is, but there *is* something about you that draws me to you, and something that pushes me away. Can you understand that? You to need to figure that out, and when you do . . ." He dropped his body in one graceful swoop down to the ground. He looked back up at her, shielding the sun from his eyes, "you let me know. Then, we can have an adventure."

Jude knew a little about monsters. And he didn't know what it was, but his instinct told him that if he wanted to get close to this girl who was so different from all the others—a challenge of sorts—he would have to take a chance.

And Anne, well, she knew a little bit about ghosts. She knew certain people could sense them, could almost smell them, around her. It was funny that he thought they were some sort of danger to her, but she wanted him. So she would have to put the ghosts away and see what happened.

She went to the attic later that night and gathered her ghosts, pushing the thoughts of jars and fireflies out of her mind.

See Anne, so small for her age; see her holding Ava's hand as they walk across the moonlit field to the gardener's cottage. See Gwyneth walking behind her, happy to be out in the night, happy to be outside. Twirling her white dress around in the high grass . . . touching the overgrown sage flowers that spring up everywhere this time of year, and smelling her ghost hands. Gwyneth missed being alive.

Anne opened the door of the cottage and shoved the ghosts in. "This is your new home! What do you think? Okay, you go to sleep. I will come and visit all the time."

"Little Anne," Gwyneth whispered, "Why are you doing this? Why are you putting us away? You promised you wouldn't."

"I made a friend. I made a friend, and he is afraid of you." Anne shuffled her feet, looking hard at the floor.

"Maybe," Gwyneth's voice began in Anne's mind, "Maybe you should be afraid of *him*. . . ."

"Show. Me. Sleeping!" Anne demanded, with a stomp of her foot to emphasize the word *sleeping*. She stomped it so hard her knee sock fell down. Gwyneth put her hand over Ava's face, turning it into a pale and empty place. Ava was still. Then she waved her hand in front of her own face, leaving a blank void as well.

They were sleeping. Anne left the cottage but wanted to cry. This is why I have to put them away, she thought. I'm too close to them. I miss them all the time and I count on them. I have to learn not to love them. Maybe they aren't even real.

She walked back toward the Witch House chanting quietly, "They aren't even real, they aren't even real. They aren't even real."

The next Sunday she passed him a note in church.

Dear Jude,
I put them away. I don't even know if they are real.
Anne

Jude had no idea what she meant by "put them away," but he could already sense a difference in her. She was more vulnerable. And that was just how he wanted her.

The next afternoon, he was at the Kitchen garden gate.

"Hey, can I come in?" Before Anne could answer, the gate was unlatched. He hopped on it, swinging his tall lanky body into the yard. The gate complained on its hinges, as the breeze ruffled his hair. Nan yelled something in Italian out of the back window.

"Hi, Nan! Just wanted Annie here to take me for a walk and show me where those wild raspberries are. My mom wants to make some turnovers for the church bake sale."

Silence hung in the air for a second. Nan stared at him for a moment. Then she looked at her Anne. Anne was smiling. She had a feeling about this boy. Something in her gut. He'd always made Nan nervous, the way he watched watched watched. But what harm could it really do, he was a big boy, and what would he want with her Anna? She was only eleven years old and looking no older than eight. And besides, she was smiling, such a rare occurrence, it made her look almost pretty.

"Okay, be safe. Tell your mama to let those turnovers sit out overnight. It's the only way to get the raspberry flavor into the crust. You'll tell her?"

"Will do, Nan! Come on, girl, let's go on an adventure. A raspberry adventure!" He held out his large freckled hand and Anne—who touched no one but ghosts on a regular basis—put her small pale hand into his. He had called her Annie. . . . This must be love. They walked through the backyard and then through the vegetable garden. "They are back there," she said, "by the juniper pines. It's kind of a long walk."

"Shoot, I can see the property line from here. Come on, let's run." And with that, he was off over the fence and through the meadow. Anne hesitated, but only for a moment. She quickly unlatched the garden gate and began to run after him, toward him, toward love, toward feeling, toward freedom. He waited for her on the old foundation. "This place must have been amazing!"

"It was magnificent." She was a little out of breath. "Our house was built from its pieces."

"Amazing," he said, then added, "I guess we get the rasp-, berries now. . . ."

"I guess so. . . ."

Jude took her hand in his and began to lead. Then he stopped; he stopped to look at her, he had to look down, so far down. His voice changed, got thick. "You are so beautiful, do you know that?" Anne wanted to swoon—maybe he would kiss her? A part of her wanted him to kiss her, and a part of her was afraid. He was so much older. Jude leaned in, put both hands firmly on her shoulders and pushed her hard onto the ground.

The fall knocked the wind out of her. And Anne knew. She knew what was happening. And she had no way out, no way home, and no one to hear her call out but the ghosts.

She lay there and made her mind go away. This isn't real. Nothing is real. I'm not real.

When it was over she was bleeding, but there were no other marks on her.

"Clean yourself up before you go home," he ordered. She tried to move but could not. "I am going out that way"—he pointed to the forest—"and I am going to cut around so Nan doesn't see me. You get back to the house quick and tell Nan we got a lot of berries. And no telling or I will kill your Nan, just see if I don't. And I will tell the priest you seduced me. And he will believe me because everyone knows you're crazy."

In her heart she knew he was right. He looked down at her for a moment with a look that began to scare her in a place deep inside her mind that she was not used to visiting; he was thinking about killing her.

"You should do it," she said.

"Do what?"

"You should kill me. It would be the smart thing to do. Don't think I don't know you're thinking about it. I won't stop you."

"I know you won't. Because you're brave. That's why I won't kill you. I only kill the weak ones. But trust me, after time, you may get weak, and when you do? I'll come hunting."

"Maybe I'm dead already."

"You know, Anne, I was lying when I told you I wanted to be your friend. But now . . . well, I'm starting to think it's a swell idea. We should make this a habit," he said, sneering slightly before he strode away whistling. Anne thought he looked a bit like a deranged Huckleberry Finn. It took a long time for him to reach the tree line where he then disappeared into the pines.

After he was gone, she got up and tucked her clothes under her arm. Everything hurt, but she managed to make it to the cottage where her ghosts waited to comfort her. "Let us out love," they whispered. "Let us out and we will help you." Gwyneth and Ava's words echoed in her head as they swirled around her in distress. Anne put her hands over her ears and cried out, "*No!* Maybe he will stop, and maybe he will be my friend. I don't care what he did. He thinks I'm brave, and I want him to be my friend!" And with that she left the cozy safety of the cottage, pulling the door shut tight behind her.

When she made it back to the blue-and-white house, she took a bath. In the tub, she undid her braids. She didn't need them anymore. She tried to comb out her hair, but it was wet and tangled, so she gave up. Anne wouldn't wear braids any longer. Her hair remained matted and hung thick and heavy down her back. A tangled black halo now encircled her head at all times.

But there would not be a friendship with Jude. And he would not hurt her again.

Two days after Fiona MacPhee went missing from the farmers' market after church, an anonymous tip led the police to a warehouse by the river. They found her just barely alive, tied up on a dirty mattress in the basement. The authorities took Jude away and locked him up. That was that. It was over and Jude was gone. Fiona survived but was never quite right. Anne thought about her once in a while and wondered why she couldn't just "get on with it." Shitty things just happen sometimes.

22

William on the Playground with the Truth

1952

What Anne didn't know was that as Jude attacked her, a boy named William was watching. He watched through the trees. He'd been swimming and decided to take a shortcut through the Witch House estate. He kept very quiet. He knew what this was. He lived it, too. So though Anne didn't know it, the moment she lost herself and her body to violence, she gained a soulmate and lifelong friend.

William and Anne were schoolmates but never quite knew each other because they were too busy watching everyone else around them. The only difference was that Anne was watching everyone with distrust and a touch of hate, while William was watching them with distrust and an abundance of love.

One day at the beginning of the new school year during recess, he finally got up the courage to approach her. She was on a swing, and there was one open next to her; it was kismet. They swung next to each other without speaking until he cleared his throat, clenched tight with terror, and said, "I saw you and Jude."

"So what." She knew instantly what he meant, and she wouldn't be bullied.

She didn't look up; just kept on swinging slowly and letting her feet drag on the ground.

"You gonna tell?" he asked.

"No, you?"

"No." There was a long silence between them. They were trying to figure each other out.

"Happens to me all the time," William said in a nonchalant voice that attempted levity.

They looked at each other then, deeply, knowingly, and a smile broke out across Anne's face. Soon they were falling from the swings and rolling around on the blacktop in their uniforms, laughing until they cried and their sides hurt and Sister Mary Frances had to yell at them to stop.

"Who did it to you?"

"Father Callahan."

"Does he do it all the time?"

"Nope. Just every once in a while."

"You should tell. You got a priest, I got a monster. You should tell."

"I can't. I live here. My family sort of gave me to him. Now, it's better. I have my own room, and I have food to eat. And I don't get beat by my drunk pop anymore."

Anne thought on that. "So, it's like rent. Kind of."

"Yeah."

"Well, William, you must promise me that you will not allow his abuse to ruin the inside of your heart. Your body and your soul are two different things. He can touch your body, but he can't touch your soul unless you let him." She felt very grown up.

"Deal."

From that day on, it was Anne and William, William and Anne, everywhere and all the time.

William was what they called Black Irish. Pale skin, black hair, blue eyes. And he wanted nothing more than to take care of Anne. Because her life? It was a great big ball of shit, in his opinion.

William knew he loved her. He loved the way she looked, the way the sun would put freckles on her face. He loved her angles and her deep frowns. He loved her long black mess of hair and her hard sense of humor. He thought she was full of some sort of magic. He would make Anne love him back. It would be his life's work.

They explored the world together. Anne loved broken things and she shared her world with Will. She shared her taste for the old, the cracked, the torn. There was beauty in the memory of what once was.

The factories downtown and along the industrial part of the bay were favorite haunts of Anne's. The ones in use and the ones abandoned—all had the same, dim, cracked misery about them that she loved so much. A bleakness that drew her in again and again to explore, so she might place her hands on the cold brick exteriors, feel the roughness, run her fingers through crumbling mortar lines, and peel the rust spots away from the ironwork staircases. She haunted these buildings so often that the workers in the factories knew her by name. Anne would be outside, leaning her forehead against the brick, when the end-of-day whistle would blow and the men would stream out, nodding at her. "G'night, Anne," they would say, one after the other.

William and Anne ran rampant through the empty ones turned playtime castles. Inevitably, though, each building would get a new tenant, and they would have to say good-bye. But there would always be a new one. Thank goodness for free enterprise.

Anne taught him everything she knew about Haven Port, about the tides, about plants and when they bloomed and what they were good for. They even had a special way to communicate their affection for each other. They would lie facing one another with their foreheads touching. Then they would enclose their hands together in front of their chests as if they were in prayer, palms touching, hands layered, while pulling up their knees so they touched, too. They had long conversations this way. But sometimes they would just lie silent for hours, as their breathing became one harmony.

See them, see Little Anne and Sweet William; see them like that on the beach late at night with the deep, starry night sky above them and the beach sand in their hair; see them on the grass, on the snow, on the multicolored quilt that Lucy made for Dominic, the one Anne took from the attic and put on the bed in the cottage, see them watch the draw-bridge go up and down as Frank, the bridge master, shakes his head and wishes he didn't blame the girl for being born because her existence reminded him that Vito was dead and gone for good.

Anne and William were very best friends. The only place they didn't explore was the Witch House. First, because he hadn't been invited. Second, the place made him feel funny way down in the pit of his belly. He couldn't understand Anne's deep love for this strange place, but who was he to judge?

All he wanted was a life with Anne; a full and robust life with the girl that won his heart and his mind, the girl whom he needed to save.

Anne told him her secret on Palm Sunday.

"I have ghosts."

"We all do, I guess," said William, feeling highly philo-sophical.

"No, I have real ones, Will."

"What do you mean?" He was interested now.

"I keep them in the gardener's cottage." Anne took a key out of the pocket of her pinafore. (William loved that her clothes were so old-fashioned. Nan made all of them, and Anne was never insecure about it, she just wore what was there. He loved that about her.) She fit the key in the lock and gave the door a shove. "It's me, Anne . . ." she called out.

"Come on, Anne, quit kidding . . ." William trailed off, nervous now.

He didn't see anyone but Anne inside the dimly lit space.

"You fooled me, Anne," he laughed. "For a minute I thought you were serious!"

"I am drop-down-dead serious, Will."

And then she spoke into the air. "Show him!"

The air shifted in the cottage, and William's vision blurred. He felt dizzy. He rubbed his eyes, closing them and then opening them again and then . . .

Nothing.

"You don't see them?" Anne whispered with a pleading in her voice, a desperation that made William think perhaps he should lie. He didn't want to hurt her. She looked defeated. He went to her, and in an awkward gesture that became graceful, he put his arms around her and drew her into a hug.

"Anne," he said softly, "just because I can't see them doesn't mean they are not there." He pulled her to the floor to sit with him. "Tell me about them."

And Anne erupted, letting loose mouthful after mouthful of information about Gwen and Ava dead and alive.

"So you see them?" William asked when she was done.

"Yes, I see them just like I see you, only when they are mad or upset, they change. They get ugly."

"And they can do stuff?"

"Yeah, but there are a lot of rules . . . even though they break them. . . ."

"They break them?"

"Yes, they do," she said pointedly to where her ghosts were clearly listening in. "They are naughty." She laughed before growing serious again. "They are my family, Will. Do you think you can understand that?"

"Sure I can." William looked around the house, curious once again and a bit eager to change the subject. "This place is pretty cool. We could make it a swell hangout if it didn't have such a good view of the place where he hurt you from the window."

"Yeah, but I wasn't really there."

"What do you mean?"

"I made myself go away, sort of. . . ."

"How?"

Anne decided to tell William a very private thing. A thing she hadn't even told the ghosts. But they would hear it now, too.

"When it was happening, I closed my eyes and . . . I saw Jesus." Anne waited for him to laugh. He didn't. "Like, I am on the ground, but Jude isn't on me. And the sun is in my eyes so I can't look up, but I see Jesus's feet. He had sandals on. Then I look up and see his white robes and the rope around his waist, and when I finally look up to find his face, I can't see it because the sun is making a halo around his head. And I felt totally at peace. And when I came back, Jude was done."

William's eyes were as big as saucers.

"Anne, maybe the ghosts aren't really ghosts at all. Maybe they're saints and you *are* seeing Jesus, and saints . . . which would make *you* a saint!"

Anne laughed.

"No, Will, the ghosts are not saints. They belong to me and

to this place somehow. They are just as real to me as you are. I told you, they can do stuff."

"Jesus can do stuff," said William.

"Oh, yeah? Then why didn't he pull Jude off me when I saw him, huh?" Anne asked, half joking.

"Well, he sort of did. Didn't he, Anne? I mean . . . you thought about him and what Jude was doing just . . . just went away?"

They were both very quiet; but in that moment, they both began to believe in God. Anne would waver throughout her life, but William wouldn't. William would devote his life to God, or Anne, whichever would have him first.

"Share everything with me, Anne," he said. "I will never leave you."

"Do you want to come over tomorrow? Into the Witch House?"

"I thought you'd never ask!"

"What are you doing?" asked Nan. She had woken in the night to hear ripping noises and climbed the stairs to find Anne in the attic, her feet shuffling around in torn paper and kicking aside doll heads.

"I am cleaning out the attic, sort of. I've invited Will over."

Nan frowned, then walked away. Anne watched her go before continuing to rip and scrape at the walls.

"Anna?" Nan was back.

"What?" Anne asked.

"Here."

Nan held out a bucket full of warm soapy water and a large bag to put the garbage in.

"Do you want me to help you?"

"No, thank you."

Nan watched her for a moment, and then went back to bed.

The next day Anne practically dragged William back to the Witch House after school.

"What is it?" he asked.

"Wait and see! Wait and see!" Anne said.

When they got to the house, she ran in the front door. William couldn't help but stop to put his hands on the massive doors to feel the ornate carvings.

"Ouch!"

"What happened, Will?"

"Just a splinter." William put his finger in his mouth.

They went upstairs to the attic, Anne hurrying him the whole way.

"Come on!"

It was very clean.

"What was it you wanted to show me?"

"This . . ."

She walked him up to the cupola.

"Oh, Anne, it's beautiful!" Outside he could see the day was getting stormy.

Anne took down a massive rectangular book from a shelf.

The scrapbook was leather bound and contained thick black pages filled and overlapping with newspaper articles and photographs.

"This is my Nan's Black Book, a sort of memory book."

"Does she know you have it?"

"Of course. She gave it to me."

Anne placed the book between them and opened it. The pages and binding groaned, always the prelude to a good read.

"See?" Anne said, putting her finger on the first photo. "That's Haven House."

"Wow. Look how big. . . . It really was the most beautiful house." William couldn't believe it. It looked as if it had come right out of a fairy tale. There was no angle that wasn't covered in fancy woodwork, and the corners turned into rounded rooms and then straight back up again into pointy towers. It looked impossible.

"I know . . . I wish I could have lived there," Anne said, wistfully.

"You do, sort of."

"I guess . . ." Anne positioned herself on her stomach and put her legs in the air behind her, crossed at the ankles. She liked to get as close to the book as possible. The rain was coming down outside now, but it only made it cozier in the attic.

Anne turned the page. "These are the Greens. Archibald and Isabelle. They are drawings because they are so old. These particular Greens built Haven House. It was the very first house of its kind. Before it was built, this whole area was a small fishing village called Dragon."

"That's a funny name," William laughed.

"The Native American tribe that lived here before the settlers came called it Dragon because of the sounds the sea lions made mating on the riverbanks. I guess they called to one another and sounded like dragons." Anne paused.

"Actually, Haven House took up the entire area of land that was the old village. That is how big it all is! Anyway, Archibald and Isabelle had six children. They all died, William, all of them. And then they had one more, Gwyneth, and she lived." Anne turned the page. "Everyone said that Archibald sold his soul to the devil in order to have a child. And his punishment was crazy Gwen. But she's not crazy at all. She's lovely. But I think that most rumors have some truth hiding inside, don't you?"

William nodded.

"I think Archibald did bad things. When Gwen was small, she was naughty. She used to sneak out into the gardens at night and find Archibald in the gatehouse in all sorts of compromising positions. Very odd."

"How do you know all of this stuff?"

"I just know. And also, Ava, and Gwen, too . . . Here she is! This is the wedding portrait of Gwyneth and Reginald Green," she proclaimed proudly. "They were so lovely. If I ever get married, I want a dress like that. Reginald was her cousin. Can you believe it? Gwen didn't have to change her name or *any-thing*."

They lingered on this photo. Even though there were only two people in it, they made you forget everything else. She was very fair with thin features and a frantic look that danced behind the still picture. He was her opposite, dark and dapper. Black hair and a black mustache. And deep, inset eyes. He was almost handsome.

"They had so many babies—six or seven, I think—but they

all died, too, just like Archibald and Isabelle's babies. But you know what?"

"What?"

"Gwen hired someone to take pictures of them."

"Of course they did," said William. "That's what people do. They take pictures of their babies."

"Oh, yeah? How about pictures of them *dead*?"

"What?"

"Yep, she had pictures taken of them when they were dead. She kept them in frames in—" Anne returned to the first page she showed him, putting her finger on the rounded turret of the west side of the house. "—this room. The turret room. You can't tell, because the picture is black and white, but see those windows? Those windows were all different colors of stained glass. It was Gwen's collection room.

"They weren't very nice people. Especially Reggie. He was very mean. Everyone in town was afraid of him. Before Nan came, he locked himself up in the east wing of Haven House and hardly ever came out."

Anne flipped to a series of photographs of Nan and Reginald, Gwyneth and Ava. "Wasn't my Nan pretty?"

"Very. I can hardly tell it's her."

William looked at the pictures; they made an odd sort of family. Gwyneth sitting on the lawn on a blanket, her arms stretched out to Nan, Nan on her way to the embrace, Reginald looking on with a contented smile, Ava playing with a jump rope in the background.

Anne began humming something, a soft yet familiar melody,

while they looked at a picture, blurred in action of Reginald spinning Nan around in what looked like an impromptu dance.

William began to sing the words.

" 'Let me call you sweetheart, I'm in love, with, you!' I know that song."

"It was Reggie's favorite. He sang it to Nan and Gwen all the time."

"I thought he wasn't nice?"

"He wasn't . . . but he was nice to them. After Nan came, anyway. . . ." Anne trailed off and turned to the last pages in the book, tore out a newspaper clipping from the back, and ran for the door. The storm was over and the sun was peeping out from behind the clouds.

"Come on, Will, this next part I want to show you! It's better that way."

He followed her down the stairs and then outside and onto the old foundation. The air was fresh and earthy. William inhaled deeply and blinked as the world began to blur. He grew dizzy. He shook his head and looked up. Anne was standing on a two-foot wall of crumbling rock and pointing up.

"That is where she was when Gwen lit the lighter. The turret room. The stained-glass windows exploded in, and the next morning they found her." Anne held out the newspaper clipping that captured the grotesque image.

"What *is* that?"

"Ava."

"Jeeze, what happened to her?"

"The room exploded and the heat from the fire melted the glass onto her. It encased her! It was amazing! No wonder

Gwen and Ava are still earthbound. That's what Father Callahan calls ghosts . . . earthbound spirits who have sinned or who were sinned against."

Will was a little horrified, but Anne was right, it was amazing.

"What do you want to do now?" asked Anne.

"Everything," said William. And he meant it.

He did anything she wanted him to do, all the time, and all too soon, their trying yet adventurous childhood was behind them.

23

William on the Beach with
Coppertone and a Kiss

1957

The summer after they graduated from high school, Anne and William's relationship took a turn for the romantic.

He'd gotten a job working at Bodine's Apothecary in town and was living in a rented room above the store. Meanwhile, Anne was spending all her time reading on the beach, learning as much as she could about her family's dark ways and flat out ignoring Nan's protests to leave all of that be.

"But really, what's stopping us from just getting married?" William asked after another endless day at the beach in late June.

"We haven't even kissed. Married people have sex. Really,

Will, be practical," Anne replied, without looking up from her black book.

"It's not like we can't kiss. You're just being stubborn. I can tell you'd like to kiss me."

Anne snorted out a dismissive laugh.

"I'm serious. . . ."

"Okay, fine," she said, closing her book and flopping down on her back. "Where would we live? What would we do? Tell me, Will, really . . . what would a life like that look like? I'm not exactly June Cleaver."

"We could live in the gatehouse. Your aunt Lavinia's moved closer to the prison, and Nan hasn't rented it out yet, right? She wouldn't mind. She loves me. And Lucy would be happy to get you out of the house altogether."

"Will . . . I'm never leaving the Witch House. You should know that. I belong to it, and it belongs to me. Anyway, you're missing the point. Besides the fact that we've never kissed, don't you think that with our shared past we may be ill-suited to marriage? Think about it, William."

Will smiled and leaned over, kissing Anne on the cheek.

"You taste like Coppertone."

"That's because it's summer. That's what summer tastes like. Now, stop trying to manufacture this romance and lie back down, you're blocking my sun. Rude is what it is."

Later that night, Anne wrenched her windows open, seeking relief from the stifling humidity. That's when she heard it.

Music. Rolling in on the sea breeze.

She followed the sound through the ruins of Haven House, stepping on her own past with a sure foot as the music coursed through her, making her inner strength even stronger.

When she came through the juniper trees, the beach lay in front of her. It was a stunning night. The moon was high in the sky, almost full, and the water was full of phosphorus, so the foam crashing into the beach was fluorescent green. In the center of the beach, William stood smiling by a bonfire. "Would you care to dance, m'lady?" he asked, bowing.

"What the heck is all this, Will?" asked Anne, trying to act as if the whole thing weren't delighting her.

"I thought we could pretend to be strangers. Start again. A better kind of start."

"You want us to fall in love. . . ."

"Yes. I do. I think I'm owed this one farce. Come on."

"Oh, fine. Who are you supposed to be, anyway? And where is that music coming from?"

"Old man Bodine let me use his new transistor radio. I am a fisherman washed up from the sea. And you are a saint . . . or a mermaid. Or just . . ."

"Have I told you lately that I am worried about your confusion between devoutness and paganism? A gypsy mermaid witch virgin. How's that?"

"Perfect."

"You are from the house, no? On the hill?" asked William, putting on a terrible accent.

"Yes," Anne said, trying not to laugh. "That would be me. . . ."

"Good, good . . . You must stay for the celebration."

"And what are you celebrating?"

"Life, love . . . and vino." Will brought out a bottle of wine and two glasses from a bag at his feet.

"Oh, you are naughty, Mr. Fisherman. I like it!"

Anne and William drank a lot of wine that night and danced, spinning in tipsy circles until they fell into one another. Then, they swam naked in the sea.

"I have always loved you, Anne," said William, swimming closer to her. She could feel his breath as he spoke. The salty water lapped against her bare, moonlit shoulders.

"Are you going to kiss me, Mr. Fisherman?" she asked.

"Forever," he said.

Anne understood that the feelings awakening inside her were real, and she knew it was what William had felt all along.

She didn't want to argue with herself, or with him. And she took it as a good and valuable sign.

Her body soon found his through the water, and for their first kiss, every inch of them pressed together, electrified that nothing separated them. Soon, with the humid night air pressing against them as they lay on a blanket by the dwindling fire, Anne and William became lovers.

"We will do this all summer!" Anne said, as she kissed him long and then quick before running back up the rock wall steps.

"We will do this all our lives," he called after her.

By October, she was pregnant.

"Marry me," said William. They were lounging by the empty ruins of the Haven House pool, wrapped in blankets to abate the crisp October day.

"Don't be ridiculous, Will. When has anyone in my family ever done the right thing?" she said, shielding her eyes from his look with sunglasses and turning her head toward the gray, sunless sky.

"Anne, I love you. Please. I know we're young, but your mother was married close to this age, it's not such a big deal. Marry me and we can run away to New York or California, just *somewhere*, and we can have a life. Together." William felt the earth shift under his feet. He felt a moment of fear. The trees whispered out a warning. His get-out-of-jail-free card had expired. *You won't take her,* he heard just underneath a ticking sound that grew louder and louder until his ears rang. *Tic tock tic tock tic tock. Tic.* He gulped and shook away his fear. Screw that wicked house, he was taking Anne.

Anne looked at William. He was so sincere. His blue eyes told her he meant what he said. She knew this was a defining moment in her life.

"I can't leave here. I don't *want* to leave here. But . . . yes, I'll marry you. I suppose it's the right thing to do. The Christian thing or what have you."

"You will?" he said.

"Of course. Just as long as you don't have me wearing an apron and making perfectly portioned meals and all that. And

I don't know the first thing about being a mother. So don't get all worked up about it. I plan on making a ton of mistakes. We'll be weird, Will. We'll be outcasts. Are you ready for that? Because out of all the things I hate about the women in this family, that's the one thing I'm proud of."

"Terrifying the community at large?"

"Precisely. And I'm not wearing a white dress, just so you know."

"Listen here, I know I'm young, but Will loves me, and you of all people should understand. . . . No. . . . that's not right. . . ."

Anne was in her bedroom, practicing her speech in the mirror. Her nervousness was rattling her. Why tell them? They probably won't even notice, she thought.

The real truth was, Anne was secretly hoping her mother would finally open her arms and her heart to Anne. That she'd see Anne doing the same type of thing she'd done with Vito, and that similarity would let Lucy finally show love toward her daughter. And maybe Nan would be warmer and less strict with a new baby. And even Dominic might come home. Anne felt like perhaps she could right all the wrongs with this one act of normalcy.

But just when she had worked up the courage to call Lucy and Nan to a meeting and was coming out of her room, she heard the kitchen screen door slam.

"Nan! Where are you going? I need to talk to you," she called out as she ran down the stairs, letting her fingers fly across the stairwell walls, her imagination tossing around romantic ideas of a reformed happy family. She rushed into the kitchen and hugged Nan tightly.

"I must tend the garden, Anne. You know that. You have become too lazy with your books this summer, young lady. What do you want?" asked Nan, trying to free herself from Anne's embrace.

"I have news. Big exciting news! And I want to tell you and my mother together."

"You think I don't already know? You're with child. You intend on marrying William, yes?"

"You know?"

"Just because I wish the ways away, doesn't mean they go. Of course I know. But you mustn't tell your mother. Not yet."

"Why?"

"Because she's been drinking since morning. Because you are too happy. Because she will be angry. Don't do it. Come with me outside instead and tell me of your plans while I pull the weeds."

"No, I need to have some lunch first." Anne knew that would get Nan to leave her alone. Nan liked to see her eat.

"There's focaccia with olives in the oven. Eat and then come outside."

Anne kissed Nan on the cheek. But once the screen door was shut and Nan was inside the vegetable garden, Anne ran upstairs to tell Lucy.

It did not occur to Anne that Lucy might not be immediately emotionally available simply because Anne was finally ready for a relationship. Other people rarely occurred to Anne at all. In this way, she was like her mother.

She found Lucy sitting in a chair at the end of the second-floor hallway, smoking a cigarette by the window. She didn't even look at Anne. She took a drag of her cigarette and said, "You're pregnant. . . . I can tell. I can smell it on you. I see your breasts. That pansy boy. That God lover. Did you let him do it? Or did he take it from you, like the other one? You let him, I know you did. And you want me to be happy. Yes. I see it all."

"Mother . . . Lucy. Mama . . . I just thought maybe we could look at this as a new beginning."

Lucy laughed. "You are a shadow." She laughed harder now, with a wicked singsong lilt to her voice. "Who are you? I can't see you, you ugly little ugly shadow. You weren't even supposed to be born. You were a *demon* inside me. . . . So was that man. . . . Just shadow demons . . . the two of you." With that, Lucy began to move toward her bedroom door.

Anne watched her walk away, and then, quietly, without meaning to, or without even expecting her mother to hear, said, "Gavin wanted us. You chased him away. He might have stayed with us. It could have been good, you could have married him, and we could have been a family."

Lucy snapped around with some sort of fierce wildness to her eyes that Anne had never seen—it was scarier than even the faces of her ghosts at their most warped. Through clenched teeth, Lucy railed at Anne. She said all the things she never should have said. The things no child should ever hear. She made a very bad mistake.

"Let me tell you something, sweetheart. I had a family. I had a family that I lost. Vito, dead. Dominic? Gone, never writes, never visits. All because of *you*. I thought if you were anything, you were smart. He didn't leave us, I didn't chase Gavin away. I *forced* him. I *made* that demon leave, and I *begged* him to take his spawn with him. But guess what? He didn't want you! He wanted me . . . *only me*. Not you. Who would want you? *Hmmmm* . . . who would want you? *No one*. You are one hundred percent unwantable."

Lucy had drawn closer and closer to Anne, and she was practically on top of her when she spit out the word *unwantable*. Anne wiped Lucy's bourbon spit from her face, and then something unfamiliar happened. Anne broke open, and the anger she had held deep inside unleashed. It lit like wildfire, fast, furious. Anne didn't even know she could feel such a pain in her heart, that she had feelings that ran that deep. A primal scream escaped her, and she slapped her mother across the face with such a force it threw Lucy backward. When Lucy got up, her eyes were open inhumanly wide. She rushed at Anne, and terror sent Anne running back down the hallway to the stairs.

Anne turned around to look at the wild hate in Lucy's eyes, knowing everything was different, and then Lucy just . . . pushed . . . just pushed her a little bit . . . and down she fell, backward, hitting the curved wall, before falling forward again. The moment she landed she knew two things for certain:

She was done trying to love Lucy.

And she knew she'd lost the baby.

She hit her head at the bottom and blacked out, but only for a moment. No one came.

Lucy wasn't running down the stairs. She was crying at the top of them, saying, "I'm sorry, my little Anne, I'm sorry, I'm so sorry," over and over again.

Nan didn't come running inside.

And of course, Gavin wasn't there to help her either. He'd been gone forever and always would be.

There was no one to protect Anne. She would have to stop letting herself get hurt. She would have to be a soldier, and her ghosts would be her guns.

At the same time that Anne decided to not listen to her Nan, instead setting off a whole slew of disastrous events that might have otherwise been avoided, Nan had gone to work in her kitchen garden. The garden was just beginning to push up sprouts. The day was warm for early spring, and Nan began to daydream of what a life could be like here if the three of them could reach some sort of peace and just love one another. It occurred to her for the first time that they were all so similar. Maybe this was the time. The time to let the past be the past. Maybe it wasn't too late. If Anne was brave enough to reach out to Lucy, why couldn't she, her own mother, reach out as well?

She knew Anne could make a connection with Lucy, if she tried hard enough. Anything was possible with hard work. And she knew that this pregnancy, however inconvenient, could be the thread that would knit this little family together.

Nan knew she was not a girl any longer; it was time to put her thoughts into action. She opened her eyes, ready to begin anew, and started at the sight of a child at the end of the garden path.

She tried to blink it away. This was a phantom child, not a real one. But the child held fast. And then Nan knew. It was Ava. And instead of holding out her arms, which she longed to do, had longed to do since that painful day at Haven House when everything collapsed around her, Nan got scared.

Her whole body recoiled in horror and shame. She didn't mean to—in reality, she was in a repair-damage kind of mood that day—but the ghost was so vividly frightening to Nan that her reaction was involuntary. Ava's little ghost heart broke in that moment. And so she left as quietly as she'd appeared.

"Wait! Ava! I'm so sorry. . . ."

And it was too much for Nan. Her heart broke too. "Ava . . . if you won't come back to me, I guess I have to follow you. Like sardines. Like we used to play . . . ready or not. . . ."

William, (who had decided Anne needed company when she broke the news to Lucy and had returned too late), was the one who found Nan. He started yelling for Anne, who stumbled out of the Witch House hunched over in pain, blood on her head and on the seat of her dress.

"Anne!"

"Will Will Will Will!"

"No, Anne! No!"

Anne didn't think she'd ever stop hearing their own screams.

"It's over," she said when she reached him. "Everything is over. It's over. It's over. It's all dead. Everything is dead now."

Lucy looked out the window and screamed with them.

The house screamed, too.

Tic tock tic tock tic tock. Tic.

24

*Cupid in the Garden
with a Hatchet*

SATURDAY, SEPTEMBER 5, 2015

10:00 A.M.

Eleanor was in the kitchen on the phone with Anthony. Maj and Byrd were told to leave, but they hid in the hallway, listening on the other phone.

Eleanor: "Are you planning on hanging up on me again?"

Anthony: "You used to do it to me all the time."

Eleanor: "Yeah, but you said I was crazy. So unless you've become just like crazy ol' me, you need to be the one that doesn't do it. Right?"

Anthony: "You sound different."

Eleanor: "I am different. I think. Well, I feel good. There's a teenage girl here, a cousin. She's like Maj. I'm home."

Anthony: "I was thinking I'd come for a visit. Now I'm sure I will."

Eleanor: "Why?"

Anthony: "I don't know. . . . To see my kid? To see you? To figure out if I have any place in your new '*home*'? To meet a strange girl living with you? God, Elly. . . . Why do you need to make this hard? I'm telling you I miss you. It's been two days, and I miss you. I want to see you. Isn't that what you want from me? Some epic love song? This is it. Take it or leave it."

Eleanor: "Are you bringing Josephine? I need to know how many vacuum bags to buy. It's easy here, laid-back. You'd hate it. And here's a piece of news: *I can live wherever I want.* You have no say at all. She's not even yours, remember? You have no claim."

Click, dial tone. He'd hung up on her again. Like always. But this time, Eleanor didn't try to call him back.

"Mama?" asked Maj from the hall, still holding the receiver in her hand. Byrd's eyes were full of regret.

"I didn't know," said Byrd. "I wouldn't have helped her listen in if I knew you'd go all truthtastic."

Maj ran upstairs.

"Should I go after her?" asked Byrd.

Eleanor wanted to run after Maj, too. But she was too damned angry. Angry with herself, angry with Anthony. Angry with decisions.

Tic tock tic tock tic tock. Tic.

"I don't know. How would you like to be treated after a damaging secret is revealed? She's like you. More like you than me. I need a drink."

"Then leave her. She probably already knew. She'll come down, and you can tell her the whole story."

"There's more to it, you know."

"I figured."

"She may have known, heard, sensed that Anthony wasn't her real father. But as far as I know, she has no idea that her real father was a borderline sociopath who tried to kill us."

"Damn."

"Love is evil, Byrd," Eleanor said, furiously buttering toast.

"You may not believe me, as I sure do love myself some evil . . . but I don't agree. Love is love. It's its own damn menace, but it isn't evil." Byrd shrugged.

"And what exactly would *you* call something that made you do things you would never do? Act how you would never act? What would you call something that could make a peaceful person rage or a well person sick? A natural disaster is what it is. Like being caught under a mudslide suffocating while in the last stages of rabies. And here's the kicker. . . . When someone offers you a way out, you smile and tell them to fuck off. That's love," Eleanor said.

"Well, when you put it that way," laughed Byrd.

Maj came back into the kitchen, and without a word, Eleanor picked her up and walked outside.

They were quiet with one another.

"I know all the things, Mama. I just am scared I'm like him. I've always been scared of that. But then we moved here and Byrd was here and I'm like her. And you, too. So I'm not scared now."

"Are you angry?"

"No. I was more surprised. Then, I went upstairs and Anne told me a secret."

"What did she say?"

"It's a secret." Maj smiled.

The phone rang again. Maj popped up and ran back inside the kitchen to grab it. "Hello, the Witch House residence, Your Majesty speaking. Yes, okay, hold on. . . . Mama, some man named Amazing Andy says he needs directions. He can talk to ghosts."

"Curiouser and curiouser," Eleanor said, walking back into the kitchen. Her step was lighter than it had been for years. She'd not realized how much that secret had weighted her down. And just like that . . . it was all out in the open and cleaned up. No fuss, no muss.

"Ah, that would be for me," said Byrd. After a short exchange she hung up, turned to Eleanor and said, "Our psychic is lost. I just can't stand it when interesting things turn alarming. And they just always do that, you ever notice? I mean, whoever heard of a lost psychic? I SWEAR."

11:30 A.M.

Eleanor sat on the bottom step of the porch with Byrd, watching Maj try to play with Delores (who was old and tired and slept the days away under the Willow tree) while waiting for the lost psychic.

"Byrd, so far Anne's story is sitting right in my throat like a scream," said Eleanor.

"It's hard to hear. And I'm a lot like her, which is hard to say," said Byrd.

"I just keep thinking about it, then looking at Maj. Then thinking about it. It makes me think maybe the decisions I made weren't so bad. Nothing like that happened to you, did it, honey? Like what happened to Anne?"

"Things happen to everyone."

"Bad things?"

"The way I figure it is this: I had to have the bad things happen for the good things to happen. History is history, as far as I'm concerned. This is a new start."

"Byrd, do you trust me?"

"I think I do."

"I think I trust you, too."

"There's some kind of sissy words comin' next. I can feel 'em."

"Well, these women sure knew how to avoid their feelings. Got to be honest with the ones you love."

"Oh, sure, one slip of the tongue and an entirely too forgiving red-headed daughter and now you're the queen bee of honesty."

"Very funny, Miss Byrd. Very funny."

1:00 P.MM

Amazing Andy toured the house. He walked up and down the stairs, into each room and out—and he did it all walking like he'd been born on a horse. Afterward, he met Byrd and Eleanor in the library.

"So?" asked Byrd.

"Well, y'all, I'm afraid what we have here isn't a haunting. It's a hostage situation," he said.

"What does that mean?"

"It means you got spirits here that can't move on. The house won't let them go. Usually we got to rid the house of the ghosts. In this instance we got to rid the ghosts of the house."

"And I thought this would be easy," sighed Byrd.

"So what's the next step, where do we go from here?" Eleanor asked.

"Where do you go from here. . . . That's tricky. Truth is, this thing scares me. And there's too much to lose. Death is a sort of occupational hazard."

"Ghosts can kill you?"

"No, nothing like that. I mean high blood pressure, embolism, heart attack, demonic possession. You know, your garden variety ailments."

"Oh, I see," Eleanor said seriously, trying not to break out into hysterical laughter. This guy, wow, she thought.

"I know it sounds ridiculous, but any kind of energy can cause all sorts of things in a body. Ain't you never heard of people fryin' themselves to death in a tub just 'cause they wanted to listen to music at the same time? Or say they had an angry relative wantin' to toss a hair dryer in with them? The point is, I'm always prepared for death, because I'm sure of the peaceful nature of what lies beyond. Death doesn't scare me.

"But this house? This house traps the dead."

"And it seems that it traps the women who live here, even as it kills or sickens or drives mad the men who're foolhardy enough to decide to love them.

"So I'd rather not get too attached to this house or its ghosts or even to you purty young fillies. *Comprende*?"

"Are you from Texas?" asked Byrd.

"No, why do you ask?"

"Just, you . . . there's a cowboy thing. Never mind."

"I was a cowboy in my last life."

"I see."

"And I'll be damned if I let this Frankenstein house trap me here and rob me of my next reincarnation into what could be untold wealth.

"My advice to you both: run."

1:45 P.M.

"Are you sure you're all done? Shouldn't you walk the ex-tended property, check out the gatehouse?" asked Byrd while Eleanor wrote him a check.

The color drained from Amazing Andy's face. "You . . . you mean that house at the front of the drive?"

"Yes."

"Well, I, uh, I didn't feel much at all as I went by in the car. I'm sure it's fine. And really, I'm late for another appointment." He grabbed the check from Eleanor as she was signing and ran, leaving a line of ink in his wake.

2:00 P.M.

Eleanor slapped some cheese between slices of bread—cooking was always her Mimi's specialty, not hers—while Maj and Byrd sat at the kitchen table trying hard not to laugh.

"So, do you think he was downright strange or what?" asked Byrd.

"I think he was stupid. Not strange. And I'm a little aggravated that he couldn't tell us more. No. Scratch that, forget that reincarnated old cowboy, I'm mad that we can't pool together *our* resources, our magic, and figure this whole thing out quicker. We're almost out of time. Really, are there no happy people in our family? Not one single solitary happy ending? This isn't very promising for either of us. Or Maj," Eleanor said, glancing at her daughter.

"Mama, I can just draw my own ending. I have all the colors," Maj said, taking a big bite of her sandwich.

"Anyway," Byrd said. "All good stories have interesting beginnings. And we might not be able to find a happy ending, but damn, we got the interesting beginnings down pat. And even though a lot of bad things happened to those who came before us, there's got to be a happy ending. I think. Because that's what you're missing."

"And what is that, exactly?"

"What happens after any ordinary happy ending?"

"More beginnings. And more endings. Oh, I see what you're getting at. Because the only ending would be death, and in our case, that isn't actually an end." Eleanor sighed. "Oh, Byrd, I don't know which way is up anymore."

"It just all depends on how you look at it, Elly. I mean, we're all dyin' every day. Some days it worries me, and some days it don't. I'm just going to come back and haunt you all anyway."

Eleanor smiled. "Maybe it's time you finish telling me Anne's story. Maj, why don't you go play? But no wandering off to high clifftops this time."

"Okay, Mama. I'm gonna go to the attic to finish my new drawing with Anne."

"Love you, baby girl." Eleanor brought Maj in for a quick squeeze before letting her skip away. She briefly wondered what picture Maj was working on but let the thought get lost as she turned to Byrd. "So, Nan is dead, and Anne just lost whatever chance she had at her own happy ending. What happens next?"

"Nan's funeral was a disaster, evidently. There was Lucy having relations with the funeral director, and Anne catching them in the act. And then there was the fact that Anne had avoided William since she got out of the hospital. He wanted to talk to her, you know . . . kiss and make up. Talk about the baby they lost. Things like that. But she wasn't having it. So the night of Nan's funeral, she decided to kill herself."

"Well, she obviously didn't do it. You're here after all."

"Cousin Eleanor, there are many ways to die."

Eleanor raised an eyebrow. "How dramatic, young Cousin Byrd."

Byrd ignored her and continued. "As you hear the rest of this story, I dare you not to believe that a big huge chunk of Anne, my crazy great-grandma, died in that fall. Because as strange as she was before, as downright evil as people thought she was, she got exponentially crazier after that terrible day."

25

Anne in the Garden with a Train Ticket

1957

Anne sat on the beach, staring at the waves.

Just three hours earlier, Nan had been buried at that shit show of a funeral. She shivered and raked her hands through the shell-peppered sand. Periwinkles, moon snails, coquina clam, oysters.

A storm must be off the coast, she thought. A man-made stone pier stretched out into the mist on her right, most of its rocks already submerged. The waves slapped angrily against them. In the fading light, everything had become gray, the sea and sky one. But dark clouds had rolled in, breaking everything into a living, breathing, undulating black-and-white photograph. Anne was awestruck by its intensity. She often felt a want, a deep longing, to be inside of nature, part of the actual process, to feel the whole thing. She felt it in the fall when the leaves would change. She wanted to be able to experience the whole vivid display of reds and oranges and yellows all at once instead of one or two trees at a time. She wanted it all to crash over her, through her. It seemed to her that human eyes had a very limited existence. There was so much more to see and not enough windows in the body.

Anne took off her shoes and walked thought the sand, cutting a sharp diagonal to the left to walk on the rocks. She was going to walk out to sea. If she was going to kill herself, it had better be cinematic.

The rocks were cool and wet beneath her feet. She knew to avoid the dark spots of slippery seaweed and the barnacles—they drew blood, and why shouldn't they? They were alive, and her feet would hurt them, too, as she made her way slowly out to the very edge. A perfect stillness came over her even as the waves crashed all around her. She could hear the roar of the ocean, the crush of the waves on the rocks, the sucking in of the tide, the rushing out of the tide, until the wind rushed in, filling her eardrums with its whistles and ghostly screams. Then just as quickly, it would retreat, and the sounds of the ocean would pummel her again. She felt the mad sea spray on her face, God's spit, God's blessing, it slapped her, burned her, made her unable to see. She closed her eyes against it and raised her arms up so that the wind could just take her, and for a moment, she thought that the earth, the sea, the rocks, the horizon, the clouds, the sky, would all just swallow her up, because for one moment she felt she had achieved what she had spent so long searching for, a "oneness" with the planet.

It's time, thought Anne.

"Anne!"

William's voice rose above it all, and Anne's spell was broken. She would not, after all, be swallowed up by the sea. She felt torn: throw herself in and end it now (begin it?).

All of a sudden she was a bit cold, and a little off balance on the rocks (the water was up to her ankles now), and she felt a feeling she didn't like. She felt afraid.

"I'll not die afraid," she said. "I will walk from this earth with a straight back and a fearless disposition if it kills me." She turned toward William. "Keep your pants on, Will. I'm just thinking. Why don't you just go on home?" she called.

"Anne, please talk to me. You owe me this much."

"I owe you?" she said, rushing back to the beach to face him.

"I lost the same dream you lost."

"Fine. What do you want?"

"Marry me. Just marry me and let's try again."

William had tears in his eyes. He tried to hold them back, but Anne saw his Adam's apple moving back and forth, choking down the hurt.

If he'd just waited a second longer. If he'd been brave enough to let those words of love and support linger inside of Anne, let them take hold, this story would have a much different ending. But instead, he said, "I'm going to seminary, Anne. If you won't have me, I have to go."

Amore women never respond well to threats.

"You want to be a priest, Will? You?" She laughed in that cruel way she learned from her mother. "And when will you start diddling little boys? *Hmmmm?* These things are, what did

Gwen say? Cyclical, you know. . . . It happened to you, you will do it to someone else. . . ."

William stared at her in disbelief.

"You don't get it, Anne. You don't get it and you never will. After I met you, those things never bothered me anymore. Every time it happened, I thought of you. I thought about us, escaping, being a family. Like it was the price I had to pay. But I am done paying, Anne, especially for something that I can't have. If I can't have you, then I don't want anyone, and the only thing left for me is the only thing I know."

"Don't you do this to me, Will. Don't you make me say this. I will hate you for it. You know who I am, you know *me*. I can't love you! I can't leave here!" Anne wanted to throw up. If William was asking this of her, then he really didn't know her. Which meant no one did, no one at all, except for ghosts.

He looked at her for a long time. He let his eyes linger over her pale face and angry, beautiful eyes. In his mind, he saw himself touch her hair. She smelled like roses. Had he ever told her that? Like wild roses. He walked away from her.

Anne was alone.

William wrote to her. But Anne never wrote back. He'd done the unforgivable.

He'd left her. That was all there was to it. And Nan had left her, too. Death was no excuse.

Everyone left her.

Anne didn't like to dwell on how much she thought about

her father. How many times she'd daydreamed about him swooping back in and taking her away. Protecting her.

The more she wanted it, the more she fought feeling anything at all.

That's when she decided to go find him.

And Lucy couldn't be bothered to care enough to stop her.

Lucy said. "You will terrify the entire gulf coast with your pale skin, and how do you know he even wants to see you?"

"He doesn't have a choice."

Anne stood outside the streamliner to Florida, thinking about just how amazing the world outside her small Witch House reality actually was. She wanted to watch the rushing people for hours. But her train was boarding. The streamliner was more art than transportation. Bulletlike, smooth. Gentle as well as dangerous. It astounded her. So Anne put her palms on the cold steel, but it was a new train. It didn't have many stories to tell her fingers yet, so she let the tide of people move her into the coach.

The train ride took a day and a half. Anne was rapt the whole journey. It's one thing to know that the world has all sorts of different places in it, to see pictures; it is another thing entirely to know it with all your senses. As the train went further south, the doors would open to let passengers on or off, and the smells that would come in were different from anything Anne was used to. Spicy and sweet. The smell of salt marshes and pine groves mixed with date palm and the heady perfume of tropical flora intoxicated her. The ground also became flatter, the stops less congested, the people friendlier. It was an amazing voyage. But then it was over, and it was time to do what she came to do. She stood before the open train doors, unsure of what to do or where to go next.

Trust yourself, she thought.

She got off the train, and the heat smacked into her, heavy and damp. Anne walked until she came to a street lined with tall live oaks and dripping with Spanish moss. Each tree was placed with care in front of an amazing brick dwelling with wrought-iron fences. They unfolded, magically, one after the other, as she walked by. They were close together and similar in architecture, but each house had its own flavor, its own character. They liked her well enough, but they weren't *her* house, nor were they the house she was looking for.

She stopped in front of the house. There was a sign on the gate:

Magnolia House.

Gavin had just finished shaving in the sunny front bathroom on the second floor. He looked out the window and saw her right as she looked up. They locked eyes. He knew her instantly.

Gavin wiped off his face quickly, motioning for her to go around. Anne came through the gate and headed to the back of the house, taking in the stonework walkway and the lush tropical gardens. It was all so rich-seeming, so luxurious. Excess met with restraint. This is Southern charm, she thought: restrained excess.

The back of the house was one massive screened-in porch with several sets of wide planked whitewashed wooden steps leading to different entrances. Anne walked up the stairs feeling only half herself. She was not as nervous as she was excited to see Gavin. She paused, taking a moment to look the grounds over. Palms mixed with deciduous foliage and other fantastic shrubs, dotting the emerald green lawn. The landscaping pointed downhill, like perspective in a painting, to the dock and a sailboat and the river behind that led to the sea. Anne felt her world shift to Technicolor—the world of her father, her own personal Oz.

"A river . . ." she whispered. It was late afternoon, and the sun had bathed everything, Anne included, in a wash of golden light. She turned back around to knock, but Gavin had already opened the screen door. Her hand wavered midair, her jaw slack for a moment, and then she walked past him.

"Well now, this *is* a surprise. Come on in, my girl!"

"I'm already in," Anne said. Of all the first words to her father, these were not the ones she expected to say.

"I know . . . just tryin' to lighten up the air a tiny bit." He shut the door, turning to greet her properly with an open hand. Gavin watched an internal struggle play across her face. She moved toward him stiffly with her arms open, as if she were going to embrace him (which would have been surprising, yet fine with him), but her face was contorted in contempt and her neck strained backward against the rest of her body. Gavin had heard of mixed emotions, but this was ridiculous.

"Okay, *fine!*" Anne burst out, stomping her foot before she shot toward him, flinging her arms around him. Gavin hugged her tight. She smelled like Lucy, like roses. God how he missed her.

"*Shhhhhh . . .*" he hushed. "I'm right here, it's okay now,

Pap's got ya'. I'm right here. Now, what brings you all this way, honey? Not that I am displeased to see you, but I would have liked to prepare for your arrival."

Anne pulled herself away, mad at herself for touching him—for seeming weak.

"Look," she said "I don't even know why I'm here. I should probably just go."

"Don't be silly. Why don't you just sit down out here for a second?" He swept his arm in an arc. Her eyes followed, seeing the porch in all of its magnificence for the first time. The wide, whitewashed, well-worn plank floors were covered with the richest-looking Oriental carpets Anne had ever seen. (And Nan and Lucy weren't exactly cheap decorators.)

"Child, you think these are pretty, shoot . . . out here is where we put the old used-up ones! Wait until you get inside!" Her eyes got even bigger when they latched onto the beautiful white wicker rocking chairs and sets of deep, comfortable-looking sofas covered in delightful floral fabrics next to tables set up for dining or cards. "Where would you like to sit?"

Anne thought maybe he was fishing for some kind of compliment—she could see it on his vain, still handsome face. But she shouldn't give in. So it was beautiful, so what? He didn't build it, he inherited it. He was just the fucking caretaker.

"How about here?" Anne immediately looked disinterested and plopped herself down on the first couch she saw.

"Okay then . . ." Gavin said, suddenly uncomfortable and confused, "let me get you a beer—do you, um, can you?"

"I can, and no thanks."

Gavin went to the kitchen. He opened a beer bottle and

leaned on the sink, putting the beer to his lips to take a drink, and then to his forehead for some cooling support. Back out on the porch, he pulled up a chair to face her, his past. After all those years and miles, now there was only a small round glass table with wicker supports sticking out like spider legs standing between them. Gavin leaned back into his chair, took a drink, and then took a good, solid look at his kid.

Anne could only guess what he saw.

- She was damaged. Her eyes screamed the words *lost* and *vulnerable*.
- She was dangerous, like Lucy—he could feel the hate and bitterness coming off of her.
- She was weird, with a flair for the dramatic (not that he would have expected anything different). Anne was dressed all in black, had straight black hair like her mother's only not, and was barefoot. What looked like Chinese slippers dangled between her fingers.

"Why don't you tell me what this is all about? Do you need somethin', child?"

This was just too much for Anne. Did she need something? Did she *need* something? She might have to kill him.

"I need the bathroom." she said.

But what she really needed was Proof of Love.

"There are far too many of them in this damn house. Feel free to poke around. I'll wait for you here, if that's alright."

———

Magnolia House was breathtaking and huge, as most Southern mansions are. It boasted ridiculously high ceilings and gleaming, recently waxed floors. The walls—the ones she could see, at least—were painted pale blue with white trim. They reminded her of her own house, only inside out. All the trim was white, except for the dark natural cherry of the double front doors. The whole house smelled faintly of cigarettes and bourbon. Anne felt at home here. It unnerved her.

"Everyone keeps secrets in closets. Let's go look, lady," she whispered to herself.

The front hall was really a room unto itself, with an impressive set of carved wooden doors and massive floor-to-ceiling windows of etched glass flanking them. The nearest closet was vast as well: she figured it could hold two hundred or so coats for some kind of fancy soirée or something. Anne looked up and let out an annoyed sigh. "There must be a million boxes in here!"

Noticing a step stool in the corner, Anne took the liberty of using it to go up and down twenty or thirty times and, in the waning light summer, arranged a whole lifetime of memorabilia around herself as she sat on yet another wonderful Persian carpet.

A picture of her mother stared up at her from the first box she opened. This was her box. She'd hit the jackpot. There were pictures of Lucy in many stages of her pregnancy with Anne. Beautiful, artistic photos that showed just how much Gavin had loved her, probably still did. She didn't want to keep looking. It hurt her heart. But it was a good kind of hurt, so she did. There was a picture of Nan and Dominic in the vegetable garden and a picture of the Haven House ruins. Had he loved them as much as she did? And then she saw a slip of paper. It was yellowed and folded over many times—a telegram.

GAVIN <STOP> I DO NOT WANT YOU <STOP>
STAY AWAY DO NOT RETURN <STOP> COME
GET THE GIRL <STOP> SHE BELONGS TO YOU
<STOP> YOU ARE BOTH DEAD TO ME <STOP>
LUCY <STOP>

Anne couldn't breathe. Lucy hadn't lied to her. He really didn't want her. He only wanted Lucy, and when he couldn't have her he just stayed here. And he knew how unloved Anne would be. Lucy was right. She wasn't anyone to anyone. Not until William. And now he was gone, too. And the baby . . . her throat began to close from swallowed grief.

Anne shook off the feeling and walked back out to the porch.

"Find the bathroom okay?" Gavin asked.

"I sure did. I found it, and a shitload of other stuff . . . not the least of which is this." Anne waved the yellowed paper in front of Gavin's face.

"Shit." Gavin put his head in his hands.

"*You left me there?* What the fuck kind of person are you?"

"Cool it, little girl," begged Gavin. "I can't take all this right now, I don't know how to wrap my mind around this. . . . Your mother . . . your mother was the most wonderful and most horrible person I ever met. And when she didn't want me, I . . . I swear I never thought you would grow up, I thought I still had time . . . I thought—"

"You thought!" Anne interrupted his rambling harshly. "You

thought. . . . Stupid man . . . you never had a thought in all your days that was worth thinking. I swear, you are going to sit here and try to make this whole thing make some sort of sense to me? You want me to feel sorry for you? My goodness, you *are* bold. You should get on your knees, you hear me? You should get on your knees and beg forgiveness from me."

"Anne, this whole thing, this was never about you. You come from a long line of mistakes and missteps. I don't know why you are here, or what your purpose in life is, but now is not the time to begin to break yourself into tiny pieces, girl. You don't strike me as a person who can fall apart just like that. Do you honestly care about what you can't undo? What is done is done. No matter how you shake out the bedding. What matters is how you go forward. How we gonna go forward, darlin'?"

"I don't know."

"How about we just sit and talk for a spell? You can say anything to me. You can tell me everything, all the bitty secrets."

"Why would I do that?"

"Because you don't have anything to lose when it comes to me. I owe you."

Anne thought that was sound reasoning.

They talked all night. Anne told him about her life. She told him about William and Lucy and Nan and the lost baby. She talked about the sea and the garden and how she belonged to the house. She told him she had never had a dream, not one, because Gwyneth absorbed them all somehow, and that she was now afraid to go to sleep. What she didn't tell him was how Jude stole her childhood.

In turn, Gavin told her about his adventures, his violent childhood. He told her how he fell for her mother and how he felt when Anne was born. He told her how often he thought about her, and Lavinia, and Jude.

What he didn't tell her was how, after he received the telegram, he got halfway to her, but—waylaid by a woman and the bottle—never made it all the way. How once he sobered up a few days later, he felt it was too late. How the regret of those actions kept him tied to the alcohol. She needn't have that burden as well.

He asked her when she was planning to leave.

She told him she'd be leaving the next day. Her head was hammering. *Tic tock tic tock tic tock. Tic.* And she was homesick for the Witch House already.

By the time they finished talking, it was very late. An awkward silence fell over them both. "You ready for bed?" he asked.

"Ready as I'll ever be." Anne shrugged.

The dimly lit house veiled her eyes that were already so heavy. She barely noticed there was a bed at all. She sprawled across it and fell into a deep—but for the first time in her life, not dreamless—sleep.

Horrifying dreams found her. One after the other, like machine-gun fire. She dreamt of a trolley barreling into her when she couldn't move. She dreamt about a baby eating her ankles until Anne had no more feet. She dreamt she was on fire in the middle of the beach and William only pointed and laughed instead of helping her. She dreamt of another child, of dancing in the garden with Jude. She was very happy to wake up.

Anne woke up in a house very different from the Witch House, though the room looked eerily like her own: wallpapered in millions of little yellow flowers dancing all over; whitewashed floors. She got up and went to sit at the little dressing table. She lifted a silver hand mirror to her face.

Anne inhaled deeply. She smelled bacon and coffee coming from downstairs.

"My father made me breakfast." She tilted her head at her reflection.

As she made her way downstairs, she got a better look at the house. Somehow it seemed even more incredible than it had the day before. The walls of the hallway were half plaster, from the floor up to a chair rail, and then wallpapered in some design just short of Victorian. And there were so many pictures, lovely paintings of people and places that looked exotic, covering every wall. Everywhere she looked she saw something that delighted and intrigued her. There was a whole world here for her to explore. The formal staircase was a double one: one for coming up and one for coming down. Anne felt like the whole Witch House could fit right there in that grand hallway with those staircases. The walls here were all painted linen with white trim. Refinement at its most refined. Anne was beginning to love this house, and it made her feel like she was betraying someone, something. So she stopped exploring and found the kitchen; it was surprisingly small and unlovely, and that made her happy for some odd reason. Her father stood by an old-fashioned stove flipping pancakes—and drinking a beer already. She felt she didn't really know him yet, and she couldn't tell if she wanted to.

"How did you sleep?" Gavin asked.

Anne let go a sudden, loud laugh and clapped her hand to her mouth. Gavin looked at her quizzically.

"Inside joke with myself," Anne explained.

"Anything you want? Anything you need before you go? We have some time. . . ."

Anne considered this. There was something she needed.

"I want to learn how to drive. I will need to drive when I get back."

Gavin flipped the last pancake and finally blurted out the words he had been forming in his mouth all night.

"You can stay with me," he said, not looking at her. "You belong with me."

"A little late, no? I have to go back. All I have is the house. Besides, Lucy needs someone to watch her drink herself to death. That woman is nothing without an audience." *Tic tock tic tock tic tock. Tic.* He heaved a sigh and turned around. His girl was stubborn, but he had to give it his best shot or he wouldn't be able to live with himself. He couldn't regret this, too.

"That is the point: here, you have me."

"What? So I can trade in taking care of one old drunk for another for the rest of my life? No thanks."

Gavin was hurt. But humbled. She was a smart one. He liked her.

"Suit yourself."

And then she surprised him.

"You could come with me?" she offered.

"No way, little girl, you take your seasons. . . . I'll take the sun and my beer." He toasted the cloudless sky through the one tiny window over the kitchen sink. He couldn't see Lucy again.

So instead, that day, he did what he could do. He taught her to drive. She was a quick study, and he found himself a mighty proud daddy, but there was no way but awkward to show it.

Then, back at Magnolia House, they ate a delicious dinner he made of fried fish and black beans, before she went off to bed to dream again. This whole dreaming business was going to take some getting used to.

The dreams were bad, but not as bad as the night before. And then something interesting happened. Gwyneth was there. Anne knew it was a dream, but somehow still real. Anne was right there in the bed in Magnolia House, and Gwyneth was next to her, stroking Anne's forehead. "Little Anne," she whispered, "I will always be with you. I am the butterflies." And then she was gone. And Anne woke up for real.

In the morning Gavin let Anne drive to the train station. After she shut off the engine, they sat there for a while. It is hard to say good-bye when you don't want to. They both struggled with it.

"You ever gonna put on your shoes?" Gavin grumbled through the silence.

"Only when I must." Anne smiled and looked down. Her hands and fingers traced the steering wheel. "Huh, okay, well. I guess this is it. I'm just going to go, okay? I am just going to go and get on the train."

"Anne. Stay. Please, stay."

"No!" Anne flung the door open and jumped out of the truck

and pulled her bag from the back before she could change her mind.

And then Anne did something neither of them expected: she put her palm to his cheek. His face melted against it, before she pulled it away. "Bye, Dad." She turned her back on him and walked toward the platform.

"Be safe, my girl." His voice broke. Lord, he needed a drink.

Gavin moved over to the driver's side and started the engine. Anne took one last look at her handsome, graceful, sort of a father, then took a deep breath and walked to the platform. His tires on the road echoed in her head for miles and miles and miles.

Anne got on the shiny streamliner, found her light blue leather seat, and leaned her head against the train window. It was dark outside, so all she could see was her reflection. She looked sad. She *was* sad. But it would be better this way; there would be less to feel. Anne wanted to be home at the Witch House. At least, she thought she did.

Anne got colder on the trip back north. Every stop seemed to bring more discomfort and more layers of clothing. She thought she was coming down with a virus, but in reality, she would carry with her a shiver the rest of her life, a permanent reminder that she should have stayed with her father.

When she got home, she freed her ghosts. She didn't want to live alone with Lucy.

26

Anne in the Moonlight with the Trick

1960

The years went by. William wrote to Anne. She read every letter, but she never wrote back. She studied her magic and even took a correspondence course toward a college degree. But she was bored and lonesome. And Lucy was driving her crazy.

Anne's trip to see her father had freed her in many ways. But in others, she became more caged than ever.

"I swear, I feel like a lizard, or a frog. Just cold and lifeless inside. Nothing makes me happy anymore," she told her ghosts while pruning the garden roses. "It seems to me that the issue was that damn baby dream. That's what got me the happiest. The thought of a little baby to care for. Will was a nice addition to that, but when you sit and think about it, that couldn't have lasted or worked. The house would have killed him or chased him away sooner or later, it always does."

"So, you felt the best when you were planning the baby, not the marriage. I understand. I felt that way each time I—well—never mind, it was so terribly long ago," Gwyneth said, swishing through the weeds.

"Maybe I should get pregnant again." Just saying the words made Anne feel better. Yes, that was it. She needed to right the wrong that Lucy had committed. "But I would have to get married. Who would marry me?"

Gwyneth screeched, exasperated, "You don't have to get married, child. Nan raised Lucy, alone. *A. L. O. N. E.*"

"Okay. I will have to have sex, though, you smarty-pants, unless you have some weird ghost rule up your sleeve that I don't know about. Who will I make this baby with?"

"What about William?" Ava peeked out from underneath a large zucchini plant.

"He's gone to God. And I hate him for leaving me, even though I told him to. That's the kind of crazy you get when you mess with a girl whose father left her. Does no one read novels anymore? Who else?" Anne threw down her shears and lit a cigarette. "Damn. I can't think of anyone else. Being an outcast is all kinds of fun until you need to get inseminated."

Then Anne figured it out. It came to her so fast, and with such clarity, that it was like the memory of something that had already happened.

"What about Jude?"

Gwyneth got real quiet, before she said, "Anne, he hurt you. Why would you want that?" But she was intrigued, Anne could tell. (After all, we *are* talking about the ghost who blew up Haven House.)

"He's in prison, anyway," Ava added.

"No." Anne pulled some loose tobacco from the tip of her tongue and spit it out. "I heard he is coming home. And I bet he'll need somewhere to live. Aunt Lavinia made new friends out in Richmond. She won't come back, I don't think."

"He only likes little girls," said Gwen.

"I've never been convinced that's true. I think he likes power. And power is just easier with little girls. But it doesn't matter, I can still be a little girl."

"Oh," said Gwyneth. "I see. You will trick him."

"Yes," Anne said, a cold glint in her eye, "I will trick him, and I'll kill him."

Gwyneth eased herself down on the bench in one languid movement, her smile wry. "Interesting . . ."

Ava giggled.

The three of them were silent for a bit, scheming together in their minds . . . and then Anne broke the silence.

"Gwen?"

"Yes, dumpling?"

"If I kill him, will I go to hell?"

"I don't know, Anne. But I do know that if he goes to hell when you kill him, and then you go to hell when you die, then you get to scare the pants off him for all eternity, and that doesn't sound half bad."

"Did you go to hell for what you did?"

"I don't remember. But I do remember waking up and taking care of you. And if that's hell, then I don't care one itty bit bit."

Ava growled.

"Don't blame my ghost for my crazy human brain, Ava darling. I've watched over you, too. Penance can be downright warm and cozy."

The very day Jude came slinking back, she put her plan into action. First, Anne gathered jimson weed from her witch garden of poisonous plants. (Jimson weed causes terrible hallucinations when concentrated and injected into the bloodstream.) She was fond of that garden. Proud of it, even. After Nan died, Anne didn't mind making the Witch House a real and true *witch house*.

Next she bathed in witch hazel, primrose, and pennyroyal to help boost her fertility. Then she gave her mother an extra dose of medication. Then she waited until the full moon, when she knew she was at her most fertile. That night, she gave her mother an extra dose of medication and made sure Lucy was fast asleep, before Anne bound what little breasts she had with a coarse bandage, let her hair down, and put on one of Nan's old white nightgowns that was two sizes too big, making herself look even smaller.

She went outside under the poplar canopy in the moonlight, where she waited with infinite patience.

Jude was in bed trying to figure out how to stop thinking about little girls. But he didn't want to stop thinking about them. He was a monster, and he knew it. It was too hard to fight it. It was exhausting. He got out of bed and shoved the window open to get some air. And there she was, smack dab in the middle of his view, standing like a ghost. Just staring at his window. He knew she was older now—a woman. But she looked eleven years old again standing there, and he couldn't help it. He felt the monster get hungry.

"I know you're looking at me, Jude. Come into the night garden. We can talk. It's not good to be all alone. Let's let our monsters out together. Like old times, what do you say?"

"You're crazy. Why do I want to waste my time with you?" he said.

"Because, Jude, I'm the only one who ever really understood you. We were friends, did you forget? I loved you. Besides, I gave your sorry ass somewhere to live."

"After everything I've done, you want to stroll with me in your yard in the middle of the night?" He squinted at her.

When she saw him turn away from the window she knew he would follow her, pursue her. She began to walk, moving faster when she heard the door slam, and then breaking into a run through the garden gate and into the Haven House fields. She ran and he chased her. He became all animal. Though she couldn't see him, she imagined him coming after her on all fours like a wolf, a great white wolf, and she was Red Riding Hood, all alone, running through the forest. But this was her fairy tale; she was in control of it.

She led him in a wide circle around the meadow, taking him on a tour of their violent past, and ending up back where they started. She ran up the back porch steps of the blue-and-white house and disappeared into her sanctuary.

He chased her right into the house and up the stairs. The doors, save one, were all open and candles were lit in every room. He found her in Nan's bedroom. Anne's birth room. Nan's statues of saints still held court over the room, and there were roses strewn across the bed, thorns and all. (What kind of Amore woman would only use the petals?)

Jude was surprised. "What the hell is this? What do you think I am?" he yelled, "your *boyfriend*?"

Anne stood near the bed. This was going to be the trickiest part of the whole plan. To avoid getting pricked by a thorn. She'd dipped them all in the jimson weed oil. It happened fast, so fast, and because he intended to kill her he didn't have to be careful, so he beat her and pushed her down, he scratched her and bit her, and flipped her over so he could take her from behind. Years of rage and lust and craziness had built up inside of him, and he was inside her before he even made a conscious decision on how to go about it. This was his mistake. He was kneeling on the thorns.

Before, when he stalked his prey, he was usually more thoughtful. He knew that this was going to end badly, but he didn't care, as long as it ended badly for both of them. How he hated this girl who he felt was his match.

When he finally came inside of her, he arched his back and slammed into her so hard that he actually forced her off of him. She fell forward and scurried quickly into a corner.

He walked toward her, and she didn't try to get away. She tilted her neck a little so he could get a good grip around her neck with his long graceful fingers that had delivered her so much pain.

As he began to squeeze, he started to hear a low hum that grew to a loud pitch: a deafening pitch, a growing cacophony of screams so loud and painful he had to remove his hands from

Anne's neck and hold his ears. Hunching over, looking around desperately, Jude couldn't figure out where it was coming from. Not from her. Her lips were sealed in a silent, frightening, crooked smirk. She looked up and pointed at the ceiling.

"Look, Jude, look at my friends." Anne's face broke into a grin.

He looked up then and saw a sight no human should ever see, one that could make a sane person crazy. (Luckily for him, Jude was crazy already.) He saw Anne's eyes roll into the back of her head as the entire room seemed to shift around him. The walls bulged and wavered; the closet door was opening and slamming shut, opening and slamming shut. Anne focused back on him and opened her mouth. Her teeth appeared to grow into sharp, needlelike fangs as she unleashed an unearthly sound that began low and then rose, channeling all the emotion from the girls he had murdered; death screams made of the memory of so much pain he felt himself breaking from the inside out. He backed away, feeling for the wall; it rushed at him, like a magnet to metal.

Jude was pinned against the wall, wrecked and sobbing, trying to pull his hands free to hold them against his ears to shut out the piercing screams—and then, it just stopped.

Standing directly in front to him was a battered Anne, looking more fiercely beautiful than she ever would again.

It was time for her to finally win. She'd made him docile with the jimson weed, and now she could kill him.

She held out a handful of pills with a small smile. He tried to wrench his body from the wall to no avail. Trapped, he knew he had no other option.

"Take them," she whispered, holding them closer.

"I won't."

"Take them and sleep. Don't you want to sleep, be released from it all?" she asked.

"No. I won't."

This time she hissed. "Take them, or I call the police and you will go away for life this time. How do you like it in there? All locked up. Do they hurt you? Rape you? That's called *karma*."

Anne moved her hand closer and closer, until finally he chocked the pills down, pasty and toxic, eating them out of her hand like an animal at a petting zoo. And in a way, he was relieved as he fell into a hazy half sleep.

Each time he blinked, everything around him was distorted again. Blink. Anne sitting with her legs crossed and childishly playing with a tooth he must have knocked loose. Blink. Anne playing ring-around-the-rosy, holding hands with the air. Blink. Anne pressing her face so close to his that all he could see were her crossed green eyes. Blink. Anne kissing him. Blink. Anne laughing with wild abandon. Anne was enjoying this. She looked just like he must have looked to all those little girls, bigger than life—a monster. And in that moment he loved her, which scared him more than dying. And Anne? Anne watched him, hating him. And the ghosts? The ghosts were there, too, surrounding her, keeping her safe, soothing her as they always did and always would. Finally, he took one last tortured breath and was gone.

Now, what to do with him? Anne pulled off her torn nightgown and threw it aside. She was little, but her adrenaline surged. She pulled his arms over his head and dragged him out of the bedroom as best she could (and not without bumping into a few things along the way, but that served him right) and pushed him down the steps. He tumbled down, just as she had once. She ran down after him and dragged him by his feet out of the front doors, down the porch steps, and around the back of the house.

Outdoors, he felt even lighter. Anne alternated between dragging him while she walked backward and dragging him with her hands behind her back, facing forward so she could see her destination—the large raspberry patch by the tree line of the Haven House meadow. The closer she got, the bigger her smile was.

Anne felt strong.

Once she got him to the end of the property, she ran to the gardener's cottage to get a shovel. It felt so nice, running naked in the moonlight, the pine-scented breeze cooling the sweat on her body. The cottage glowed in the moonlight and offered her a comforting nod that she had done the right thing. You couldn't feel this good if you did something truly wrong, could you? She grabbed the shovel and ran back to the body and to the ghosts who were overseeing the whole adventure. She pushed back a section of the raspberry thicket. It scratched and scraped her, but she didn't even notice. When she found a portion of earth that was free of roots, Anne began to dig.

See Anne. See Anne dig. Her skin glistens in the moonlight, her small breasts, one with a bite mark, move as she throws the dirt over her shoulder.

Anne looked at his body in the hole. Such beauty wasted on such a monster. She sat, propped up against a tall pine with her knees pulled against her chest. She stared at the grave, into the night, into the forest. The ghosts danced in the meadow. She watched them. Gwyneth twirled, and Ava leapt at fireflies. Playful and laughing. Happy.

Anne got up. What is done is done, she thought. No looking back. She pushed the earth on top of him. It smelled so good and clean. Full of loam and pine mulch. She was finished. In truth, it crossed her mind that she had something inside her, something deep and dark, much like whatever demon Jude lived with. But in the end, she decided, it was all about survival.

And now there would be a baby. A bright spot amidst all the horrible. Nothing would rob her of this second chance. No one would rob her of anything ever again.

She'd sacrificed a little bit of her humanity. It was a fair price.

27

Anne in the Field with Spiders in Her Hair

The very next day, Lucy came storming into the kitchen, yelling, "They won't stop screaming! I have to cut them out!"

She grabbed a knife and ran back to her room, wild-eyed. It took Anne an entire afternoon of sitting next to her mother's locked bedroom door to convince Lucy not to kill herself. And even then, Lucy opened the door just enough to throw the knife out into the hall, then locked the door again and said, "I hope there's something good for dinner. Also, I need another bottle of rye."

Anne rolled her eyes, then went and made fresh linguini with a quick sauce, just like Nan taught her, and left it next to the knife in the hall and pounded on the door.

"I didn't put the knife back, you know, just in case!" Anne called. "And don't choke on the pasta."

On the back porch Anne sat with Gwyneth on the swing. They watched Ava play near the juniper. Anne wondered if Ava was stomping on Jude's grave.

"Gwen, I didn't think this whole thing through properly. I can't bring a baby into this house with Lucy. It wouldn't be safe. She's unfit."

"Oh, and *you* are the model of sanity?" Gwyneth smirked.

"*Shhhh.* I'm serious."

"So am I, child, so am I."

"Maybe she went ahead and cut herself to shreds."

"I don't think so, honey. It's more about attention than anything else. Your mother, she's just a sad old drunk. You, on the other hand . . ."

"A witch can hope, can't she?"

Anne climbed the stairs that night with two worries. That Lucy was dead. That Lucy was alive.

Lucy was alive.

There had to be a way to suspend her mother between both of those two states. Not dead (because who kills their own mother?) and not quite alive—something not unlike the bourbon-soaked purgatory Lucy herself had chosen years ago.

Anne had to plot.

It wouldn't take much to make her already crazy mother fall off the edge of reality. First, Anne just needed to get her mother to really, truly trust her. She could do that. At least, she thought she could. Lucy's defenses were long gone. Her backbone had died on the streets of New York with her husband, and whatever was left to prop her up had died in the garden with Nan. Lucy was just a ball of near madness now. This would be easy.

Lucy began to respond to Anne's plan almost immediately. This Anne wasn't scary at all. She was clumsy and still looked like some sort of odd sick bird, but she had taken care of Nan's funeral, as well as all the cooking and cleaning and worry. The first thing she did was ask Anne to call her Lucy.

"If you want to be my friend, then be my friend. I don't want a daughter. Call me Miss Lucy and I might like you better."

Crushed, Anne managed a fake smile and simply said, "Yes, Miss Lucy."

And Lucy's fate was sealed, because until that moment, Anne hadn't *really* meant to get rid of her mother. It was more theory than fact. An idea that amused her and helped her make the best of a bad situation.

But everyone has a breaking point, and Lucy was our Anne's weakness.

And that was how it went. Anne made Lucy depend on her. She fed her, washed her clothes, picked up her prescriptions from the Woolworth, and even had long philosophical talks with her, when she had been drinking, about love, life, and even death. Each of those talks specifically manufactured to erode Lucy's sense of safety one neuron at a time.

"Well, smarty, what do *you* think happens when we die?" Lucy asked one day after Anne dispelled the notion of reincarnation.

"Well . . ." It was time to push her mother's sanity right off the cliff. "Well, Lucy, I'm not sure I believe in that whole 'heaven is a warm cozy place where the ones you love come and get you' idea, whatever that means." Anne paused for effect. She glanced at her mother. Lucy was beginning to squirm uncomfortably under her pretty bedclothes. Despite Lucy's hard edges, she had a rather old-fashioned idea of horror, and Anne knew exactly what to say next. "I think there is nothing when we die. Just blackness . . . and bugs. Bugs crawling all over us and eating us clean through."

"What?" Lucy asked, duly horrified. "What do you mean? You can't *really* think that." Her voice trembled; Anne had scared her.

"No. Not really. I was just kidding, Lucy." But the way she patted Lucy's knee did not make Lucy feel any better, not better at all. "Here, I brought you another bottle. I know you were swearing off, but you've been so good, I thought you needed a reward."

"That was thoughtful of you. Is there a glass?"

"But of course!"

Anne left the bottle and the glass for Lucy and waited until she was fast asleep to leave her alone.

Later that night Lucy wanted, needed, her tea. Her head was pounding, her eyes watering. And, as she'd been frightened by her talk with Anne, Lucy thought some sleeping medication might be nice, too.

"Anne! Can you bring me some tea? Now! I need my pills, too. You and your talk of bugs. I don't want to talk about that ever again. It wasn't very nice! You know how I feel about bugs!"

But Anne did not come. The light next to Lucy's bed was on, but outside it had grown darker as she slept, and the rest of the room was pocketed with shadows. She didn't like this feeling . . . this feeling of falling asleep in the daylight and waking at twilight. Everything felt . . . off.

The walls looked like they were—she shook her head, trying to blink it away—breathing. In. Out. In. Out. A tiny buzzing sound filled her ears, a low unnatural hum. Lucy twitched, slapping at her ears.

She heard Anne whispering from behind the closet door. Wait, was that Anne? Suddenly she wasn't sure. There was a little hollow giggle.

Then a clear voice. Anne's voice.

"It's almost done. I'll almost be sorry when it's over."

"*Shhhh*, I think she's waking up," said a second voice, Anne's when she was a little girl. No. Impossible. Something was wrong.

Lucy had to get out. Something bad was going to happen here.

She got up and went to the door. Her hand shook as it reached for the doorknob. She pulled it back a few times, scared it would open, scared it wouldn't.

"Get it together, Lucy!" she hissed.

"Get it together, Lucy!" the voices echoed.

She turned the knob. It opened. Lucy didn't hesitate: she jerked the door open and ran down the front hall steps and out the doors (which she'd expected to be locked) and then around the house, escaping into the back gardens.

She fell to her knees, gulping in air. She was still dizzy, but the air felt good.

"I'm free. She tried . . . I know. Laced my rum. And the house . . . But I'm out now. She can't cast that dark magic here."

"Miss Lucy," Anne called out from nearby.

Lucy scrambled up, her feet flying across the slate stepping stones of the vegetable garden and then over the low fence into the meadow. If she could just get across, just make it to the trees, she could take the cliff steps and get to the docks where there would be people. She just had to get to the beach.

She made it over the fence, but the hem of her white night-gown caught. A piece tore off, a flag of surrender.

Once in the meadow, Lucy could hear the trees. They whispered and danced. They laughed at her.

"Just keep going," she told herself, her breath hitching, "just keep going." As she stepped into the high grasses, the light changed. She was caught between some time and space she didn't fully understand. Haven House was in front of her. Whole again.

Tic tock tic tock tic tock. Tic.

A man and two women, one fair and one dark, appeared out of the dusk. They were tossing a large red ball back and forth between them, like children in a schoolyard, and laughing. There was a little girl, too. Lucy knew her. It was the girl from

Nan's photo. All four were dressed in old-fashioned bathing outfits and laughing together. The man looked up, and shielding his eyes from the sun, called out to her.

"Why, Lucy, darling! We have been waiting for you. Come now, don't keep us waiting, we must get to the beach!"

Time and light stood still. The earth stopped rotating, trapping the clouds motionless in the sky. The two women and the child all looked up at the same time. She heard their whispers in her mind.

"Yes, Lucy, we waited and waited and waited." Lucy blinked. The little girl was no longer a girl but a body shining in the stagnant sun, a prism of melted glass.

"Lucy!"

Startled, she turned around to face the back of the Witch House. Anne stood there. The house rising behind her.

Anne's hair, a mass of black, whipped around her face and— were those spiders? Dear God, spiders crawled out of her hair, her mouth as she called.

Anne stretched her arms out to Lucy, and the house wrapped itself around her, warping everything near it and reaching out from Anne's fingers in an impossible semicircle of gloom.

Lucy screamed.

She turned back to the mirage. It was still there. She tried to break sideways to avoid both fates but fell, scraping her palms on gravel left over from a long-forgotten driveway. Tears ran down her cheeks as she gazed at her hands, bleeding as though they bore stigmata. With choking cries, Lucy began to claw at her face and body, pulling at her hair and nightgown.

She would not remember anything else from that night besides the red ball bouncing toward her.

Anne hadn't realized how scared Lucy would be. The terror on Lucy's face as she pulled at the door made Anne stop the creepy mimicking. When Lucy flew down the stairs and left the house, Anne found herself worried that her mother might actually hurt herself. Might fall and break her neck. Which wasn't the plan. Lucy was supposed to drink the jimson-laced glass of rum, hallucinate just enough for Anne to call the doctor and get Lucy committed. She would never hurt Lucy. Not really. Lucy was her mother, after all.

But as Anne followed Lucy out into the garden, something felt out of her control. The plan had taken on a life of its own. Anne had never felt guilt before, and she sure as heck didn't aim to ever feel it.

"Mama?" she yelled, trying to bring Lucy back to the house. "It would be just like you to pitch yourself over the cliff. Don't you dare!"

Lucy didn't turn around. So Anne tried, "Miss Lucy!"

And that was when Lucy turned around. And she looked at Anne with such disgust, such horror, that Anne felt the way she had when she was in that bathtub after Jude . . . and when she found that telegram to Gavin . . . and right before Lucy pushed her down the stairs. Every horrible, sad, angry, unforgiveable moment crashed into her all at once.

Anne turned away and went back to the house. She called the doctor and sat in the dark kitchen. Alone.

———

The arrangements were already made. Everyone had known that though Lucy once held such promise, though she had been well-loved, she would one day succumb to mental illness. No one questioned Anne's assessment of her. Lucy was crazy; it had been only a matter of time. And time was now up.

Lucy watched the house recede in the moonlight through the back windows of the ambulance. She was calmer now. Then her breath caught in her throat.

A black bubble was emerging from the chimney. Lucy tried to sit up on her gurney, straining against the straps. The bubble was narrow at the bottom now, and then, pop! It was free. A black oval floating in the sky, with a long string attached. It followed the ambulance, dancing through the violet clouds. A balloon. The house was celebrating. Lucy opened her mouth in a silent shriek against the night.

With Lucy gone, really, truly gone, Anne thought she would feel some sense of loss. But she didn't. The guilt lingered, of course, a teeny layer of filth that needed to be washed off, but really, Anne thought, being alone is better than being lonely, and it is much lonelier to be around people who can't stand you than it is to be alone in a house that loves you, with a family, however ghostly, to keep you company.

Anne went to her mother's record player and put on one of Lucy's favorites, as a tribute: "La Vie en Rose."

And then she danced. She spun and danced and touched

everything in the Witch House that Lucy had touched or used or called her own, trying to connect with her. To feel a little bit human. To feel the loss she should have felt. While Edith Piaf sang about love, Anne danced around the kitchen. She danced through the gardens. She was free.

She danced through her mother's bedroom.

Oh, her mother's dressing table. So lovely with its frilled fabric skirting. So lovely with its piles of soaps and oils and creams and sweet-smelling things. How amazingly difficult it must have been to remain so lovely. In one great, sad, and wonderful afternoon, Anne began to understand her mother, to forgive her—to become her.

Anne sat at the kitchen table and made a list.

How to become my mother:
1. *Curl my hair.*
2. *Take medicine.*
3. *Smoke cigarettes.*
4. *Drink coffee and wine and bourbon.*
5. *Play solitaire and laugh and cry all at once.*
6. *Be beautiful and interesting and tragic (how?)*
6a. *Ask Gwen.*
7. *Curse more than usual and be generally hateful.*
8. *Go crazy.*

Anne went to bed with her hair pinned up with bobby pins and curlers. In the morning, she sat up and stretched out and looked around. Lucy's room was like a foreign country to her now. She remembered it from when she was a very little girl, but she had not spent any real time in here for so long. She thought of her mother crying in the meadow. Anne felt a twinge. It passed quickly.

The sun was filtering in through the curtains, a soft yellow, and a not unpleasant smoky smell mixed with perfume hung in the air.

It was her mother's scent. Smoke and Chanel No. 5.

Today she had important things to do. Important things to be. Anne needed new clothes if she was going to be Lucy. She went to the attic to dig through two old steamer trunks in the back she knew were filled with clothing.

"Those belonged to me, and Reggie, and Nan." Gwyneth said, hovering close. She had taken to following Anne almost everywhere lately. Anne liked the attention.

"And me, too," said Ava.

"Yes, my darling girl, and you, too."

"Look, Gwen! It all fits, and it's all pretty!" She twirled in front of the chevalier mirror. There were piles and piles of skirts and blouses, colorful and flowing. None of it looked right on Anne, it looked too forced. And her hair, springy with irregular curls from the pins, mixed with the oversized clothing made Anne look more unstable than usual. But she felt beautiful.

"Her shoes don't fit, though. And I have small feet, too. Hers must have been really tiny," Anne said with a frown.

"Evolution of the species, my dear," said Gwyneth.

Anne shuffled through the men's clothes and pulled out a pair of black boots. She put them on; they were a little big but comfortable.

"How about these?"

"You look fantastic." Anne thought she heard a placating tone in Gwyneth's voice. Maybe she was lying? It didn't matter. Anne thought it was all perfect.

Anne decided to try out her new look. She took the black silk shawl with the embroidery on it that her mother always wore, wrapped it around her finished outfit, applied some dark red lipstick, and went down the hill to the corner grocery to buy some tobacco and rolling paper.

She looked in the front hall mirror before she left. A success, she thought. She looked just like Lucy. Except . . . she didn't. She was Anne, and she didn't enjoy the same social standing that Lucy once enjoyed. Society didn't simply accept Anne as odd. It never had much patience for her.

When Anne walked down Grand Street Hill, she made her debut, and it did not go well. Everyone was staring at her. The grocer asked her if she was all right. She looked at him and gave him a smile. "I am absolutely *fine*," she said, quickly trying to shove all the tobacco and rolling papers into one of Lucy's satchel bags. Things kept dropping everywhere, and she was tripping on the shawl.

By the time she returned to the Witch House—it was obvious to Anne that she wasn't going to make it as Lucy. She took a pill.

"You are not alone," Gwyneth reminded her gently. But she felt alone. She missed Nan. She missed William. Anne took another pill.

Weeks went by. Anne began to descend into a state of malaise. And no one stopped by to check on her. The house was legally hers. Nan had left everything to Anne in her will. But, house or no house, with what money would she buy food? How would she survive?

She found the answer on the back porch, waiting for her the next morning in the form of two covered dishes of food with envelopes taped to the top. Anne took the dishes, one stacked on top of the other, inside.

One dish contained a meat pie, and the other, a whole mess of cookies. Anne ate quickly; she didn't realize how hungry she had been. Those pills she'd been taking, how did Lucy function on them? Once she was full, she opened the envelopes. Nan would have told her that it was rude to eat the present before opening the card, but Anne did not care. Nope, she did not care one bitty bit.

But they weren't cards. They were cash. Each envelope had cash inside. *Well, that'll do,* thought Anne.

And it did. For years, there would be food and money left at Anne's back door, even after she didn't need it anymore. There never was a note, only money. When she was saner, when the haze of being Lucy was a memory, when the baby grew strong inside her, Anne would discard the food. But the money was lovely. It gave her freedom. Almost.

28

Eleanor in the Library with a Pencil

SATURDAY, SEPTEMBER 5, 2015

4:00 P.M.

Maj bounced downstairs, interrupting the narrative, holding a big black book in her arms.

"What's that, baby?" asked Eleanor.

"*Something important*," Maj singsonged.

Eleanor, Byrd, and Maj sat at a table, flipping through the book. It was separated into parts. Some looked like recipes. Some looked like stories and scrapbook pages with photographs. Others were split up among the women. The Book of Nan. The Book of Lucy. The Book of Anne.

"This would have been a hell of a lot easier than the way I figured it all out. Thanks for a whole lot of nothing. Damn ghosts," said Byrd, looking up at the ceiling.

"No," said Eleanor, reopening it to the first page. "This is different. Let's look through carefully."

"It's a book of spells. Dark magic, Mama. Deep dark loss magic. It's a book of loss and shadow and secrets," said Maj.

7:30 P.M.

"You better be taking a bath, Maj!" yelled Eleanor.

Maj rolled her eyes at Crazy Anne.

"Did you take out the worst spell before you gave them the book?" asked Anne. Her hair was always moving, as if it were in the wind, only they were inside in Maj's new room.

"Yep."

"Did you place it in the attic by the candle?"

"Yep."

"Did you take the matches from the kitchen drawer?"

"Yep."

"You should say yes, ma'am."

"Nope."

Anne's ghost face flickered for a moment. It's hard for ghosts to laugh, but she was trying.

"Before we burn the spell, can we use the Death Life Wither Wander spell one more time?"

"I told you it was too dangerous. Those fools downstairs would use it, sooner or later. Trust me."

"I want to use it. I memorized it. I will use it."

"Oh, hell. Fine. Get the dog."

"Because she is old!"

"Yes. But there will be consequence."

"Yes, ma'am. Hopefully a dog who never ever ever ever dies."

8:00 P.M.

"The book is interesting, but there's nothing in it about murderous secrets, sadly," said Eleanor, braiding Byrd's hair. It felt good to mother her. It felt right. "Unlike the fact that there's the body of a monster buried out by the Juniper trees. I guess we found our bones. And, Johnny won't go all the way back there. He's more focused on the house, and the foundation of Haven House. So, that's that. Mystery Solved."

"I'm not so sure. I feel like there's way more to figure out. It's creepy and sad. The whole tale. I wish I'd known her. My great-grandmother. I wish she'd show herself to me," said Byrd. She sighed. "That feels good."

"It's impossible to get Maj to put those curls up. But I loved it when my Mimi used to braid my hair. You know what? I was about your age when I really started to know her."

"Elly, do you think we're going to figure this out by tomorrow?"

"That depends."

"On what?"

"On how much we can remove ourselves from these stories. On how far away we can get. It's all about perspective."

"Yeah, I guess. . . . Do you like it here?" Byrd asked suddenly.

"I love it here."

And Eleanor did. There was something about the way the light fell. About how she could always hear the ocean. It was peaceful.

"It's the kind of place that makes you feel like you are the only thing it loves," Eleanor continued. "And isn't that what we all want? To feel like one person's beloved? That's what the women in our family wanted. That's all I ever wanted. Actually, speaking of wanting love, whatever ended up happening to Lucy?" asked Eleanor.

"Oh, man, listen to *this* one."

29

Lucy in the Mental Ward with a Match

1960

SAINT SEBASTIAN HOSPITAL,
FAIRVIEW, MASSACHUSETTS

The hospital wasn't half bad. Lucy began to feel strong again. Clean. The house and its demons were far away. The medications they were giving her took the haze out of her mind and emboldened her. She felt unafraid for the first time in a very long time.

Charming Lucy, as they began to call her, soon became a favorite of the staff, the doctors, and her fellow inmates, and soon the favoritism she had enjoyed throughout her years as a schoolgirl became the norm. The staff even did her small favors that weren't allowed. She was smart and coy, asking only for small creature comforts that were easy to deliver, yet had a big impact . . . extra baths, nice brushes for her still-beautiful hair, nail polishing sessions with her nurses, and, most important, she was allowed to smoke. Orderlies let her go to the courtyard to smoke, and her doctor let her smoke in their therapy sessions. Yet Lucy knew this was not a wonderful hospital. Terrible things went on around her every day: shock treatments, lobotomies, ice baths, straitjackets. But Lucy avoided all of this. She had a light shining from the inside. She became the person they all believed they could save, so they tried very hard to save her.

As she thrived on attention, this was a healthy environment for Lucy. She was given the right cocktail of drugs, was treated well, and began to feel like she had a really good handle on what steps she needed to take next in her life. The doctors, nurses, patients, and staff of Saint Sebastian Hospital all took note and patted each other on the back, thinking, "We did it!"

One of her doctors in particular, Dr. David Crowley, took a special interest in Lucy. It was evident that he found her attractive. Everyone still did. She was beautiful and fragile, vulnerable in her hospital gown. Once after a session with her, he looked down at his notes to find he had written only three words the whole time: *A Beautiful Chaos.* Dr. Crowley decided to write a book on Lucy, documenting how they took a schizophrenic and were able to cure her. This would put him and his hospital on the map, and the fact was, she *was* cured. She had come into the hospital bloodied and raving about ghosts and demon houses and how they asked her to hurt herself. Classic symptoms. And now? Nothing. This kind of illness could not be faked, nor could the cure. She was sane again. This would be monumental in the world of psychiatry. It would change the way patients were treated. Dr. Crowley could practically see the future awards on his walls.

During what would be their last session, Lucy told Dr.

Crowley she had a definite and clear plan on how she wanted to proceed. He nodded and smiled, without really listening. Lucy had a habit of twirling her hair as she looked at him, right into his eyes, and he couldn't help it. He would get lost in his head visualizing fucking her, not with gentle love and kisses, but with animalistic abandon. "Well, Lucy, I guess I can sign the papers and release you to your daughter next week."

"Anne?"

"Well, she has custodial rights. . . . She is of age, is that a problem?"

Dr. Crowley immediately wondered if he could get rights and take her home, like a pet he could keep, one he could groom and—

"No, no, I see, yes, Anne . . . home," said Lucy. Keep it together, she thought. Keep it together and stick to the plan.

"Good!" Dr. Crowley said. "So this is it!"

As they stood up, he put his hand on her shoulder a little too long, a little too tightly, and she looked at him. Lucy knew all along the secrets to this place, to this life.

Lucy knew he would love to have his way with her if given the chance. Just as she knew the nurses wanted to become her and the orderlies wanted to marry her. She knew how to work this system, just as she had known how to work the nuns, priests, and other kids back in school. She worked everybody; she was good at it, until Anne. She knew that house had wanted her out. It let her wither there as long as Nan was alive, because— as Lucy now understood, too late—Nan loved her, and the house wouldn't hurt Nan. Lucy also knew she was, in fact, crazy and probably always had been.

It was all clear now. There had only been one chance, one chance at happiness, and she lost it. When Vito died, she should have tried harder to keep it together, to be the mother she knew she could be, to have the kind of relationship with her son that she pretended to have.

But Dominic hadn't come to visit her. Why would he? He had his own life now, and Lucy hadn't even tried to keep up with him. How long had it been since she had seen him?

The only person she still felt she knew was Anne. And Lucy was convinced, now more than ever, that Anne was a demon, a demon like Nan always said lived inside Lucy, a demon that came out in the form of a child.

A demon born from a demon house.

Lucy had a hard time figuring out how her life had gone so wrong, how she had ended up on this end, the losing end, of things. It couldn't have been all Vito, her entire future could not have hinged solely on him. Could it have? Shouldn't there have been a way for her to find the path home? Back to the safe home inside her head, inside her skin? Her crazies and the high-pitched *hummm* had been on for so long that, now that they were calm and she was clear, it all seemed so sad. All that time just gone, lost, simply "poof," and she's old and crazy and her family is gone and she has lost her way.

Lucy was sick of remembering. She needed to get out of this hospital and back home. Back to her real home. She thought of that childhood rhyme they used to sing at recess: "Ladybug, ladybug, fly away home, your house is on fire, and your children will burn." It used to scare and delight them; now it made Lucy weep. But the fire . . . the fire . . . Lucy got an idea. Maybe she could have a second chance after all.

It is terribly difficult to kill yourself in a mental institution. They make sure of it. No sharp objects to cut yourself with, no loose sheets to hang yourself with, and no unmanned baths to drown yourself in. But Lucy, she thought outside the box. One option was left and was perfect. A perfect death. The absolute perfect solution in so many ways. She danced around the common room laughing and clapping on the day she conceived the "fire" part of the plan.

Fire purifies, and she was in dire need of purification. She needed to meet her Vito on the other side, and she had to wash off Gavin and Anne, burn them right off. Burn the skin they touched. The womb Anne grew in, and the breasts she sucked on. All of it.

Joan of Arc died on the pyre, and she became a saint. (Would they saint her? Maybe Saint Lucia, patron saint of putting up with horrible mothers?) Lucy remembered reading somewhere that once the initial horrific pain burned through the nerve endings, it wasn't a bad way to die. Even the smoke inhalation could knock you out while the fire did the work. The trick was, not to survive. She also read that surviving burning was intolerable, so this was not an option.

Once she decided on the method, she just needed to figure out the implementation. She played the games, gave peeks to those who were peeking, allowed the crazy Dr. Crowley to look deep into her eyes; she could practically see him wiping the spit off his chin.

Nurse Nancy was a sympathetic one, a lonely, washed-out

kind of a girl. Lucy had divulged to Nancy many secrets about how to keep her husband happy in their marriage bed, and Nancy was extremely grateful. Nancy was the one with the beautiful nails. She offered to paint Lucy's nails once, and they had had so much fun. Lucy just let her yap on and on all the while. It had become a weekly ritual. This week while they painted nails, Lucy made sure that Nancy knew she was going home. "Nancy! Be a dear and give me the polish and the remover so when I get home I can have my darling Anne continue our tradition?"

Nancy didn't even hesitate. She got up and got a small paper bag from the pharmaceutical repository, popped both bottles in, folded the top over, and handed the bag to Lucy. She was crying. "I will miss you, Lucy."

"Oh, Nancy, don't you worry, you will think of me in bed!" They both laughed.

Fire starter: check.

Matthew, an innocent yet sexually charged young man who was the night orderly in her ward, would take her out for a midnight smoke. And she'd get her matches.

In the courtyard, under the moon, Lucy smoked her cigarette, listening to Matthew whine about his insufferable mother whom he still lived with. As if he had the monopoly on insufferable mothers! Please! And then she did something out of their script. She asked for another cigarette. And she asked to be left alone to smoke it.

"I don't know . . ." he stuttered as she approached him. He stood very still. She reached her hand in his pocket; she could feel he was already excited. While she wrapped her hand around the cigarettes and matches, she let her fingers find him as well.

Fire: check.

"I am getting out of here this week, Mattie," she whispered, so close to his ear that her tongue flicked it. He shivered. "Give me this time to collect my thoughts alone, and I'll make sure and have you visit us in Haven Port."

He simply nodded his head, and slowly, very slowly, she removed the hand from his pocket with the pack of cigarettes and the matches.

She took her time and smoked the second cigarette. Then pocketed the matches. Matt never noticed.

Lucy removed her gown and piled it up with the bedsheets and pillows and old newspapers she'd stashed.

Her plan was to set a fire and die of smoke inhalation. She lit the pile of fabric and stood in the corner of her room and thought of her life on the river with Vito in their little fisherman's cottage and of her real, true baby, Dominic. "Dear God," she prayed. "Please bring me back there. I want everlasting life back there. Amen."

She was not afraid. She had no fear. She was going home.

The smoke was thick. Her plan was working. The fabric was smoldering.

When poor Mattie came running down the hall and saw the smoke billowing out from under her door, he—who now believed he was truly in love with her—made the terrible and reckless error of opening the steel door that was containing the blaze. The fire exploded into the hallway, and everything went crazy. Crazy like Lucy. She took the whole wing down with her.

That woman could sure make an exit.

30

Dominic in the Kitchen
with a Crucifix

1960

"What?" Anne asked.

"Your mother, Lucy, is dead," said the now impatient doctor on the other end of the phone for the fifth time.

What what what what what what what? *What?*

"She is dead, Anne, and I need you to hear it. There are things that need to be done."

"So what am I supposed to do about it?" In truth, Anne, the Anne that was capable, the Anne who was not trying to become her mother, knew what to do, because she had already done the whole thing once before for Nan. Her mother was the one who was incapable, who didn't understand what she didn't want to understand, the one who didn't hear what she didn't want to hear. Anne understood now what a luxury that was.

It was time for the madness to end. She needed to be stable, secure, and upright. She had to know what to do all the time in every situation. She had to become Nan.

Almost immediately she began speaking to the doctor differently. "Yes, doctor. . . . Yes, I see. Yes, I will make all the arrangements. Who should I call to have her body shipped? Yes . . . I will be here when the certificate arrives. Certified mail? Of course."

Lucy's funeral was an odd one, as funerals go. Anne ordered all the flowers that came to the funeral parlor out of the wake room and replaced them with roses. Lucy hated roses.

She sat quietly in a musty, stained pink velvet chair with her hands in her lap. She didn't want to hear the stories that chair had to tell.

When Dominic walked in, he sat next to her and tried to take her hand.

"You got old," she said.

"You got pregnant."

"You left me."

"You tried to kill me."

"I was only a little girl."

He was quiet then, and Anne noticed his eyes were puffy and swollen. He'd been crying.

Later, she'd overhear him at the house while everyone ate all the food she'd stayed up all night preparing. . . . Jell-O molds with walnuts, ambrosia salad, pasta, bundt cakes, and the like. She was outside the kitchen, smoking a cigarette and hiding, when she heard him pouring out his sad story to one of them damn church ladies named Beverly Bodine.

"I looked at her, Bev, and I swear . . . I wanted to be glad to see her, to connect with her. We shared a mother, for Christ's sake, but her eyes were vacant. She stared right through me. And inside that look I could feel everything she feels about me. Like, I left her and how she suffered because I wasn't there. I can't stand it. I've always assumed she was crazy and strong. But now, I'm starting to believe she may have needed me. Christ, Bev."

"You can't take on all that guilt, Dom. It's not fair. She's just a demon child. Born *wrong*. Poor Nan. Poor Lucy. You did the only thing you could, son. You ran. Good for you, honey. Good for you."

"But I wonder if I shouldn't stay closer now, with the baby coming."

"It's sinful, is what it is. Everyone says it belongs to the devil himself."

"Go big or go home, I guess. But either way, I owe it to my mother and my grandmother to watch over her and that baby. I should be closer to Anne. Keep an eye on her."

Anne couldn't listen for one more second.

She walked in, letting the kitchen door slam the way Nan used to when she was mad.

"Oh, Bev, *darling*. Don't you worry. He always walks away. He isn't like those stories people told about his father, Prince Vito the Valiant!"

Anne needed a Valium.

"Anne, I—"

"Don't worry. My goal here is to make the both of you feel as uncomfortable as humanly possible."

"You did good, then, little sister."

Anne rolled her eyes and went into the front parlor.

There were a lot of tears in that room.

What are they all crying for? Is it that sad to lose the town drunk?

They are crying for themselves, not for my mother. Not for me.

Anne wouldn't cry. Lucy was free now.

It was, Anne was convinced, far better to be dead than to be alive. Killing herself was the one thing Lucy ever did that made Anne proud or even made her feel connected to her mother. She was not going to cry over a woman who had lived a bad, sad life. Lucy was weak. And she left Anne, just like everyone else. "I should give out certificates in 'Leaving Anne,'" she said aloud without realizing. Everyone turned and stared her way uncomfortably.

"Okay, party over. Everyone get out of my house," she said. No one moved. "I said, grab your things, and your pity, and your envy, and your lame lives and get the fuck out of my house. Now. Or else."

Dominic was by her side then, his hand on her arm, "Anne, Anne . . ."

"You get out first. And get your hands off me before I kill you. Don't tempt me, I swear."

"I'll go, but I'm not going far."

"We'll just see about that! *Get out!*"

People say the house shook with her scream. They say shutters clapped open and shut and the staircase swayed. They say that those who ate the food threw up for days. They say it was the

Witch House, not Anne, who ejected them. But no matter what anyone believed, Anne had her own truth.

They left. They listened, and they left. Because everyone was always leaving Anne, except her ghosts. The ghosts did not leave her, could not. She was sure of it. And not the house. Her house would not leave her. It was her cocoon, her true love, her sanity.

The next day Anne sat at the kitchen table and made a list.

> *How to become my grandmother, Nan:*
> 1. *Switch rooms, again.*
> 2. *Tidy hair.*
> 3. *Attend church.*
> 4. *Maintain the garden and do all chores with glee.*
> 5. *Be pragmatic.*
> 6. *Be orderly.*
> 7. *Be strict.*
> 8. *Lie about the things you don't want to admit.*

Ava sat at her feet playing peek-a-boo with a stray cat she had tricked into coming inside, but Gwyneth stood in the shadows.

31

Miss Anne in the Kitchen with the Mushrooms

1960

She'd begin with William. She had to reestablish her relationship with the church.

Besides, Anne wanted William back. She missed him, though she'd never tell him that. It was William who should be the priest at Our Lady of Sorrows. Maybe she could talk to old Father Callahan? She knew, from William's letters, that he was interested in coming back to his old parish but that there was "no room at the inn." Anne decided to have Father Callahan over for dinner. She called the rectory.

"Why sure, Anne, I'd be delighted. I always wanted a look-see inside Nan's house."

Anne bristled at "Nan's house." It was her house. Always her house.

"And," the priest continued, "I am thrilled you are finding your way back into God's graces. Thank you, I will see you on Sunday after mass. You will come to mass?"

"No, Father, I don't think I'm ready quite yet. Maybe when you come for dinner you can hear my confession and then I can come the following Sunday?"

"Of course, Anne."

Anne prepared roasted beet salad and pasta and sausage, and she uncorked a bottle of her Nan's dandelion wine. The smell brought her right back to early spring. Then she went out into the gardens to visit with her ghosts—she'd been working hard bringing Nan's garden back to life. It was amazing how one season allowed the wild right back inside.

As she surveyed her work, Gwyneth surveyed her Anne.

Hair pinned back, her apron tied neatly around her waist. She was still wearing those old boots loose and untied; the whole outfit made her look a little like a deranged prairie girl might. One hand was holding Ava's hand, and in the other, she held a cigarette. Gwyneth sat on the garden bench.

"Anne, darling, you have to give them all up. All of Lucy's habits. You look ridiculous in this here garden wearing Nan's clothes and smoking." Gwyneth slapped her knee and laughed. "And just look at your lips, you need to wipe off that bright-red Lucy lipstick. Nan would never have worn whore's red. At least, not the Nan you knew."

"Well," said Anne, taking another drag of her cigarette and ignoring the leading edge of Gwen's last words. "It's boring being Nan. It's funny, really: by being both of them, I can fully appreciate how they could never get along. I can't hardly get along with myself now. How am I supposed to go back to this? How am I supposed to just give up all of that freedom?"

"Nan did it."

"Nan had people to take care of, it was easier. She was . . . I don't know! Busier!"

"Have you looked down lately, honey?"

Ava patted Anne's belly.

"You're going to have someone to take care of really soon. Now put down that damn toxic gas, wipe your mouth, and get some practice shoes. You got a priest coming for dinner."

"I do indeed, Gwen. And I need a few special ingredients."

Back at the house, Anne added a few mushrooms she'd collected to the pasta and watched out the kitchen window as Father Callahan fumbled with the side gate.

She grimaced. He was a fat man. His hair stood up at an odd angle and was combed to the side in an unsuccessful effort to hide the pale, shiny top of his head.

Anne met him at the gate and helped him with the latch.

"Why, thank you, Anne. My, how big you've gotten! I don't believe I've seen you in what? Four or five years?" The priest lumbered past her. He wanted to see the house. She could feel his excitement.

"You really should have come to the front doors, Father. It is a grander entrance to the house."

"Oh, no, this is fine. I have seen the front doors a thousand times. This is less formal."

Anne didn't like the way he said "less formal." His voice was thick and muffled by a flabby throat. Anne visualized what the inside of his larynx must look like, all polyped and chubby, catching phlegm and food. She was disgusted.

The priest made a lot of "*Hmm*'s" and "Oh my, yes's" as he entered the house and began looking around. He touched everything. Anne wondered if his hands were dirty.

"Father, would you like some wine?"

"Oh, yes, please. Do you have red?"

"I think I may have an old jug of Chianti, but I uncorked some of Nan's famous dandelion wine. It is the most absolutely lovely thing. Would you like some?"

"That sounds delightful," he said, coughing. He pulled a handkerchief out of his pocket, spit into it, and then put it back into his pocket. Anne gagged. What a foul man. This is the man who had touched her William? This man had heard her confessions? And her Nan's confessions. This man was dirty, unholy. She left him to explore the house.

"Anne?"

"Yes?" she called from the kitchen.

"May I go upstairs? I would love to see Lucy's—I mean, the portraits."

Anne strode across the living room with two glasses full of light yellow wine.

"Oh, Father, I am so very sorry. Upstairs is so untidy."

Father Callahan took his glass of wine and raised it. "Here's to your return to the church, Anne."

These Irish with their toasts, thought Anne, as she clinked her glass to his. "*Salute*, Father."

She took a dainty sip. Father Callahan took a gulp and a thin line of yellow leaked out from the chapped, inflamed corner of his mouth.

"How about we eat? The pasta is getting cold."

"Yes, please, sweet Anne." He reached out to tuck a stray wisp of hair that had fallen from her bun behind her ear. "You really look so very young. You could be a child still."

I believe you have forgotten you prefer boys, she wanted to say. But she didn't. She had a mission. She needed to convince Father Callahan to retire.

At the table his behavior was even more inappropriate and grotesque. He drank the remainder of the wine and let food fall out of his mouth as he chewed.

"Anne, I do believe we should find you a husband. It just won't do. God forgives many things, but people are not so forgetful. Surely there is a nice young fellow for you to marry, now that you have come to your senses." A mushroom fell out whole onto his lap.

"I suppose. . . . Father? Have you ever thought of retiring?"

Father Callahan gave a little snort of a laugh and a half-chewed piece of beet fell back onto his plate. "No, ma'am! I will die on the altar, just see if I don't."

Anne pushed her food around. She wasn't fond of mushrooms. She sipped her wine. It was now or never.

"And what would happen if the diocese found out that you raped little boys?"

Father Callahan dropped his fork. "What—what did you say?"

"Surely you heard me, Father."

Father Callahan was sweating. He stood up, and his chair fell backward onto the floor. The sound was louder than it ought to have been. He couldn't think. He felt vomit rising into his throat and ran to the sink. He heaved, but nothing came out. He heard his heartbeat in his ears. Something was wrong. So much more wrong than just this simple girl with her simple threats.

"Anne . . . help . . . call help . . ." he gasped, grabbing at his throat.

The firemen came. They were there fast. It was good there was a firehouse so close by.

Father Callahan was dead three days later. First there was the vomiting, then the diarrhea, then the splotches that turned into bleeding sores all over his skin.

The doctors thought it was surely some type of virus brought on by the incision Anne had to make in his throat to remove the mushroom he'd choked on. Her quick thinking saved him, but nothing could save him from the infection he must have picked up at the hospital. Anne's status began to shift in Haven Port that day. I truly am becoming Nan, she thought. Nan overcame her heathen ways, and everyone loved her. Now I'm going to do it, too. Smiling, she rubbed her belly while reading a new book on poison herbology.

32

Anne in the Kitchen with a Smile

1960–1970

With William as the new pastor, it was safe for Anne to go to mass. She entered the church after mass had begun already and somehow let the side entrance door slam behind her, so everyone turned around to look at her. Anne was sure she heard a collective gasp, and then Father William coughed and all attention went back to the altar. Anne had forgotten how much she loved this place. The thick smell of incense, the dim light, the profoundly moving statues . . . artifacts. How Anne loved artifacts. Everything came right back to her. Stand up, sit down, Amen. She did not take communion. She really needed to make a confession first; for all she knew, the communion wafer might set her on fire.

After mass she walked out the front doors of the church into the bright sun. And her sweet William, now handsome Father William, was at the foot of the steep stone steps, his robes floating in the breeze. William's hair shined dark black, and his profile mesmerized Anne for a moment. It occurred to her that she missed him very much, more than she had realized. In her reverie she bumped into an old woman and almost pushed her down the stairs by accident; the old lady cried out in surprise, and a nearby boy caught her and helped her regain her balance—but it was too late for Anne. Everyone was staring at her now. There she was, centered at the top of the steps, and as she walked down, the people parted like the red sea, all murmuring and full of speculation. William found her with his eyes. Those light eyes so like her own, only more blue than green. He was smiling at her. She walked toward him, and he met her at the base of the steps. "Anne." He took her hands.

"Want to come over and play?" she asked.

William laughed an easy laugh. A relaxed and relieved laugh. "You bet!"

Anne went home to make Sunday dinner for William. It would become their weekly habit. Things were coming back together. Everything was going to be fine after all.

"You look handsome in that collar."

"I will help you. With the baby."

"Really?"

"Yes. Anything you need."

"I won't tell you about her father."

"I don't want to know."

"I need you. I'm afraid to love this baby. I'm afraid to lose her. I'm afraid I'll be cold like Nan, or crazy like Lucy."

"Or clever like Anne," he said, smiling. "Besides, you have me." He knew he would finally have a family. It was like winning a prize: he seemed to have been able to achieve the impossible. He was a priest, and now he would be a "non husband" and a "non father." It was perfect; he would have her now. She would be his, forever.

William loved being a priest. It didn't bother him that he lived in the same house, serving on the same altar where he had been abused as a child. In a way, it helped heal him. He had power in a place where he had once been so powerless. And he loved hearing confessions, becoming an amateur historian for his parish and Haven Port, presiding over both the beginning and ending of lives, the general feeling of responsibility he had for humanity, especially for those who attended his church or sent their children to his school.

And then there was Anne. When he finished seminary, the church had approached him to do work abroad. But when he declined, they were gracious enough to offer him a place back at Our Lady of Sorrows when Father Callahan died. And more than anything, he wanted to go back to his home, to his school—to the community he loved, back to Anne.

He knew she had been through rough times while he was gone. Her mother . . . that horrible tragedy at the mental hospital . . . all those poor souls, dead, and at Lucy's mad hands. Anne needed him. The ghosts couldn't be her only companions forever. The only question was, how would he get her to trust him again?

But it turned out he didn't have to do anything; she came to him. He was only just back, and there she was, in the back of the church. She looked as if she had just gotten out of bed: her hair was standing straight up in the back and full of snarls; she wore an odd, ill-fitting dress; and she was tripping over a pair of untied black boots. She was just about the most beautiful thing he had ever seen. His heart had a home again.

He began to visit her. He came to dinner.

He blessed the Witch House, tried to rid it of the madness. They prayed together. (He didn't think she was paying much attention, but every little thing counted.)

He knew she still consorted with the ghosts, who he had decided were either demons or Anne's own psychosis. And that bothered him, but she would not budge on the subject. They were her family.

And then there was the house. The house only tolerated William, he sensed it. But even through its tolerance, when inside, he always felt as if he was walking against the wind.

Pictures of Anne. Oh, look at Anne there, in the sunny kitchen that she painted turquoise while she carried Opal. Just look at her! Bathed in the sunlight, her hair carelessly piled in a bun, her white nightgown, another of Nan's, wide at the neck, exposing her slender shoulder. See the blond cherubic baby sitting in the wooden highchair and playing peek-a-boo with a clean white dish towel.

Look at them! There they are in the garden, weeding and watering. The baby is laughing and pointing to the rainbows that the water spray makes in the sunlight. See Anne teach her all of the things Nan taught her. She is sharing garden magic. First to an infant tied to her chest in a brightly colored makeshift sling, then to a toddler who continues to pull up new spring shoots, and then to a bored child who would like to be doing other things. See Anne's garden grow. See Opal grow.

See them there! There she is in the rocking chair in the living room, rocking her baby to sleep, nursing her, singing to her with a lovely voice. The baby is half asleep, touching her mother's cheek with one chubby hand. The ghosts are with her, Ava helps rock the chair, Gwyneth lounges on the sofa, softly singing with Anne. There is so much peace here, so much love. Anne is happy.

There's Anne again, she is playing the piano with the baby in the Moses basket, and then with the toddler sitting next to her, banging on the keys to drown out her mother's music. Anne is laughing at her willfulness, her desire to be the best at everything so early on. And now, the child alone, her hair in perfect ringlets, sitting at the piano with her teacher, the metronome swinging. Hear how perfectly she plays, see the serious look on her perfect round face. Anne doesn't play much anymore. . . .

See Anne, downtown with the baby in the carriage. Everyone thinks she is such a pretty baby, and she is. Her blond curls, her china blue eyes! What a picture. And Anne! "How lovely Anne looks," they would say. "Perfectly lovely, just like her mother." Anne loved the *validity that Opal gave her. It was a gift, the icing on the cake. The normalness was a constant, pleasing surprise for her.*

There she is with William, and the baby is all smiles. Who took that photo? They are in the garden in late summer; it looks like the tomatoes have taken over the whole patch! And there are baskets and baskets of raspberries in front of them. This is the day Anne makes her first batch of raspberry jam. Look at William, he is looking at Anne, and she is smiling, the chubby, pretty baby has mashed raspberries in her tight fist. William's eyes are full of devotion; he looks at her like a man who never needed anything else but to be right there, frozen in time.

Here they are making cookies. Anne is caught in a silent laugh. There is flour everywhere . . . then there are cookies being cut and baked. Serious Opal has her tongue between her teeth at the corner of her mouth in deep concentration as she mangles the dough. And then the decorating: sprinkles and icing and licks of many mixing spoons and bites of crumbled cookies.

There is the Christmas tree. It looked the same every year. They would go and cut it down together, back in the pine forest, and for every one they cut, Anne insisted they plant another. "You have to give some back," she would say. The ornaments would glisten in the fire-light, colored blown glass, painted silver spheres, little trinkets that Opal would make at school. And the star. A store-bought star. Expensive. William bought it for them the year Opal was born. "A star for a star!" he said every year as he held her up to put it on the tree. And even if she put it on crooked, they would let it stay that way, because it was hers.

And there is Opal in the Christmas pageant! Father William always cast her as Mary. No one in the parish even got mad anymore. It was just expected. She is so beautiful with the scarf around her head, kneeling in prayer in front of the baby Jesus, one of her very own favorite dollies. See how the fake snowflakes made from powdered soap fall all around her head, and a light is shining on her from above, making her glow just like an angel.

There is the picture of Opal and her mother on the morning of her first communion. Anne looks stunning, so does Opal. Anne is standing in the front yard at the gate. She is wearing one of Lucy's too-big green silk dresses. It is a bit old-fashioned, but Anne fixed it with a pretty jeweled belt and turned it into something remarkable. She never felt so lovely. Her hair, still holding the wave it picked up while she was pregnant, is pulled over to one side and floats down over one shoulder. She is holding Opal's hand. Opal is looking coyly into the camera. She knows she is lovely and this is her day, but she is also proud of her mother, who has planned a nice party and who looks so beautiful. Anne has even taken the time to clean the garden soil out from under her fingernails.

Opal has a wreath of baby's breath in her hair, which is down and curling perfectly, just brushing her shoulders. Her dress is white satin. She looks like a miniature bride, with overlays of lace on the skirt, a wide satin band with a huge bow in the back, a beaded bodice, and a lace collar. Anne had it made especially for her. She has lacy ankle socks and a pair of wonderful new shoes. Little white patent leather shoes with a buckle that kept them on tight, because they had a little heel.

Opal begged and screamed for that little heel. Anne tried to hold firm, tried . . . for once . . . to hold her ground. She contended that Opal was too little to wear heels, no matter how low. But the girl cried and banged and begged for the shoes for days. Every other word was about those shoes, and finally, Anne gave in. She just didn't want to hear about them anymore.

They were the picture of normalcy that day . . . the two of them smiling into the camera, obviously smitten with themselves and each other. They had their whole lives ahead of them.

33

William on the Porch with the Truth

As much as he loved Anne, it was his love for Opal that won out. From the moment she came shooting out of Anne into his hands, as if she couldn't stand to be inside for one more second, William was taken. She looked at him with her big blue eyes and made a cooing sound, his little dove.

He loved her for who she was, for how she loved him, and for how she changed his Anne. This was the Anne he always knew existed. He was so proud of her. She was pretty, competent, organized, and logical. She lost a little bit of the wildness that had always intrigued him, and she had also lost a bit of her dry sense of humor. But raising babies is a busy business, if you want to do it right, and Anne didn't have a lot of time for joking around or running wild in the meadow.

He didn't mind the gossip. Of course there were people in in his church who assumed the child was his. Why wouldn't they? He was a little flattered, but he knew it was a good thing, that the math didn't work, and she didn't look a lick like him, or there would be issues with the bishop. But he liked to pretend she belonged to him, so the talk helped validate his dreams.

Everything in their lives was going well. Anne was growing more respected each day. There was even a mysterious someone leaving her money and food on a monthly basis, so he didn't have to worry about her income. And the baby? Opal was growing up strong and beautiful. William visited them almost every night and even stayed over some Sundays as well as on Christmas Eve.

But then, Opal—always precocious—began to talk. And when she began to talk, his whole world began to unravel.

Opal was interested in the most unchildlike things, like dead animals on the side of the road.

Anne wouldn't believe it . . . or maybe she did . . . that was what bothered him the most. He couldn't figure it out.

"Did you tell Mommy about your bad thoughts?" William finally asked one day when Anne was out. It was just him and Opal eating egg salad sandwiches out on the front porch.

"I tell Mommy all the time. I tell her and I tell her. She says my thoughts are one hundred percent normal."

Opal was quiet. She looked at her sandwich. The sun was shining down onto her sweet head. It made the gold shimmer in her hair.

"What is it, Opal?"

"Sometimes I hear voices that scare me." She began to cry. William couldn't stand seeing her cry.

"It's okay, honey. Finish your sandwich. I will talk to Mommy."

Opal threw her arm around him. "Oh, thank you, Father! Thank you!"

William laughed. He had egg salad in his hair.

He didn't talk to Anne right away. He needed to think about the whole thing. He began to believe that Anne was keeping her past from Opal as a personal keepsake, holding onto her past, not letting Opal, or William, for that matter, in on a secret that kept a little bit of who she used to be intact. William could not understand why she would do that. He soothed Opal as much as he could, with words, pure unadulterated affection, and gifts, but it didn't help. She was growing ever more distant, aloof, mean, and afraid. The demons that had plagued Anne had obviously been passed down to Opal and were now attacking her very spirit. Or (and it wasn't the first time he'd pondered it), she may be like the mysterious father Anne wouldn't talk about. This situation needed rectifying.

Right before Opal was to make her first communion, he felt he had an argument that Anne would respond to.

"She is seeing things, Anne. And I'm not sure if the things she sees and hears are there or not, but it scares her."

"Suddenly you are so sure you know everything about us? About me? About voices and demons and . . . ghosts? You didn't believe me."

"I always believed you, Anne." William was staying calm. "I always believed *you* believed it. Which made it real to you."

"But you never told anyone. You never stood up for me. *Never.*"

This statement hit William hard. He wondered if she was still talking about the ghosts, or if it was Jude. He wanted to hold her, shake her, kiss her, cry. Instead he just sighed.

"It doesn't really matter, does it? If they are real or not? Maybe it is some genetic thing? Maybe a toxin in this—*this house*? You were born here, right? And so was she. In the same room, for God's sake! You belong to the house, and the house belongs to the two of you. Both of you, you and Opal, could be suffering from some sort of malformation of your brains, or poison. Or, simply psychosis!"

Anne stared at him in furious disbelief. Mad that he was saying such a thing and angry with herself for not figuring it all out on her own. Of course it was psychosis. Opal belonged to Jude.

William was still talking. ". . . so you owe it to her to come clean. Remember, this may be something we can fix. Opal is your child. She is alive. She needs you. By ignoring her issues . . . the same ones you have suffered with . . . you treat her like, well . . ." He paused. "Like others treated you."

"How dare you!" Anne seethed. She picked up a crystal ashtray. Anne chucked it at his head; he ducked.

"I knew this Anne was still inside you. I can't say I've missed her," said William.

"Shut up, Will, just shut up."

William tried a different approach. One that would hopefully keep her from harming him. This Anne could be lethal.

"Just try, try to be honest with her. Just love her, Anne— you can't fully love her unless you let her in, let her into you. Tell her *your* story. It belongs to both of you. Let her in."

Anne hated when he was right. She thought about consulting with Gwyneth, and then, given their current conversation, just felt insane.

"Oh, fine. I will see what I can do."

"That is all I ask, Anne. That is all I will ever ask."

34

Anne on the Stairs with a Dress

1970

For months all Anne could think about was falling down the stairs. She dreamt about it, she saw it in her mind. It reminded her of something she couldn't quite put her finger on. She would be washing dishes and all of a sudden she was tumbling down the back porch steps. She could hear the sound of the fall and the impact. She could feel the cracking of bones, the hot twisting of ankles. She thought maybe it was because Opal was growing up and she was somehow reliving the death of that first baby that lived in her womb. But still, Anne became very wary of stairs. She didn't want to fall and ruin Opal's first communion.

On that perfect Sunday morning in early May, the kind where it was not quite spring and not quite summer, that Opal was to become a true child of Christ, to receive his body and blood and begin her journey to confirmation, Anne had everything just so. Opal was whimpering and mad as usual, but it couldn't wreck the day. The dress was perfect, the flowers perfect, the day perfect. The church hall was set for the party with the help of the Ladies' Guild (they invited her to join, joy!), and Dominic was even going to make an appearance. She had William call and invite him and his family, and they all said yes.

Everyone was gathering at the front of the church, waiting to go in. They all got there early to get the best seats. The children had gone in already, but the massive doors opened, and Anne saw Opal come out to the top of the steps, frowning. She motioned for her mother to come. Anne ran up the steps to see what could be wrong.

"Mommy . . . I am sorry I was mad this morning. I was just nervous."

Anne laughed, relieved. "I know, sweetling. Don't worry, Rome wasn't built in a day."

"What does that mean?"

Anne laughed, "You will find out. . . . Never mind, go back inside!"

Opal turned to go, and Anne began to walk down the steep steps (being extra careful).

"Mommy!"

Anne was startled.

"What, dear?"

"I just wanted to tell you . . . I have the prettiest dress!" Opal did a little twirl and then gasped.

Anne felt her fall. Felt the air go before it even went, saw Opal's little hands try to grab (and actually graze) the hem of Anne's green silk dress. Then Anne was watching her fall. Opal had somehow lost her balance: her shoe slipped, and she fell sideways, landing hard on her side. Three or four ungraceful somersaults later, she was at the bottom of the church steps, and by the angle of her pretty head, she had to be dead.

Anne's heart frosted over. William was screaming. He had been screaming, she realized, for a long time. He broke free of the panic paralysis and ran down the steps so fast he slipped on them, sliding down the last few like a bumpy fair ride.

He crawled to her and lifted her wobbly head onto his lap.

"It's okay Opal, I'm here. It's okay. It'll be okay."

Anne sat down at the top of the steps, unable to move. She spoke the Death Life Wither Wander Spell in her head like a prayer. Over and over. She watched as everyone but her crowded around her child. Her baby. Someone cried, "Give her some air!"

"Air?" she murmured.

The crowd cleared. William held Opal still, but she was very much alive.

"It's a miracle!" William cried.

"Mama?"

William began to carry Opal up the steps so Anne could touch her daughter. Feel how close they'd been to losing her. To see God's love at work.

"Take her to the hospital, Will. Take her away from me," Anne ordered.

"Anne, don't you want—"

"Now."

Alive.

Then dead.

Then alive. Was it the spell? Was it a miracle? Would she be Opal? Or would she be empty? It didn't matter.

"I don't deserve her. I never did. I don't want her," said Anne.

Her voice surprised her. She hadn't heard that particular tone— that dead tone—in a long time. Opal had to go. She had to be away from Anne, away from this house. Away from this town.

Anne, not knowing what else to do, went home, sat at the kitchen table of the Witch House, and opened the cards that had been sent in celebration of Opal's first communion.

One in particular caught her eye. It was postmarked Fairview, Massachusetts.

Dear Anne,
Send her to me. My mother, Evelyn, arranged it long ago. You toyed with fate. *You lost.*
Vivian Pratt

"Fairview? No . . . Fortune's Cove. I remember from the book." Anne went into the library and pulled down her big black book. She went back to the Book of Nan and skimmed the entries and clippings.

Evelyn Pratt to read fortunes at Haven House.

"Thank you, Nan," she said.

———

William took charge of gathering Opal's things and accompanying her to Fortune's Cove.

He came back a different man.

"I knew it was just a dream," Anne said, pruning roses.

"It wasn't a dream, Anne, it really happened. And you sent her away. You must tell me why. It's not right. She's not right. She's empty. She didn't even cry for you."

"She is gone. I'm not an idiot. Having her at all was the dream. I wasn't good enough to have her, to keep her. She couldn't stay. She wasn't really real, she wasn't really here."

"Shut up, Anne," he said, his voice choked with anger. "It was you. You and this suffocating house! You stole her from me, because you couldn't bear to actually lose her. That split second of loss almost killed you, so you sent her away, and you sent me to do it! You are a demon after all. You stole my heart, and now it's broken." He broke off in a sob.

They stood in the garden by the roses for what seemed like a lifetime. It was very dark now. William was quiet. All tears shed.

"Don't you have anything to say?" he asked, wiping his face with his robed arm, Father William still. Only Father William now. His pretend family was dead.

"What do you want me to say?" Anne asked, flippantly.

"Fuck you, Anne. Fuck you and your ghosts and your house. I am done. I am finally done with you, Anne."

She knew what William had said was true. He'd even cursed.

327

That his language amused her was what finally broke her free of her carefully manufactured "numb."

"Well, praise the Lord, then, Father William," she said.

Anne went to Opal's room. She opened the closet and found a box of paper and her set of crayons. No, not a set of crayons—a box containing many of a single color. Too many of a color called permanent geranium lake.

As she boxed up the life of a little girl, a little girl she dressed in that very room a week before, a nine-year-old who belonged to her but whom she always felt disconnected from, it occurred to her that she didn't know if she was sad because her child was gone or that now she would not have much to keep her busy anymore. The numb seemed to take hold again. Maybe she was a sociopath? Maybe she couldn't feel anything. Maybe William and her mother had both been right all along.

But then, her eyes fell upon a blanket that Opal had wrapped around a stuffed animal, pretending it was a new baby, and it just so happened to be the very same blanket William wrapped Opal in right after she was born. A plain, white blanket with satin binding. Opal had carried it, slept with it, loved on it for her whole life. Anne lifted it to her face and breathed in her daughter. The world ended. There were no words. There was nothing but bright, shiny, black pain.

She could not feel this.

She refused.

But it swallowed her whole. She fell asleep on the floor of her lost child's room amidst a sea of lost child's belongings with the lost child's infant blanket draped over her own lost face like a shroud.

Anne sent the blanket to Opal the next day, never expecting to see her daughter or the blanket again.

And then one day, in 1984, there it was.

Wrapped around her granddaughter, Stella.

35

*Gavin in the Witch House
with the Letter*

1971–1998

William couldn't stay away. He was back within a year. When they reunited, the loss of Opal had taken its toll on William; he was ill. His eyes would go dark and distant mid conversation. He'd look right through her.

Anne didn't mind. Company was company. Her ghosts had left her, too. Opal's fall changed everything.

Sometimes, when she allowed herself to remember those sweet years, she pictured it as she would a movie. Then she would sigh, wipe a tear off her cheek, and, as she was known to say in town, "Move the fuck forward, for fuck's sake."

That was that.

And then, in 1984, fourteen years after Opal was sent away, Stella arrived in a basket on the porch of the Witch House.

She was a proper baby, with black hair and pink cheeks. A baby Anne recognized as one of her own. Not blond and perfect. Another kind of perfect. A clever sort of perfect.

She knew it was her granddaughter, even though there was no note, just a little scrap of paper pinned to a pink sweater that said: Stella.

"Of course there wouldn't be a note, Miss Stella," Anne said, carrying the basket inside. "For all anyone knew, I could have been in one of those moods where I don't leave the house at all. You may have starved out here, or frozen. Or worse. But no, no, not you, little one. Not you with all that sun shine. Now, let's get you settled."

A stilted phone call came a week or so later.

"I don't want her. I guess it runs in our blood, giving up children," said Opal.

"Well, I suppose we can make that end here. As it began with me. No one else did that. I was the one, Opal. I loved you too much to keep you."

"You're wrong, we all leave each other. You were the one who actually did it *almost* right. Nan left Lucy by dismissing who she was. Lucy left you with all her hate and drinking and so on. Must have been harder to have your mother leave you over and over again each day. You didn't love me, Anne. You loved the idea of me. I know that now. And I'm too busy for a child. If I'm cold, you created me. Bury her in the backyard or what have you. See if I care."

Anne was almost proud of the cruelty.

"Do you want me to tell her about you?"

"I want you to tell her I'm dead. Because I am."

The line went dead.

Cold and surgical. Anne thought about crying, but she'd brought it on herself.

"Rule number one, baby Stella. You can't cry over it if you built it," she said.

She took a job working for William at Our Lady of Sorrows parochial school. She taught third grade science. Her classroom was a beautiful and peaceful place. Anne was strict, but despite everything, she did have a way with children. They trusted her. The large windows in the room let in plenty of light for her students' seedlings to take hold. She used the entire year to teach them about the growth cycle of plants and their relationship to the earth and to the sun. She loved Mother's Day especially, when all of her little children would take their baby plants home as gifts to their mothers. It was always a happy day for the third grade. The third grade was also the year where she prepared them for their first communion. Though this could have been a difficult task, what with her losing Opal on the day of that milestone, Anne liked living the day over and over again. It helped her remember her lost girl from a safe distance. And it helped her remember her lost girl's dead father. Some wounds bring strength.

1988

Dear Anne,
I wonder if you ever guessed that I was the one who left
you money and food all these years. I am not telling you now

because I want your gratitude (if you are reading this,
I am dead anyway) or because I need your forgiveness:
after all, I am your aunt. I wasn't a useful one until I got
sneaky. What with everything that happened, I didn't know
another way. I just thought you might not have known it
was me, and this would clear up the mystery. I don't like
mysteries or surprises, which I suppose is ironic, given my
son. I want you to know that I always knew what he
was doing. What he did to you, as well as to the others,
and there were many others. That is my sin. And I'd like
to say I was able to help him, but we all know that would be
a lie.

I did love him, Anne. And I wanted to protect him from
himself. I didn't do a good job.

I am not mad that you killed him. You are family, after
all. And for all the crazy on your mother's side, there's a
homicidal gene pool on your daddy's side that you can't
escape, I guess.

I don't know why or how, but you must have. You dispatched
him, and I am grateful. . . . I would have gone back to my
family straightaway, but then I saw you in the garden with your
belly, and I knew I had to stay . . . stay and try to keep
helping you.

Anyway, the long and short of this is that I feel I still owe
you a debt, and I have nothing to give you but a secret. You
will find a key with this letter. A key to a trunk in the attic of
the gatehouse. Do with it what you will.

Please know that I am very sorry.

Opal was a lovely little girl, Anne. She reminded me so

*much of him. I'm sure wherever she is, she's happy. You were
brave and right to send her away.*

    Best,

    Aunt Lavinia

Anne turned the key over in her hand. It had been a long
time since she'd thought of Lavinia. She thought about Jude.
She thought too much about Gavin. But chubby, insipid aunt
Lavinia, who never said much and should have showered more,
wasn't on the top of her urgent thought list.

She gave Stella lunch and went directly over to the gatehouse.

Tic tock tic tock tic tock. Tic.

Time to enter the lair.

The attic Lavinia referred to was a tiny crawl space with exactly enough room for exactly one thing in it. A steamer trunk
chock full of cash.

Filled to the brim.

She smiled a little and then, thinking maybe there could be
more things hidden inside, Anne considered wandering around
the gatehouse. She'd never spent too much time there.

But Lucy had.

And before her . . . Reginald Green had.

And before him . . . Archibald.

She had Nan's keys on the big silver ring. Keys to places in
the house that would have been locked up since before Haven
House was destroyed.

Anne knew the stories, and it occurred to her that perhaps

she'd missed something quite simple all along. Some darkness that tainted all their lives.

She never spoke or wrote much about that day. All anyone knew was that she was seen nailing boards against the windows as if a storm were coming.

"No one will ever live here again," said Anne. As if it were an opposite curse.

She didn't need the gatehouse for money anymore. She had a big old pile in a steamer trunk. And it was cheap, living just the two of them. Besides, that house never did well with renters anyway. There'd been a series of tenants, mostly people who were new to the area, but terrible things seemed to happen over and over again. It became almost comical to Anne. But not to Stella, who, as she grew, had much less of a sense of humor. She was delicate and very clever. But she felt the hurts of the world.

There was the university student who fell down the porch steps and, in the opposite of a miracle, broke his back, becoming paralyzed from the waist down.

There was the man who felt the house was suffocating him and the only way to loosen the pressure in his head was to put an ice pick in his ear and pound at it with a mallet.

There was one botched abortion, at least three lost limbs, and always, each and every time, a broken heart.

It was as if the property was spitting them all out.

Stella, who was just a tiny thing when most of the terrible

gatehouse events were happening, used to say, "I do not think that our Witch House likes the way these tenants taste. It only likes you, Gran."

"We don't have to worry about that anymore, Stella girl. No we do not."

Stella and Anne were always seen laughing, skipping, and pointing at the sky. Stella was a happy child. She loved her house. And she loved her Gran.

Slowly, as the perfume of her past wore off, or at least grew fainter, Anne's status in the community improved again. Perhaps because the raspberry jam she made was so sweet, Anne became beloved.

Most agreed, however, that it was really Stella.

Her change could have been due to Anne wanting to give Stella the security she never had. It could have been many things. But mostly it was love. And fear.

She'd seen Stella's future in the girl's eyes. That she would die in childbirth. Anne convinced herself that the only thing to do was to keep Stella safe and sound at the Witch House. There would be no baby.

In some ways Anne actually took over Nan's role in the community; not the way she'd tried before, by acting the part. No, this time she became a sort of *strega* and wise woman. People would come to her for advice, at the markets, after church, in the schoolyard, but not to the house, never to the house. Sometimes, on New Year's Eve, people would ask her over to their houses to ring in the new year, and inevitably, once it was known that she was going to be there, a line would form in front of her, full of people wishing to have the *malocchio* (evil eye) taken off of them. Her grandmother had taught her how to do this odd trick, and somehow people seemed to know she had the "gift," so she would hold bowls of water over their heads one by one and drop pure olive oil into the water to dispel the curses. It didn't matter to her if it really worked or not, but it seemed to matter to the masses, so she was happy to oblige. The people of Haven Port were falling in love with Anne, not just for what she could help them with, or how she taught their children at school, but also for what she could make.

Anne fell into a thriving seasonal business. Her raspberry jam was so popular she began putting up other things that her garden gave her. She had preserves, relishes, pickles, and all sorts of wonderful things to help bring summer to the table during their cold winters. The farmers' market, more popular than ever, was a place where she sold much of her canned goods, with little Stella in one of those old-fashioned aprons by her side.

Stores and markets in the greater Haven Port area sold them as well. She needed to have a good way to get the jars safely from place to place, so she bought herself a truck, a 1950 GMC pickup truck, turquoise and chrome. It was a wonderful investment and quite a fun toy. Anne and Stella became fixtures driving it around town, dressed all in black, with their long black hair flying free (Anne's streaked with silver as the years wore on) and the windows down and jars and crates of something or another clattering and clanging in the back when Anne took a hard corner. And people liked her, they liked her style. Her black capes, her black combat boots (new ones that fit), her cigarettes. Her wild hair. Stella wore hers wild, too. And she was smiling, always smiling.

1990

"Gran! Gran! There's a letter for you. The postman came all the way up the road. He must be new, because he didn't look one bit scared, not one bit. I had to sign for it. Like a grownup! Gran?"

Anne was standing in the doorway to the kitchen, afraid to touch the letter in Stella's hands.

She'd woken in the night, shivering. Knowing her father was dead. It seemed a cruel blow. She'd somehow thought that he'd come back for her, finally. She'd never stopped waiting. Finality is always hard, but harder for a witch. No spells are strong enough to raise the dead. Well, fine. There are those spells, but they are best left undone.

"Leave the letter there, darling, and go play. I need to be alone when I open it."

"What is it?"

"It's bad news. And it's the ending of something that I never had a chance to start. Those are hard things to figure out. That's why I need you to go play and let me be brave here on my own. Gran will be fine."

"I'll go study the big black book. I've almost memorized the

338

reckoning spell. And now I want to find out what the house is saying when it's worried."

"What the house says?"

"You know, Gran. *Tic tock tic tock tic tock. Tic*," she said, singing its eerie beat as she skipped up the stairs.

Anne turned to the letter in her hands. She felt the outline of the folded paper under the triangle seal. She noticed another outline, too—a photograph, perhaps.

Lord, I'm not ready for this. She thought.

Dear Anne,

I am old now, and unwell. I guess my time is about up. I wanted to write you a letter, to give you the farewell you deserve. I don't expect you to come on down here; I'm probably already dead and buried. I just figured I needed to make my peace, and I hope you don't find all this too selfish. So here goes . . .

I never said I was sorry. At least, I don't think I did, and if I did, I didn't mean it, but now I do. I really am sorry, Anne girl. Sorry for what I did, for what I didn't do, and for who I was never able to be.

I don't say this to force you into a position to forgive me, I don't deserve it, I don't need it, and I don't even want it. I know what I did. I have to make some sort of peace with it on my next trip 'round this crazy place. I just wanted to give you something, maybe a little something to hold on to, to make whatever time you have left on this planet a little more bearable. (Am I giving myself too much credit? Probably, but I'm a goner, girl, so cut me some slack.)

The point is, I love you. I loved you the minute I saw you. I loved you each time I came back, and I loved you when you brought your crazy ole self here. I just love you. For real. Whether you know it or not, whether you will believe it or not, you have always belonged to me.

That is what I wanted you to know. That you have always been a part of me, living all on the inside of me. You. Belong. To me.

I tried to make my way back, but I just didn't get there. No excuses. I just didn't.

I shouldn't have left you there. I knew it that day on the stairs. Do you remember that day? I should have picked you right up and run away. They wouldn't have cared, would they? I don't think so. So that is what I am doin' right now, baby, right now as I lie in bed and write this, I am making up a pretend.

I am pretending that you ran down the stairs, and instead of promising you pretty things and skulking off, I stopped, and I held out my arms, and you jumped down the last two stairs right into them like a little kitten. I pack up your stuff, no one stops us. I promise them I will take real good care of you, and Nan packs up some food for the trip. When we get outside, I put you high on my shoulders and we walk on down that damn hill straight to the station. We are singing, baby, "Froggy Went a-Courtin'," do you remember that song? And we are just the two of us, the two musketeers.

Is that okay with you? Can I pretend that for a little bit? Just enough to get me through . . . is it selfish? Probably.

I missed you, baby, I missed you all the time. And I never

wanted anyone or anything more than I wanted you, not my
own mother, not the booze or the women, not even Lucy. Just
you. You have always been the home I have been trying to find.
Somehow, I just couldn't find my way. I didn't try my hardest
or give it my best and for that I will be eternally sorry.

Try to do your best, girl, God knows I didn't.
Much Love,
Your Daddy,
Gavin

Anne wiped the tears off her cheeks. She hadn't even known that her eyes were leaking. She folded up the letter and put it back inside her apron pocket, along with the picture. Later she would find a pretty frame and put it up on the mantel where Ava's used to be. A prime spot.

That photo . . .

Anne didn't have a lot of photos of herself. You need a loving family, or celebrity status, or friends in order to collect pictographic images.

"How funny that the very moment my life turned weird and took a turn for the worse is caught here on film."

She remembered that day. Not the circumstances, but the day. Gavin had taken her downtown. Anne had ridden on his shoulders, and he was so handsome and she was so proud. He had bought her ice cream, and she kept asking him if he was going to stay this time. He wasn't answering her. He would keep putting her down, taking pictures of everything with his fancy camera. When they got back home, they all sat out on the patio and ate a delicious lunch. Anne remembered eating tomatoes, how they would squish between her teeth, and drinking ice-cold lemonade. She remembered Gavin asking Lucy to take a picture of them together. Lucy must have, Anne remembered the flash.

Later, they had fought . . . Lucy and Gavin. There was a lot of yelling, and Anne had hidden herself on the back steps. Gavin came running from the yard, shooting by his daughter. He paused at the screen door to take a look at her, and she held out her arms and said, "Don't go, Daddy, please don't go? Promise you will come back?"

And Gavin had placated her with promises of more ice cream and rides on his big boat and even a camera of her own so they could take pictures together. And then he was gone.

She thought of this for a long time and tried to figure out if she would have, in fact, preferred his pretend ending to their story. Most people say that if they got the chance, they wouldn't change a thing, that it makes them who they are.

But not Anne. If given the chance, she would have taken him up on that alternate ending.

It put her life into perspective, and she would live the rest of it with the guiding premise that it was a life that never should have been, a mistake for sure. Not that Anne herself was a mistake—that was what Lucy thought—but that it was Gavin's mistake that could not be undone. It was what it was. It was easy to live in the mistake. It would help negate the bad things, help her to embrace growing old. Everything would be okay now.

"Gran? Are you okay?" asked Stella.

"I'm fine, my darling. Come, let me look at you. Would you like some jam? On a spoon?"

"Gran, I love you so much. Past the moon and speed of light. I will never leave you."

"And I will never leave you, my darling. Now, shall we watch the night come out from behind the sun? Later can we practice sleeping spells."

And they ate jam from spoons and walked through the gardens while looking up to find dinosaurs in the clouds. Anne had never been happier.

1998

If only the solemn vows of nine-year-old girls could be trusted. But they can't. It's not their fault, though. At nine years old, the world is more beautiful and safer than it ever was or ever will be again. At nine years old, you can learn to make your own ice cream and eat it alone with no regrets.

Our Stella couldn't stay nine forever. She did what most of us do. She grew up. She fell in love, as ought to happen to a young, beautiful, mysterious girl. And she decided to finish high school early and defy her grandmother by not going to college.

Defy could be a strong word. Because Stella understood the risk. But she did it anyway. She left her happy little enclave of Haven Port in Persimmon Point, Virginia, for Magnolia Creek, Alabama, where Patrick Whalen lived.

"There is nothing bad about being in love or leaving home.

I love Paddy, Gran. I love him with all my heart," said Stella, trying to reason with Anne.

"You lie! And what if you have a baby? I swear!" said Anne, her graying hair blowing in the wind. She clutched her black book of memories and magic against her breast on the front porch of the Witch House as the car waited to take her Stella away.

"If you have any children in any other place than this, you won't live to see them grow! This house is your lifeline. This is your destiny! You are breaking fate. It is suicide! Don't say I didn't warn you!"

Stella left the Witch House and grandmother she loved with a bitter taste in her mouth and a growing fear of her own past.

36

Anne in the Witch House with Despair

1999

When Stella left, Anne placed herself, along with the Witch House property, in some sort of snow globe and decided to get old. Her life seemed lived up, used up already. It didn't matter that women with her lineage lived longer than most. *I've had enough time. I've done enough damage. It's time to be old now,* she thought.

It was the first and last time Anne Amore would be reflective. The two years that passed between Stella leaving and Anne dying felt like the longest she'd ever lived. Which seemed silly, because during her life men walked on the moon, telephones became cordless and then, eventually, wireless. Everything had gone electric.

But Anne had gone backward instead of forward. She got

rid of her television set and even her radio. She had an emergency wind-up radio in case she felt a storm was coming and also for the occasional interest in news (which would inevitably lead her to putting the thing away again in disgust).

She stopped her canning and selling; if the people missed it, she wouldn't have known, because everyone was starting to move out of Haven Port. There was money to be had in America, and none of it involved staying in a town with no industry. Slowly, everything around Anne became very, very quiet. And she liked it that way. She would wake up, say the rosary, and make a strong pot of coffee on the stove. On milder days, she would take her coffee outside into the garden, to feel the morning sun on her face. Then she would go inside and make breakfast and get on with her day. She loved this newfound quiet. Just her breathing and the sounds of the house and the birds outside. And in the winter, when the world was frozen, so frozen it seemed it would crack, it was very quiet, too.

She thought of Lucy.

"It's quiet, Mama."

And those were the days, as she got older, that she loved the most. The coldest, quietest, dimmest days. She would sit, and read, and cook a bit, and think, and pray, and clean. And, of course, sit with William. Because he was dying, too.

She could tell when he was saying mass. He had paleness, a gray tone to his skin that Anne had begun to notice around people who were near death. She went to the rectory after the service to talk to him.

"You are ill."

"You noticed?" They shared a knowing smile.

"Is it bad?"

William nodded. Anne was startled, and she thought it had been a while since he had come to the house. She was so busy—time went by fast these days. He was too thin. She knew, being up close to him, that it was only a matter of when, not if or what. Nothing in her old spell books could undo it.

He bent his head and began to cry. Anne felt the heat of sorrow burn up her throat. She was not accustomed to having all that pain she pushed hard down inside her come back up. It made her furious. But instead of running away, scratching at her eyes, she patted his shoulder instead. "Don't worry, Will."

Anne asked the rectory for permission to bring him home, and they asked the bishop, who agreed. She knew the house would end it quickly for William. He knew it, too, just as he knew it was time to go. She moved him into the Witch House and put a sickbed in the open living room. As they had both predicted, he quickly took a turn for the worse. The house shifted, letting a chill in through its cracks, and as the cold air made its way to his lungs and his phlegm thickened, William began to suffocate.

One night, he called out to her in a hoarse whisper, "Anne!" She came quickly to his side. "Anne, lie next to me the way you did when we were young."

Anne laid her head on the pillow and looked into his eyes, taking his hands in hers so it looked like they were praying. Anne noticed William's eyes didn't look sick, or old. They were still young as ever and sparked with humor. But it didn't matter.

At that very moment, Anne's soul felt very, very old, and so did William's.

"Do you want me to try and fix a remedy, Will? We could stay together for a while longer. An hour, a day, a week?"

"Oh, no, Anne, I don't want to stay. I don't want to be made dark or crazy. It wouldn't be the same. It wasn't right. . . . It wasn't supposed to be like that, for you or for them. For Opal." He began to cough.

"Enough with the lecturing, Will, I just thought I would ask. We don't even know if it would work."

"True," he said as he caught his breath. "Anne?"

"Yes?"

"Will you promise me something?"

"Anything . . ."

"If there is a life after this, will you marry me?"

"Of course I will."

"And will you give me Opal? Can we make her together, you and me? Out of love? Maybe if she was made in love, she could stay."

"Yes, Will."

He gasped for air. "I love you, Anne."

"I know."

William looked at her, the longing for her to say it back was clear in his eyes. But she couldn't. Anne opened her mouth and nothing came out. And then William took his last breath. He was gone. She lay there for a long time, looking at him and holding his hands as they grew cold. She closed his eyes with her fingers, and then, when he was no longer looking at her, she said the words he had always wanted so desperately to hear, the words she wanted desperately to say.

"I love you, too."

The next morning the doctor came with the death certificate, and the funeral director took him away in a shiny black death wagon. And Anne began to close up the Witch House. She placed sheets over the furniture. She had the roof inspected. Anne was very, very, busy with preparations. There was much to do before she joined him, and she knew her soul could not continue to thrive without sweet William in the world.

"Anne, would you like me to call Stella, or try to find Opal?" Bev asked.

After all these years, Anne had been struck down by stage four or stage one thousand of some kind of man-made illness Anne couldn't and didn't want to pronounce.

Anne sighed, wondering why Bev wasn't dead yet. Old hag. "No. Please. I just want to be alone with my house," she said.

Anne waited to die in the bed, now hers, that used to belong to her Nan. She was alone. Except for her house.

The house breathed around her, crying, holding her in, creating a cool breeze to blow in through the windows to make the white sheer curtains dance like magic (she had loved to watch them as a girl), and wafting in the scent of the pine trees (long rotted and removed, in which she used to climb and sleep).

And Anne understood how fully the house loved her and she cried with it, a sweet, sad, and joyful cry that expressed all the pain and pleasure of living.

And as she died she wondered, *Where do we all come from? Where do we belong? Maybe it isn't so defined. Perhaps it becomes . . . as everything else does . . . whatever it is. . . . All the clichés.* "Home is where you make it." "You get out what you put in." "If you try, you will succeed." Anne began to realize that they had all been liars, every one of them. She lied to herself about who she was. It was apparent now that she had been a sad little girl who simply missed her father. There is nothing so extraordinary about that. And Lucy, she had been a beautiful widow, with a damaged mind and heart, who missed her husband. Nothing less, nothing more. She led a charmed life that took a wrong turn. And Nan, she had been a dreamer who thought her dreams died on the shores of America just when everyone else's around her were coming true. But they didn't. If only Nan had known she was having dreams come true every single day. Miraculous and extraordinary things unfolded for her, like the roses in her garden, all the time, and she just did not notice. If she had known . . . she could have changed it all, she could have changed their histories. At least now there were no more of them left to harm one another. Stella was right. It was good to let bad things end. Let other people get it right; their story was over.

Anne's ghosts returned, right at the end, good now, not to eat her up, not angry with her selfishness, but come to deliver her home; and there was her child, not Opal as she would be all grown up, but the Opal she raised, the one she remembered. The one she loved too much. With her golden hair shining like the sun and her blue eyes clear as a blue sky, and wearing that white lace communion dress as white as a cloud on a perfect day. "Mama," she whispered, and Anne's soul just rose right up, right out of her body, and she ran. Anne ran to her lost baby and her ghosts and into a perfect beautiful place. And as she left, the house heaved with a sob of great loss, and a rumble went through Haven Port, and the church bell broke, this time for good, and the drawbridge stuck midway, and everyone in the neighborhood stopped what they were doing for a moment and forgot to remember something, then shook their heads and went back to their lives.

Nothing remained but the sound of a clock. *Tic tock tic tock tic tock. Tic.* Until one day, her great-granddaughter found her way home, turned the golden doorknob, and reclaimed the ghosts.

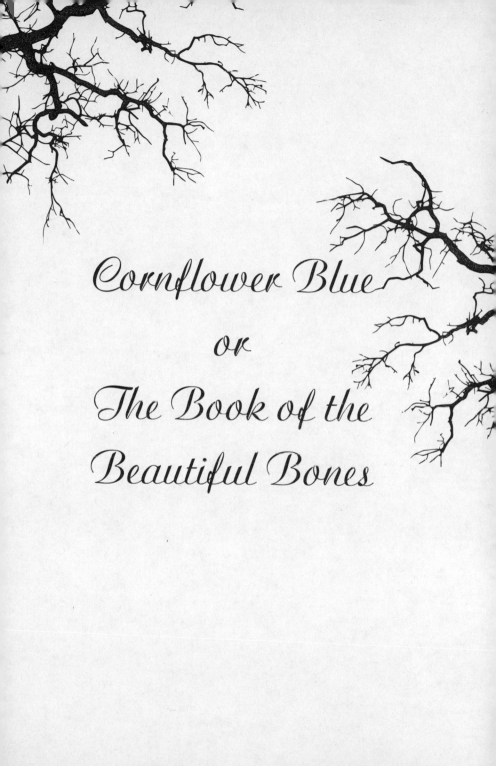

Cornflower Blue

or

The Book of the Beautiful Bones

37

In the Cellar with the
Psychopath

SUNDAY, SEPTEMBER 5, 2015

MIDNIGHT

They were in the library.

"That's it. That's where the story ends and, in my opinion, it's too damn sad," said Byrd. "I'll never get over it. The fact that I lost great-grandma Crazy Anne before I ever got to have her. I swear, there's a patent unfairness to the world that I wish I wasn't smart enough to see sometimes." Byrd wiped away her tears.

Eleanor pulled her into a hug. "*Shhh* now, Miss Byrd. It's okay. Really. You and me and Maj? We'll be just fine. No matter what happens with this television show."

Byrd wailed louder. "That's today! We didn't do it. Elly, I swear I thought we'd figure it out. I *believed* it!"

"Byrd. Calm down. Let's go to sleep and maybe . . . just maybe . . ."

"Maybe what? What else is there?"

"Maybe this can help?" asked Maj from the doorway, making them both jump.

"What on earth are you doing up, sweetheart?" Eleanor asked, picking her up to cover her with kisses.

"Someone had to figure it out," said Maj. "Byrd, look at my picture."

Byrd took the rolled-up picture and placed it on the massive desk, holding it down with an ashtray on one side and a book on the other.

"Well, I'll be damned," she said. "We've been telling and retelling stories of madness and sorrow while Maj colored us the truth. It's the gatehouse. It's always been the gatehouse. I mean, think about it. How much did we hear about Gavin and Lavinia and Jude? Not too much. But they *are* direct relations to me. Everything we heard pointed to that place. Even Amazing Andy didn't want to go there. You could tell when he said he felt nothing coming from it."

"You didn't search it?"

"It's the strangest thing. . . . I don't feel anything when we walk or drive by. Not even curiosity, which is very, very strange. Because I'm damn curious," said Byrd.

Tic tock tic tock tic tock. Tic.

"Do you hear that, Mama?"

"I do. I've heard it, felt it, like my own heartbeat since we got here. Do you hear it, Byrd?"

"We all hear it, Mama. And the gatehouse was hiding from you. There are secrets there that weren't in the stories. Our Witch House is ashamed of them."

"We have to go over there," said Byrd.

"No. Not now. Not in the dark. We'll go first thing in the morning. Together."

7:30 A.M.

Around the gatehouse, the grasses and vines had grown up over and through the porch, and the doors and windows were boarded up tight, so Eleanor and Byrd decided to try the back door.

"I DON'T UNDERSTAND WHY I CAN'T COME OVER THERE!" Maj yelled as loud as she could from where she was sitting on the lawn of the Witch House eating pie for breakfast (again).

"You stay right there, baby! We'll be out in a second."

"YOU WOULDN'T EVEN KNOW WITHOUT MY DRAWING, MAMA!"

"Just stay there and you can have more pie when we get back as a reward!"

"BUT YOU WOULD GIVE ME THE PIE ANYWAY, MAMA!"

Eleanor made a face at Maj and shook her head. "Kids," she said, turning back to Byrd.

Byrd laughed. "Well, she's not wrong. I just hope she's right about this, too."

A small, peeling, and half-falling-down entry gate stood between them and the backyard of the gatehouse. Byrd kicked it, tearing away vines and old pain. And when it flew open, they understood.

There were red geraniums everywhere. Potted and cracked and large and small. An entire expanse of the fenced-in yard simply swimming with red geraniums.

"Did we ever determine if it would be politically incorrect to call ourselves special needs psychics?" asked Byrd.

"I believe you voted for backwards psychics. I can't believe it's been right in front of us the whole time! Geez."

They opened up the back door, jingling Nan's old key ring full of keys and stepping over the thick overgrown geranium leaves and stalks, and entered the dim, hollow kitchen.

"It's too quiet," Eleanor whispered.

"I know," said Byrd.

"I don't hear the clock."

"What?"

"The clock, *Tic tock tic tock tic tock. Tic.* You know. I hear it on the grounds, I hear it in the house, by the pool, halfway up the drive, but I don't hear it now. At first it drove me crazy, but now I'm almost sick without it."

"Elly, you just figured it out. Let's investigate here, and then I want to show you something back at the house in the big black book."

They found the tables in the basement. The cage. The chains. Instruments of pain hidden behind a furnace much too large for such a small house. A house that wasn't built with a basement in the first place.

Jude's torture chamber.

Eleanor felt sick, like if she didn't get out now, she never would. She rushed out, with Byrd swiftly behind her.

"It must have been *built* for evil. Terrible intentions are the worst sort of energy," said Byrd, as they emerged back outside like a couple of deep-sea divers, gasping for air.

"Why is all that stuff still there? Don't people take those things for evidence or something?" asked Eleanor.

"I bet no one wanted to touch it. I bet they were all too afraid, so they closed it up."

"They must have known, you know," said Eleanor.

"Who?"

"Nan, Anne, Lucy . . . well, maybe not Lucy. But Nan and Anne had to know about this cellar. They used it for drying things and bottling wine."

"That doesn't matter. We are not normal folk, hasn't that sunk in yet? And I don't want to be. And you came all the way here so you wouldn't have to be. The question is, *What are we going to do?* Johnny Colder is clear on his way!"

"It's time to tell you the secret," said Maj from the staircase, her shadow tall and reaching into the cellar. Byrd and Eleanor jumped.

"Dig there in the floor for bones. And dig outside in the fenced garden for bones. There are generations of the lost and dead under our feet. They will be everywhere.

"All over the yard, under those red geraniums. There are women, children, and even babies."

As she rushed up the stairs to scoop up Maj and to hurry Byrd out as well, a clarity descended on Eleanor, "It wasn't just Jude.

It was Archibald. Who knows what he was experimenting with in his attempts to get, or grow, or tame the magic of the Haven Port Greens? And I imagine Reginald was anything but innocent, too. Who knows what he did before Nan? Those stories, our heritage, they are colored by the women who told them. Nan was in love. Monsters are not monsters when you are in love."

"Are you okay, Byrd?" asked Eleanor, concerned. The girl's whole demeanor had changed since Maj's revelation.

"I've been wrong about everything. Let's go back to the main house. I need to get away from here. I need to show you something," Byrd said quietly.

Eleanor thought of making a joke about all the things they'd just discovered, and how one more thing might tip the balance out of their favor, but when she saw Byrd's face, she thought better of it. No sass there at all, just an open wound. So instead she led both girls to the porch of the main house and sat them down.

"This is the letter from the library," Byrd spoke up after a few moments of strained silence. "The one for me. What . . . what do you think of it?"

Eleanor took it with the same reverence she knew Byrd felt and began to read.

Dear Byrd,
The sun shines bright here. And though I know I've craved this moment of tranquil gardens and peaceful, quiet days filled

with light, I'm homesick. Which is not the way I intended to tell you this story, our story, at all. I intended to fill it with all the gloom and despair I could muster, so that you wouldn't be curious about your history. I wanted to frighten you. Yet here I am, confident I made the right choice, and wishing I could run away home and end my days safe inside the toxic embrace of the Witch House. Only I don't run. Instead I sit here under this magnificent southern magnolia, knowing my time on earth is short.

I live a life I know is not my own. I build it for you, so that it will be yours without question. The story I'm about to tell you, one of aching, dark resilience, remains the comfort of my soul. Because no matter how starless a night sky may seem, those stars are still there, promising their light, if you listen.

Inside the Big House they are laughing. I'm always so impressed by their ability to laugh through the sorrow. But I shouldn't be. It isn't like we never laughed. All families must examine their broken pieces and laugh from time to time. But here, here it's different. Here they laugh and the ghosts seem to laugh with them. Back home, our ghosts take offense.

I feel, for a moment, as if I'm a ghost as well. I hear someone calling me, they are so warm here, these people.

"Stella, honey, come on inside for supper."

I walk, slowly, through my garden. The one they allow me to have, the one that reminds me so much of home. If I closed my eyes, I could be standing in the house my great-great-grandmother Nan saved, on the land she inherited from her lover.

They are ghosts and I am caught here, in an unknown place. Not dead, not fully alive. Stella under glass.

My grandmother, my mother . . . the story doesn't even start here, in the country. It begins in Italy.

There are so many tales told about the immigrant waves to the land of opportunity. Story after story about Mafia and tenements and finding their way.

The stories I heard were different. Not at all the same.

No gangsters (well, one), no hard work toiling away in dress shops. No city tenements. No, ours was a story captured in time.

And because we are who we are, each story comes from the women who raised me, the ghosts that haunted them, and the house itself. Our house. Every corner, every rafter, beam, and windowpane told me stories for as long as I can remember, reaching back far before I was born.

I belong there, in that house, on that land. I belong to the women who came before me and the ghosts they left behind. That is my life. The only one I ever knew, so I belong to it, and it to me. Which is why I left. My wish for you, sweet child, is that you will not know the ease of pain, or come to expect loss as other children expect gifts. You will not seek out the shadows, hoping to find a tragic secret. You will be as much the sunshine as I have been the night sky. It is time for our family to break free of the persistent nightfall we've come to not only know, but crave. So, I will tell you of the dark and the light, and I will hope it appeases any sort of curiosity. Because if you decide to return, even for a glimpse, the history will cast its net wide, and draw you back in.

I suppose I already know you will go there someday. And when you do, perhaps you can use this history to save yourself.

And if that doesn't work, at least you'll know there is a richness there, another layer that exists between what we know and what we feel, that is inexorably linked to life. If you choose to stay here, in the sun, your life will be filled with all the pain and joy a life deserves. And if you choose to return to the darkness, you will struggle against the peculiar delicacy of loss that, in our upside-down lineage, is mother's milk.

Remember that, baby girl. Remember it well. And know, I love you more than all the stars you can or cannot see.

Love,

Your mama, Stella

"It's a lovely letter is what I think," Eleanor said, clearing her throat, suddenly missing Mimi.

"This changes everything."

"It doesn't change anything, honey. Calm down."

"Amazing Andy was right. We are hostages. Ava and Anne and all the rest. Can't you see? You were happy once, but now you're the proud owner of a burial ground that was populated by the evil hands of our relatives. And you're here, and Anthony is there. And, well, you kind of inherited me, too. Only, I don't have to stay if you don't want me. Not that I don't feel want-able. And look here what my mama says about loss. . . . See, that sounds about right. Doomed. We're doomed. We'll live here all alone forever and we'll continue to do the strange bad things that make this family all colors of awkward. It's like . . . we've been poisoned. Like Amazing Andy said. And if that's true, we have to leave. And you will leave me, and I will go back to Alabama and I don't want to go. Don't leave me." Byrd wilted in defeat.

"Do we have to leave?" asked Maj. "I don't want to leave."

"We do not have to leave."

"What if it's cast a spell on us? What if we can't see it for what it really is?" Byrd was crying.

"Byrd. If we feel happy here, doesn't that make it a good thing? Loss or not?" Eleanor grabbed Byrd's hands between her own and squeezed. "You need to breathe. You're having an anxiety attack, which is totally fine, but hear me: I'm not leaving you. I can't be with Anthony right now. I have always defined myself by what those around me wanted. Damaged, pretty, magical . . . or weak, strong, damsel in distress for Anthony. Well, that's complicated. He wanted me to seem weak so he could feel good about himself, but be strong inside so if he failed, I'd be okay. . . ."

"Maybe it's simpler than all that," said Maj stopping the torrent of her mother's words.

"How do you figure?" asked Byrd.

"Crazy Anne told me something else. She said I'd know when to say it. She said we can trust ourselves. She said Stella was going to die in childbirth no matter what. That it was a fate you didn't want to control. She said when we try to manage life and death that it makes a hole in the universe. She said not to let your fear tell you lies. 'Every coward I've ever met thinks they're fearless. Heroes, on the other hand, are accidental,' Anne said. She told me that no spirit is trapped here, that they make their way to the other side when they're good and ready. And . . ."

"What, Maj?"

"She said Mr. Colder can't go in the house. Because of Nan's spell. Come look in the book, I'll show you."

———

Back in the kitchen, Maj helped Byrd find what she needed.

"Right here, the Book of Nan. Nan's last act of magic. She buries Reggie's watch in the basement," Maj said, finishing her second piece of pie.

"It's about intent. She probably wasn't even thinking about the gatehouse. She was protecting the old house. She was protecting us," Byrd said, smiling.

"See, Byrd?" said Maj. "It's a good place. A safe place."

"Let's go see Johnny," said Byrd, closing the book.

"Where do you suppose he's staying? He could be anywhere, really." Eleanor frowned.

"He's here," said Maj, holding up her drawing of the Stardust Motel on Grand Street, right by the highway. "Now, Mama, how's about a third piece of pie?"

"But how will we keep his sorry ass self at the gatehouse, instead of coming up to the Witch House?" asked Byrd.

"Here's what we're going to do, Byrd," Eleanor said. "We ban him and the crew for their safety, or for our sanity, it doesn't matter. We'll sacrifice what we found at the gatehouse. All of it. Johnny Colder can have his evidence. It's the easiest option."

8:30 A.M.

Johnny Colder sat in his crap motel going over the last sound edits before the live show. He was tired of Haven Port and its ass-hat coffee. Christ, he couldn't wait to leave.

At least he was finally hitting the big time.

But even he had to admit that, though he thought the whole thing was a bunch of hooey, the interview he was reviewing was fascinating. He hit play again.

"There is, perhaps, no finer example of the devastating supernatural effects 'the Witch House' has on all those who dare step foot on its cursed land than that of Matthew Makepeace. A local carpenter and devoted family man, Mr. Makepeace was, by all accounts, just your average, upstanding man, before his curiosity got the better of him. At the time of his encounter, he was twenty-five years old with a thriving construction company he built from the bottom up. Looking for new and interesting ways to recycle older building materials into newer homes, he decided to ignore the local folklore, not to mention his own childhood fears, and take a look around the house and the grounds. His ex-wife, Carly, stated:

"'Matthew walked in one person, and came out someone else. Some say he died in there—or a piece of him did, at least. Others say he was born. I guess that depends on whether or not you like a large helping of mean with your man. I didn't, so I divorced his ass.'

"That Carly is a feisty one, folks! But either way, everyone agrees Mr. Makepeace will never be the same.

"After learning all I could about the history of Haven House, this supposed 'Witch House,' it was the documented, drastic change in Matthew's mannerisms and temperament that interested me the most. Others have gone there with little or no effect. So, before I took the leap and investigated on my own, I interviewed Mr. Makepeace himself. The following is a record-ing of that interview where Matthew states, in his own words, what happened the day his life was forever changed."

[Static sounds and a thud as a mic is dropped.]

Johnny: "Sorry. Damn outdated shit, I swear, hold on. *[High-pitched feedback.]* There, good. Okay. First, thank you to the Virginia State Department of Corrections for allowing me this interview. I'm sitting here with Matthew Makepeace, whom many know as the Tangier Island Firebug. Matthew, you are currently serving a twenty-year sentence for setting fires to mul-tiple historic buildings. Now, you claim that it was some sort of possession you picked up at Haven House that compelled you to set the fires. Do you stand by that?"

Matthew: "I don't know. And I don't care anymore. The truth is, I'd like to burn down the entire world. Shit, I'd set fire to you if I had a lighter. Got a lighter?"

[Uneasy laughter.]

Johnny: "Not on me, no! Anyhow, I'd like your full account of that day. It will help me decide if I want to go see for my-self."

Matthew: "Don't go, man."

Johnny: "Convince me not to. Tell me why you went, and what you saw."

Mathew: "It was up for sale, see? And it was unlike any-thing I'd ever seen. I'd grown up in Haven Port, and the Witch House was kind of an obsession for all of us neighborhood kids. We rode our bikes past it all the time, daring each other to go inside.

"But none of us, not one, ever went in. But when I got older, it seemed damned stupid to believe something I did as a kid. It was just a house. And I wanted to see it because of my work. See, that house, it has an entirely original blueprint. It's a type of architecture nobody could place. Not Victorian, yet Victorian . . . not mid-century, not a cape or colonial. And there was a rumor of an art deco pool, like Gatsby, no joke. And you can't see the back part of the estate from the street. It goes all the way out to the end of the point. I'm telling you, it was something else. The Technicolor lushness of the gardens was over the top . . . heady. And when I first stepped onto the porch, everything seemed shrouded in mist, and it felt . . . it felt . . . *luxurious.*

"When I went inside, I was stunned. I thought maybe the Realtor had been there, but I knew the guy was out of New York and hadn't been around at all. At least, that's what my guys were telling me. But I could smell cooking, and hear music. Lights were on. You know when someone has just left a room and you can tell they were just there? A hint of a smell. It was like that. Makes me go nuts just thinking about it."

Johnny: "What was it like inside?"

Matthew: "The interior was like this glorious open maze and around every corner there was something beautiful or odd to see. Like . . . all perfect and well preserved, a museum of sorts. Maybe it was just the craftsman in me, I kept touching the molding and plaster walls. I felt home. Like I never wanted to leave. It was a paradise. It was *lived in.* Like I was the ghost, you know? Hell . . . I don't know. And it felt right. Nothing has ever felt so right. I remember thinking, 'I'll just buy it.' And that was before I went out back to see the part of the grounds hidden by the house.

"It didn't disappoint, Johnny, it was like a secret. Like the land knew it was a beautiful secret and dressed up for me. And that pool? Better than anything Gatsby would have had, and running. It was *running*. Crystal clear and well-kept. Who the hell maintains that place, right? You see anyone? I sure as hell don't. Not ever. And beyond that, the land stretches out to this pine grove, and you can hear the waves at the end of the point and beyond. And between, there is a meadow. It was like all my boyhood dreams had come true. I decided I'd run to the beach, through the pines, to see if there were really wild ponies living there. Some said there was another herd of Chincoteague ponies on the beaches of Persimmon Point. But no one had ever seen them. Well, by sea, but only by sea. I ran, happy. I swear I've never been so happy. That's when I found the ruins."

Johnny: "Ruins of what?"

Matthew: "The original house. Half of me thought that was all made up, too. But damn, I felt like an archeologist. I looked around for a while, picking up odds and ends of glass and such. Looking at the masonwork of the original foundation. Hell, I even started taking measurements. I was a kid in a candy store, but then I tripped. Goddamn, I was embarrassed going down, so embarrassed. Felt like a million people were watching and laughing, even though no one was there.

"I must have hit my head on a piece of old foundation and

blacked out. When I came to, the light hadn't changed. It must have been all of five minutes. Five minutes? How could that be? It was impossible, Johnny, totally impossible."

Johnny: "Why?"

Matthew: "Because I lived a hundred years in those five minutes; it was like the house and the property and every shadow of a memory of a thought came screaming at me. I woke up knowing things no one should ever know."

Johnny: "What things?"

Matthew: "Fuck you, man. Don't make me say it. Evil things."

Johnny: [*Muffled*] "This is family rated, watch the language. [*Clear*] Thank you, Mr. Makepeace, for an interesting interview. I'm even more curious to go, now. And I think our listeners will be, too."

Matthew: "Don't go there. Trust me. Don't go. Don't go!"

[Sound recording clicks off.]

"Interesting stuff, right, ghost hunters? So, the story ends like this: Mr. Makepeace went inside a happy guy. Happy with his new wife. Happy with his life. But when he came out . . . well, he went down to the local bar, Witches Brew, and almost killed a man who asked about a quote for a new roof. Then, he went home and beat up that pretty new wife of his. She left him, of course . . . and then he started to set his fires.

"The question remains, why do some people go inside that house or explore its acreage and come out just fine? Could it be that when Mr. Makepeace hit his head on the grounds, whatever evil lives there seeped right in?"

Johnny clicked off the recording and sat back in the plastic chair, pleased with himself. If it weren't so early, he'd have a drink to celebrate his imminent rise to prime time.

His daydream of watching that well-coiffed hack, Brad, suffer as Johnny took over his spot as anchor was disturbed by a knock on the door. He cracked it open and saw a woman, a teenager, a red-headed little girl—and one old German shepherd—all giving him the stink eye.

"Mr. Colder? We have a proposition for you."

Eleanor told Johnny about the gatehouse while Byrd and Maj sat on two orange pleather chairs. Smiling in a way that made his skin crawl.

"No way," he said. "So what if you found some old torture chamber in the gatehouse. You're telling me I can't explore the foundation of Haven House, which is why I'm going. And that I can't even go inside the Witch House itself? There is no way I'd agree to that. It's comical, really."

"You know what, Byrd?" said Eleanor, while Johnny laughed off their deal.

"What, Elly?"

"Nothing is more truly terrifying than a person who builds a plastic world around themselves and pretends not to be disgusting. You can always smell it underneath."

"You sure can." Byrd sniffed the air. "It smells of cheap sweat and toe rot."

"It smells of stale processed foods and fake gold chain necklaces," Eleanor continued.

"It smells really not good, Mama," Maj added, waving the air in front of her face.

"No, it sure doesn't, baby." Eleanor looked straight into

Johnny's eyes. "Listen to me, you poor excuse for a human be-ing. Here's what will happen, *Johnny*. I thought you would see *reason*. But I'm afraid you have *forced* the *issue*. If you don't agree, two things will happen.

"We'll call the police right now, and local news will break your story before you can. One of our crazy relatives burnt down a whole asylum in order to make a point—don't test us.

"We will curse you. And our curses, we just found out, run as deep and true and terrible as our protection spells.

"So, Mr. Colder, what do you say now?"

1:00 P.M.

When the crew got to work, Byrd and Maj and Eleanor sat on the Witch House front porch watching the progress while sketching out a new garden with colored pencils on thick sheets of paper.

The show was going really well.

"I can't believe it's live," said Byrd, delighted, before getting back down to business. "But anyway, once these fools are gone, I think we should plant okra."

"Ewwww . . ." said Maj.

"Plant it with the marigolds near the tomatoes. You got a light green pencil over there?" asked Eleanor.

Just as Maj handed her a pencil, a man's high-pitched scream broke through their peaceful bubble.

All three of the Persimmon Point Amore witches looked up

in unison. Each smiled. And Maj said, "They found the bones. I just hope they don't kill all the geraniums."

"If they do, sweetheart, we'll plant more."

4:00 P.M.

Johnny Colder stood in front of a camera crew, with the Witch House behind him, under the poplar canopy as he closed his show. Maj thought it all looked very dramatic with the police cars and sirens and lights gathered around the gatehouse.

"It's been a day full of action and adventure here at the Witch House of Persimmon Point. And now, it's time to leave with the sunset. One final note about this family of women. It seems to me that everyone lives with a glimmer of redemptive light. When that goes out . . . well, they're dead already. Rabies of the soul, they call it," he finished, before glaring at the three very amused witches sitting on the porch waving good-bye.

Epilogue

On the Night of the Biggest Doom

Byrd Whalen

It's funny, the things that people are afraid of. Like shadows and deep, dark corners of houses, or places. Pieces of wood and glass, patches of earth. It's my opinion that we make up impossible things to be scared of, because the real scary stuff is far more probable, and if we focused on that, we'd all be as crazy as great-grandmother Crazy Anne. Or batshit, as Elly's portion of our clan likes to call themselves.

That doesn't mean there's no danger in a house. Certainly this house was dangerous, and the gatehouse downright evil.

I'm convinced a house is like its own world, complete with its own peculiar rules and atmosphere. And if that's even just sort of true, it stands to reason that this house does, in fact, keep people and spirits hostage.

One of my favorite words these days is *retrospect*. It means "a survey of past events," but it doesn't really say if you have to take those events into account or not. It only implies it.

I swear, sometimes I think that everything I believe in is implied. Not solid at all. Hazy like the mist that falls over our land and at the mercy of the waves and the wind and the phases of the moon. Even the sounds of hooves on the sand.

Which explains my ongoing trust issues, I suppose.

But think about it. Do we live our lives in pursuit of where we will end up? What the tarmac will look like when we land?

If you die in an accident, was that your fate? And if that's the case, why does anyone do anything? Here's why (and don't you worry, my grandstanding is almost over):

Life is about each moment. A sum total of the impact you had on others. A collection of beauty. A retrospective. It is not changed or affected by the circumstances at the end. God, if only we all knew this epic truth. Each day, each breath inside a day, is a new moment to build love.

Just like Elly and Anthony rebuilt their love. Though it took many years and a whole heck of a lot of unnecessary moving backward to go forward. Some people just got to make things complicated.

Oh, hell, here they come. The dress is on. Let the doom begin.

Byrd closed the journal just as Maj burst through the door.

"Are you ready? Jack looks so handsome! Everyone, absolutely everyone is here! Even Opal, can you stand it? Time to tie the knot!" Maj squealed.

"Damn, was I that high-pitched as a teenager? Nah. I just had personality," said Byrd.

"Stop being grumbly, it's going to be FINE. Now come on!"

"I'll be down when I'm good and ready. Go have a drink or something, your eagerness to see the death of my whole independent, goddammed spirit is about to make me throw up, I SWEAR."

"You know you can't wait. Come on, Delores!"

The old dog got up and ran to Maj with agility impossible for her age.

Maj laughed and ran off. Byrd reopened the journal for one final thought.

I love being around people who find my offensiveness amusing. Sometimes, anyway.

But, see, before I begin this whole new kind of life, I'd like to do a rewrite on all the others who tried this very same thing and failed. Because if I don't, I'm never going to believe I can make a go of this.

Like maybe . . .

Nan walked down the aisle and married Giancarlo, who wasn't horrible at all, but handsome and caring, and somehow they fell in love.

Or even . . .

Lucy and Vito grew old together and had two more children, daughters, who loved them and respected them. And the family grew and grew and this house was filled with light and laughter and love, with every door painted raspberry.

Or . . .

Anne became a mystic in New York and wrote novels and raised her daughter Opal into adulthood. Friends with Dorothy Parker, she was.

Wouldn't that be lovely?

But best of all . . .

Stella never died. She was by my side in the night garden under the moon while I vowed to love and trust Jack, who vowed to love and trust me right back.

And so it goes.

But I guess we shouldn't really worry about a past we can't change.

JAYSUS. This whole thing's just got me thinking too much. To hell with it.

It's like me and Elly always say, the thing we figured out at the end of that long, wild weekend of searching.

There's evil and there's good. There's love and there's hate. There're things you can't change and things you can and things you shouldn't mess with at all.

But at the end of the day, we die young, or grow old. Don't have no real choice in the matter. . . .

So, leave your worries with your shoes and make a run for the ocean.

Acknowledgments

This book was the hardest and easiest book to write. Easy because the base of the story was written years ago. Written on my body and in my heart. Trapped words like tape across my mouth and seeping up like internal tattoos on my skin.

Hard because I had to take all that crazy and rewrite it . . . reform it . . . translate it into a novel.

A mighty chore. And a lonesome one. Usually, I have a list of people to thank at the beginning of these acknowledgments. That list is missing here, because I chose to keep this book close. Even when I wanted to share it, I felt the damn thing tugging on me, whispering . . . *not yet. Not yet.*

That being said, I could not have written it without the un-yielding and ever-present voice of Glitter (the glitter editor of all the things), AKA Vicki Lame at St. Martin's Press. You kept me sane this year. Sort of.

Acknowledgments

To Gina Miel Heron, my book-touring soul sister. You, my love, made this happen.

To my brave and brilliant agent, Anne Bohner, at Pen and Ink Literary. Your continued, consistent support for my crazy stories is admirable!

To my husband and three daughters: Billy, this year taught me to hold on to what I have. I'm holding on so tight to you, babe. Rosy, you flew the coop! Fly high. Tess and Gracie, DO NOT FLY TOO HIGH . . . YET. Mommy loves you.

To my mother, Terry, and my godfather, Robert. I never figured us for the Waltons, but here we are. Oy.

To my mother-in-law Margaret Palmieri, you keep trying to get me to drink that good wine. And I love you . . . but I'll stick to my Lambrusco. In a mason jar. On ice.

Thanks to my Cooper clan down South and to the Palmieris both here and in St. Louis. (Kisses!)

But most of all, thank YOU, dear reader. Thank you very, very much.

1. *The Witch House of Persimmon Point* explores the lives of five generations of women and the self-created myths of their family. How do the family stories we tell through generations change and become the narrative of our own lives?

2. The actions of the Amore women can often be seen as selfish. Do you agree or disagree and do you think their selfishness ultimately keeps them safe or destroys them? Discuss.

3. Through the timeline of the book, pivotal moments in history occur, yet the characters do not seem to experience those events fully. Why do you think Palmieri only brushed the surface of those events?

4. Each time her world collapses around her, Nan becomes stricter, more pious with her feelings and actions. Do you ultimately think this made it easier for her to move on or harder, and why?

5. In what ways do you think Lucy as a character is a product of her environment? If Nan had given her love more freely, would Lucy have been different? If so, how do you think that might have altered Anne while she was growing up?

6. Palmieri frequently refers to her novels as "Gothic" in nature. In which ways do you think *The Witch House of Persimmon Point* can be viewed as her most Gothic novel yet?

7. Relationships between mothers and daughters play an important role throughout the novel. Do you think the relationships of Nan and Lucy, Lucy and Anne, and eventually, Anne and Opal might have been different if they had not lived in the Witch House? How so?

St. Martin's
Griffin

8. Why do you think it was so important to Byrd to control the version of the truth the public knows about her family? Do you think it is easier for her to let go of control once she forms a family within a family with Eleanor and Maj?

9. Much of the action in the book centers in the Witch House, the Amore family home. Consider the idea of "home" and what it means to each of the characters.

10. In many ways, the Witch House is also a character. Do you view it as a villain or a savior? Why?